American Kitsune

A Fox's Love

Brandon Blake Varnell

Copyright © 2014 Brandon Blake Varnell

All rights reserved.

ISBN:

ISBN-13: 978-1494976729

ISBN-10: 1494976722

ACKNOWLEDGMENTS

I would first like to thank my parents for supporting me in everything I do, and all the fans who read my stories on fanfiction.net that bought this book. Without them, none of this would have been possible.

I would also like to thank Daneel Rush, whose fanfic, Naruto Genkyouien, inspired me to write this original novel.

And finally, I would like to thank tvtropes and those guys who created The 100 Laws and Rules of anime, for without them, I wouldn't have so much material to make fun of.

Chapter 1: Paper Route

The Swift residence was one of several apartments inside of the Le Monte apartment complex located in Phoenix, Arizona. More specifically, it was located on the crossroads of 16th Street and McDonald Road, though just why someone would name a street after a fast-food restaurant was unknown.

Le Monte apartment complex was a pretty nice place to live, all things considered. It wasn't very ritzy, but the grass was green, there were two well-maintained swimming pools, among other amenities, and all of the apartment buildings were clean, modern-looking structures with red roofing and white stucco walls. There were definitely worse places to live.

The apartment belonging to the Swifts was modest in size, possessing two-bedrooms and two-bathrooms, with a moderately sized kitchen connected to a living room, and an office near the master bedroom. Despite not being very large, it had all the comforts one would expect to find in a well-loved home.

Lining the walls were pictures within various sized and styled frames. The images were of a pretty young woman who didn't look a day over twenty and a boy who grew throughout each picture. In one, he was a small baby that looked like a tiny ball of fat and pudge, as all babies do. In another, he was a young boy no older than one with a head full of peach-fuzz hair, taking his first steps. In another, he was a preteen with short spiky hair and a large grin as he held a soccer ball in his hands next to an equally grinning girl with short blond, almost boyish hair. All of the pictures showed the boy as he grew up, and the young-looking woman, obviously the boy's mother.

The apartment was mostly empty of inhabitants, save for one bedroom where the boy in the pictures was currently sleeping peacefully—

BEEP!

BEEP!

BEEP!

BE—CRUNCH!

—Or at least, where he *was* sleeping, until the alarm clock went off, ruining a wonderful dream. Couldn't it have beeped just ten seconds later? He had been just about to share a romantic kiss with his crush!

Sometimes, he really hated that infernal piece of racket making machinery.

Blearily sitting up in bed and pulling his hand off the now somewhat abused alarm clock, Kevin Swift blinked his weary blue eyes, striving to come to terms with the fact that he was now awake. It was harder than it looked. He ran a hand through his tousled, medium-length, light blond hair, brushing several stray bangs out of his eyes. As his mind became more alert, the young teen found himself absently staring around his room.

It was about what you might expect from the room of a 15-year old boy. Lining the walls were posters of all his favorite bands, and his favorite sports teams, along with a number of posters showcasing his favorite *anime* and *manga*, which had become quite popular in America as of late.

Surprisingly enough, there were no pictures of bikini models, hot actresses or half naked women. Why was this a surprise? Because Kevin was a 15-year old boy. Large posters of half-naked super models were something people simply expect to see in the bedroom of a young man undergoing puberty. It was like a rite of passage!

That they weren't sharing Kevin's bedroom may have had something to do with his innate shyness when it came to women. To put it simply, he couldn't talk to girls to save his life. Any time a girl came up to him, he would freeze, his mouth unable to move and his mind unable to think. It was an affliction that affected him in more ways than one, and was the main reason he still couldn't ask Lindsay Diane on even a simple date despite the years they had known each other.

Yeah, he was pretty pathetic like that. Laugh it up. Have a joke at his expense. Not like he'll ever know.

Another key factor of Kevin's room that most would likely notice upon entering was the large book shelf. It didn't have any books. At least, not reading books. Filling the shelf from top to bottom was a large collection of all his favorite Japanese pop culture items: *manga*. Like a good number of boys his age, Kevin had a thing for Japanese pop culture, or at least for Japanese animation and manga. Thinking on it, maybe the reason he couldn't talk to women was because he'd watched one too many *Shōnen* love comedies?

Grumbling irritably about having to get up so early in the morning—the sun hadn't even come up yet!—Kevin Swift proceeded to complete his daily ritual for waking up and getting ready.

In other words, he spent a long time in the shower, staring blankly at the wall as steam rose all around him, made a breakfast of eggs, toast and a glass of milk after getting dressed, then brushed his teeth. Once his ritual was complete, he was awake and raring to go.

Not really. He was actually only marginally more alert than before he got ready, but it wasn't like he had much of a choice in the matter. There were things that needed to get done, things that unfortunately couldn't wait.

Stepping out of the apartment he shared with his mother, who was currently across the sea doing something for her job, Kevin locked the door and walked over to the bike that was padlocked to the railing. He undid the lock, grabbed the bike, rolled it down the set of stairs, and took off, pedaling his way out of Le Monte apartment complex and onto the main street.

As he rode in the bike lane on the left side of the road, Kevin mused that even in the wee hours of the morning, it was still hot as hell in this state. Seriously, Arizona had to be the hottest state in the United States, especially during the summer.

Well, technically summer was nearing its end. Just a little less than two weeks and it would be September, but Kevin had never been one to bother with such semantics. It wouldn't stop him from complaining, that's for sure!

And so, mentally complaining about the heat, the teenager continued to ride his bike along the side of the road all the way to his job.

Yes, his job. He worked to actually earn his own money as opposed to mooching off his mom's hard-earned cash. Kevin wasn't like other kids who had things handed to him on a silver-platter. He was responsible!

Well, that, and the fact that Kevin didn't really like relying on his mom for money or anything else. This may have had something to do with how she was rarely ever home, but again, semantics, he didn't bother himself with them.

Kevin's job was delivering the morning newspapers on bike to the houses along his predetermined route. He had started doing this two summers ago when he was in eighth grade and decided to continue doing so after he had started going to high school as a means of earning more cash.

Since it almost wasn't summer anymore, he would only be delivering the Sunday morning newspaper. He just didn't have time on weekdays now that he had school, homework, and after school activities. It would mean he made less money, but at least he was still making something, so he couldn't complain too much.

He actually enjoyed his job. Sure the pay wasn't great and his boss freaked him out, but he earned enough spending money to go out on weekends and still have a bit saved up. As long as he finished delivering papers by five a.m., his life was copacetic.

Of course, he hated the fact that his job required him to get up at two in the morning. That sucked. It wasn't like people would be awake around that time to read the newspapers anyway. Why would they be? How many people actually had to wake up and go to their job that early in the morning?

Not many, Kevin would wager.

After somewhere around fifteen minutes, a hot and sweaty Kevin arrived at the Newspaper Distribution Center, which was really just a fancy name for the place that received the newspapers he delivered.

The newspaper building wasn't much to look at. Really, it was just a moderately-sized, one-story rectangular building made out of drab gray bricks and possessing a flat roof. It looked boring, and the manager there wasn't much better than the building. Actually, Kevin preferred looking at the building as opposed to the manager.

Thankfully, the manager would not be there this early in the morning. Kevin supposed there was some kind of silver lining to that, but he couldn't really see it in the early morning darkness.

Kevin didn't bother locking up his bike as he set it against next to the front door, which he then unlocked with the key he had been given.

When Kevin first started this job, the manager had actually woken up every morning to unlock the door. He would then proceed to watch Kevin like a hawk while the young man loaded the newspapers onto his bike. That had actually been pretty creepy, being watched like that. It had only been after six months when he had proven himself trustworthy, or something like that, that the manager had decided he didn't need to show up every morning and gave him a key to get in.

Kevin found his papers ready as usual. The box was pretty heavy, but Kevin was able to take it to his bike in a single haul, which was much better than what he used to be capable of. He had grown pretty strong since the first year he had started. Back then, he'd been forced to make six trips. Which, by the way, totally sucked.

Once he had gotten all of the rolled up newspapers in the carrier on his bike, it was off to do his newspaper run.

The paper route he took had him traveling through two different neighborhoods near his apartment complex. All the houses there were large and nice and imposing in their ostentatious magnificence. They were mostly two-story homes with off-white plaster walls and red tiled roofs. The front lawns were all manicured to perfection with neatly trimmed hedges, perfectly cut trees, and a large variety of cacti. From time to time Kevin would see expensive cars parked in front of the garages.

Kevin had to shake his head at the wasteful use of money. Maybe it was his mom's influence, but he just couldn't see the point in buying such extravagant vehicles. They might look nice, but they cost more than they were worth, especially considering how most of them were likely custom models that required constant maintenance in order to keep them at peak performance.

And that's not even getting into the cost of those houses. Those probably had a price range of at least several hundred-thousand dollars, if not somewhere around a couple million. Why would anyone want to buy such a large, expensive house when something a little smaller and more affordable would be perfectly acceptable *and* could probably fit their entire family comfortably without all that excess space? What would they even do with all that extra space anyways? Make their own bowling alley? Dedicate a large room of the house to store paraphernalia?

Actually, that last one sounded kind of cool. Maybe he should think of getting an entire room dedicated one or more of his favorite hobbies when he moved out? A room for just anime and manga would be awesome.

Thinking of all the people who lived in those houses, Kevin

was sure they were just trying to show off how rich they were with their stupid expensive sports cars and unnecessarily extravagant houses. That honestly wouldn't surprise him in the least. While he didn't know anyone in this neighborhood personally, he knew that a good few of the children he went to school with lived in these houses. If they were reflective in any way of their parents, he could imagine them being some of the most obnoxious and snobbish people around.

He sighed. Maybe he was just being biased. He and his mom were pretty well off, even if she was always away on business. They could probably afford to live in a nice house like these, but when he once commented on it, she had simply told him there was no point in spending so much money on something so unimportant.

Yeah, his mom was frugal like that. This wasn't to say she didn't spend money on other things, like those new *Android* mobile phones that came out a while ago. Those were awesome! Or on things that were fun, like vacations.

At least once a year she and Kevin would take a vacation somewhere nice, usually out of the country. He had been to France, Italy, England, Ireland, Spain, Greece and Germany. Last year he'd even had them flown out to Japan!

Now *that* had been awesome. He used to think the Comicon that he went to annually in Arizona was the height of cool, but the anime conventions in Japan were just incredible. The one he had been to there must have had at least a couple hundred-thousand people on that day alone! And almost all of them had been dressed up in some kind of costume! He'd seen everything from *Son Goku* to Natsumo Uzukami from Shinobi Natsumo, and upwards of 100 Ichika Kurohimes from White Out.

He had also seen a good number of Satsuki's, which was not cool because Satsuki was an emo jerk who needed someone to pull her head out of her rear end.

With a shake of his head, Kevin dispelled his rather superfluous thoughts and focused on delivering newspapers. The trip through both neighborhoods took him a little over two hours. By the time he got back to the newspaper distribution building, it was about 4:30 a.m..

He probably could have finished much sooner, but Kevin had decided to make a game of trying to smack the cars with a newspaper. More often than not, he failed. Kevin wasn't a basketball or baseball player. He had no talent in throwing anything unless it was a Frisbee, and even then, not very well.

After he finished his newspaper route, Kevin re-parked his bike by the front door, went in and headed down the first hall on the left. He didn't have to walk far. Not only was the hall short, the room he needed to enter was the first door on the right.

The room was a standard office. It had all the things that were expected of an office: a desk, a chair, a file maintenance cabinet, things like that. This particular office was very spartan, possessing only the bare necessities and nothing else, not even a single picture hung from the walls. There was nothing in this room to indicate it was being used other than the stack of papers sitting on the desk.

Well, that, and the very large man sitting behind the desk. And by large, Kevin didn't just mean big. He meant *ginormous*, like Sumo Wrestler large. Kevin wouldn't be surprised to learn that this man had been a Sumo Wrestler at one point in his life, or even the reincarnation of a Sumo Wrestler.

The man in question was his boss, Davin Monstrang. He was a beefy man with a head of short brown hair, two small brown eyes, and a girth that made it look like he could eat two entire cows and still be hungry. He had no neck, somewhere around ten chins, and fat that practically rolled out of his ugly, khaki colored, button-up shirt.

"I finished my newspaper route," Kevin informed the man.

Davin grunted, still not looking up from whatever paper he was working on. "And I suppose you'll be wanting your pay?"

"Yes."

Another grunt was the answer he received. Davin wasn't one for words. The chair creaked ominously as he rolled it away from his desk, and Kevin actually wondered how long the chair had before it broke under the strain of keeping that man seated.

"Here." Davin slapped Kevin's paycheck on the desk. "Try not to spend it in all one place, brat."

Kevin resisted the urge to roll his eyes at the man. Even after all this time, his boss still seemed to think the worst of him. He wasn't like those spoiled rich kids who spent their money frivolously on things he wouldn't need...

... okay, so maybe he was. But at least he spent it on fun activities like going to the arcade and not on drugs like a lot of kids at school did. That had to count for something, right?

Grabbing his paycheck off the desk, Kevin thanked his boss and hurriedly left. He didn't enjoy being in his boss's presence any longer than necessary.

It was all that fat, you see. Whenever the man moved, it looked alive and made Kevin feel like he was staring at some kind of eldritch horror that might eat him if he stayed too long. HP Lovecraft had nothing on those fat rolls.

Grabbing his bike, Kevin was just about to leave when a noise caught his attention. It was very muffled and difficult to make out, but it sounded like a whimper from some kind of animal. A cat or a dog maybe.

Kevin had two weaknesses, one well known, one not so much. The first was a weakness towards women, which everyone and their mother knew about.

His second weakness, one known only to his best friend and

crush, was his love—obsession—for animals. Kevin had loved animals ever since his mom had first taken him to the zoo when he was five. He had gone into the petting pen and played with all the animals there. They seemed to like him, unlike some of the other kids who had been bitten, and he'd had a great time. That had been the start of his animal obsession, which rivaled his anime obsession.

Back when he was younger, he would occasionally bring stray or even wild animals home with him. It had caused a lot of problems with the people in charge of their apartment complex because of their no pet policy. His mom had put her foot down and made him promise to stop bringing in every animal he found. Since then, he hadn't brought animals into the apartment.

With the noise possibly falling into the second category of his list of weaknesses, Kevin quickly made his way toward the source of the whimper. It sounded like it was coming from around the corner of the building.

He turned the corner and stopped.

His eyes widened.

"Ohmygoshit'safox!" Kevin squee'd in a manner that was eerily reminiscent of a fangirl who had just bumped into her favorite pop idol.

You know what a fangirl is, right? They're those pre-teen and teenage girls that go "SQUEE!" when they're excited.

Squeeing, by the way, is a very shrill noise that pierces the eardrums and can cause them to occasionally burst. In severe cases, it can also induce brain hemorrhaging, in which blood and liquified brain matter ooze out of the ears.

According to Mythbusters, being near someone who is "squeeing" has a ten percent fatality rating.

If you ever decide to become a pop idol be prepared to buy ear plugs.

But you are probably wondering why Kevin was 'squeeing' like one of these fangirls, yes?

Because lying near the dumpster was an honest to god fox.

Less then a second after letting loose with his "inner fangirl," Kevin slapped a hand over his mouth. Idiot! What was wrong with him? Squeeing like some kind of prepubescent little girl? Worse still, he had "squee'd" in front of a fox! It was a well-established fact that foxes didn't like humans! They shied away from human contact and when frightened, would bite!

If he wanted to have any hope of even getting near it, much less petting it, he would need to be quiet. As in, quieter than Elmer Fudge when he was "hunting wabbits" quiet.

Luckily, the fox didn't seem to have heard him. It hadn't even moved from its spot. Now all he had to do was sneak in close.

He would become one with his surroundings. He would blend in with the shadows. He would be like a *shinobi*.

Nin nin.

Making a weird sign that looked like a cross with his fingers for no apparent reason, Kevin began slowly creeping toward the fox. As he did, he began to wonder how it got into the city. There were foxes in Arizona, of course, but they all lived in the desert, far away from any human habitat.

Though, with the recent expansion of city limits, the fox's natural habitat was getting smaller. Maybe it was forced to come here because it had nowhere else to go. Kevin scowled at the thought. No one seemed to care for how people were destroying the natural habitat of animals like this fox anymore.

As he neared the creature, he observed its appearance. The fox was very small, nothing more than a tiny kit that could easily fit in the crook of his arms. It had a flattened skull, upright triangular ears, a pointed, slightly upturned snout, and deep red, almost crimson colored fur.

He recognized the species, a red fox, the most common type of fox among its species. Strange, he didn't think red foxes lived near Phoenix. Their habitat was supposed to be the northeastern portion of the state up in Flagstaff.

Perhaps the most unusual thing about this fox was its tails. Yes, tails. Lying limply behind the tiny critter were two, bushy red fox tails with white tips.

How unusual. Kevin had never seen a fox with two tails before. He was pretty sure that foxes weren't supposed to have more than one tail.

Maybe it was some kind of government experiment? He couldn't see why the government would experiment on a fox to give it two tails, but there were always conspiracy theories about various world governments doing inhumane experiments on humans. Why couldn't they do one on a fox as well?

Another whimper escaped from the tiny red-furred animal and Kevin realized that it was injured. He hadn't noticed before because its fur was so red—and because he was so excited about seeing a fox—but the fox was bleeding from its torso. It was only after taking a more in depth observation and noticing a portion where the thick red fur was slick and shiny, like someone had splashed liquid on it, that he noticed the injury.

And now that he *had* noticed it was injured, he also saw the expanding pool of blood underneath it, along with the carnelian trail that showed it had dragged itself to this spot before collapsing.

Fearing for its safety, Kevin dropped all sense of subtlety and sneakiness—and his ninja hand sign—and rushed toward the fox.

It must have really been out of it not to notice his approach. Foxes were supposed to possess very keen senses. Even injured, he would have expected it to try running away the moment he started making too much noise.

It was only after he got in close enough to kneel right next to it that Kevin realized the reason it hadn't noticed him: the small kit was unconscious.

Growing even more concerned, Kevin scooped the small fox into his arms as gently as he could and stood up. A small whimper managed to escape from the tiny animal as the movement jostled its wounds.

"Sorry," Kevin whispered, even though he knew the fox couldn't hear him. He rushed back to his bike and, after a moments thought, divested himself of his shirt and used it as a makeshift pillow for the fox. It would become stained with copious amounts of blood, but that was a small price to pay to keep the little critter from getting injured further as he rode back home.

Placing the fox into the basket on top of the waded up shirt, Kevin took off toward his apartment, his thoughts focused solely on helping the small creature suffering in front of him.

Chapter 2: First Aid Fox

After hauling ass back to Le Monte apartment complex, Kevin quickly dashed toward his bedroom. He didn't know how much time the fox had before it bled out, but judging by the way his shirt was now soaked all the way through in the carmine liquid, it wasn't long. He didn't want to take any chances and have the fox die on him because he'd been too slow to render aid.

For an animal lover such as himself, death was unacceptable!

Placing the still unconscious fox on his bed, the high school sophomore ran into his mom's bathroom where all the medical supplies were kept. Crouching down, he opened the cabinet door and peered inside. There, he found the first aid kit sitting between a large bottle of *Zzzquill* and a box filled with various feminine products. Exactly where he recalled it being last time.

He grabbed the box and tore through the short hallway once more, heading back to his room. Sitting on his bed next to the fox, Kevin opened the first aid kit. Before doing anything else, he took inventory to make sure everything he needed was still there. It would suck to begin working only to realize he was missing an essential item and be forced to search throughout the house for it.

He found the disinfectant, cotton balls, gauze and bandages. Nothing seemed to be out of place. Good.

Quickly pulling out the supplies, Kevin got to work. If he wanted to help this fox before it bled out he would need to hurry. At the same time he needed to be careful. He couldn't rush through the process and do a half-hazard job of patching up the poor creature. Expedient yet careful, that was how he needed to work if he wanted to have any hope of saving the small kit.

The first thing Kevin did was grab one of the cotton balls and pour a good deal of disinfectant on it. Carefully rolling the fox over to make the injury on its torso more easily accessible, Kevin began to clean the wound and surrounding fur.

The fox whimpered in pain as the ethanol did its work, killing off whatever harmful bacteria surrounded the wound. Being an alcohol based disinfectant, Kevin knew the stuff stung something fierce, and was quick to apologize despite the fox not being awake to hear it, much less the fact that it wouldn't understand what he was saying even if it *was* awake.

As the blood and grime covering the fox's torso was wiped away, Kevin was finally able to see the injury more clearly.

His stomach churned.

It was a rather nasty looking gash that reminded Kevin of the time he had been bitten by a pit bull that belonged to this grumpy old man. When he tried petting the animal had quite literally clamped its jaws onto his hand and tore into his flesh. He had needed somewhere around half a dozen stitches on each side of his hand for the damage to heal.

That was the only time any animal had ever bitten him before. He still had a memento in the form of a white scar on both sides of his hand near his thumb, a jagged, white line that stood out starkly against his lightly tanned skin.

The longer he continued cleaning the wound the more he realized just how horrible the injury truly was. It was more than just a ragged gash. Whatever had done this had actually torn through some of its muscles as well, or was that just fatty tissue? It was hard to tell since Kevin didn't know much about fox anatomy. Either way, he wasn't even sure stitching the wound shut would allow it to heal properly. And even if he had the necessary supplies, he knew next to nothing about stitching wounds.

This would require professional help.

Unfortunately, the nearest veterinary office was over 15 miles away, and he didn't think he could make it on his bike before the kit died of blood loss. Maybe he was imagining things, because really, he couldn't see the fox's skin beneath all that fur, but the creature was beginning to look kind of pale.

Not knowing what to do, Kevin just kept cleaning the wound until he felt it was good enough to begin bandaging it. He ended up going through eight cotton balls because of all the blood and dirt covering the injury. Truth be told, he had expected to use more.

It was right after he grabbed the bandages but before he began wrapping the wound that his eyes caught sight of something startling.

"What the heck...?" The young teen looked more closely at the wound, his eyes squinting.

He blinked several times, then rubbed his eyes to make sure he wasn't hallucinating. With how panicked he felt, anything was possible. When he'd convinced himself that, no, he was not suffering from any kind of hallucination and that, yes, what he saw really was happening, his eyes widened. The wound was healing! Slowly but surely the large gash on the fox's torso was closing up. Small lines of skin like thread slowly stitched themselves across the fox's wound. There had to be at least six or seven of these "threads" slowly weaving through each other, leaving behind perfect, unblemished skin that began growing sparse amounts of bright red fur soon after.

"What is this?" he asked under his breath. It was a question asked in rhetoric, as there was no one who could answer him.

It was like watching a video of how a wound might heal if someone used a *Curaga* spell or something else from one of his video games. It was fascinating to watch, but Kevin wasn't thinking about how amazing the sight was. He was more startled than impressed.

What was going on? Was this fox some kind of ancient and powerful creature like those half demons he read about in his manga? Or was it some kind of government experiment that had managed to escape from a top secret lab somewhere? What if it had been injected with the T-virus and granted superhuman... um... super fox, healing abilities?

Kevin obviously played way too much *Resident Evil.*

As he continued watching Kevin noticed that the wound was still very large, *and* that the fox's breathing had become much more heavier, as the constant loss of blood took an even harsher toll on it. If this kept up, super healing abilities or not, the fox wouldn't last much longer.

Deciding to think on the strange sight later, Kevin began dressing the wound as best he could. He pressed the gauze against the bloody gash, putting as much pressure on it as he dared to keep from aggravating the injury further. After that he used the bandages and wrapped them tightly around the fox's torso to keep the gauze pads in place in an effort to help stem the flow of blood.

Several times while he worked the fox whimpered or yelped as he was forced to turn it over or accidentally pressed on the gauze and bandages too hard. Each time this happened Kevin would flinch as if he could feel the fox's pain, and he whispered apology after apology. After what felt like hours of some of the most heart stopping and stressful work of his life, the wound was dressed to the best of his abilities.

Leaning forward with a frown of concentration, Kevin checked over his job of dressing the wound. It was a pretty good patch up for an amateur, if he did say so himself. Several gauze pads were pressed securely against the fox's torso, directly over the injury, and the bandages wound around its body tightly enough to keep the gauze in place, but not so tight that it constricted the fox's breathing. It didn't look like any blood was leaking out, so Kevin believed he was in the clear.

Of course, the reason for the lack of blood might have been how the wound was healing at an astounding rate. It might be slow in some ways, comparatively speaking, but it was far above and beyond anything he had ever seen in anything less than a *Shōnen manga*. In either event, the bandage job should keep the fox from dying of blood loss until its healing ability could finish the job.

He very briefly thought of calling a vet, or taking the fox to the veterinarian himself, but in the end, decided against it. If that fox was some kind of government experiment, then he didn't want to let anybody know about its existence.

Especially because it was such a cute little thing. There was no way he would let something so adorable get sent off to the labs to be experimented upon. Not in this life or the next.

Kevin could only imagine what would happen if the government found out he had one of their experiments. He could just picture them beating down his door, arresting him for harboring a government project and taking the fox back with them to continue committing their inhumane torture on it, strapping it to a table, cutting it open and doing who knows what to it. He would never let something so awful happen to something so cute!

Cuteness is life! Cuteness is justice!

Kevin was a big fan of Sora.

He even had a *No Game, No Life* poster in his bedroom.

Sighing, Kevin rose to his feet and left his room. There wasn't much more he could do right now—it would be up to the fox's strange healing powers to do the rest—and this whole incident had taxed him far more than he had realized.

Kevin found himself walking into the living room. As was the case with most apartments, the living room connected to the kitchen via an open entryway that changed from beige carpeting to white tiles to show the shift in rooms. There wasn't much to note about the room other than the couch sitting against the northern wall near the entrance and the large, 62 inch, flat screen

TV that hung from on opposite end, complete with several gaming consoles and surround sound speakers. Between the two, but closer to the couch, sat a glass coffee table, and on either side of the television stood a pair of tall, steel lamps.

Kevin went to the couch, collapsing on it with an exhausted exhalation of breath. Raising a hand to cover his face, he closed his eyes and felt himself slowly drift off. He would just get a couple minutes of shut eye before deciding what he should do next.

He didn't know how long he had been asleep, but it must have at least been a couple of hours. When he woke up and looked at the clock, he saw that it was 12:30 in the afternoon. Having been in such a panic when he arrived home, he had lost track of the time and couldn't say how long he'd been sleeping, but it must have been a while.

A growl alerted him to the fact that it was well past the time he normally ate lunch. Not being one to ignore his stomach, he got up from the couch and walked into the kitchen where he made himself something to eat: a plain ham sandwich with a lot of toppings that he scarfed down like a man dying of starvation.

Once satiated, Kevin went back to his room to check on the fox. It was exactly where he had left it, lying on his bed, seemingly still unconscious. Walking over he noticed immediately that the bandages had bleed through and would need to be changed. Glad that his forethought kept him from putting the first aid kit away, he got to work.

As he unwrapped the bandages, Kevin saw something that made him pause.

"Oh...!" He sounded surprised. "So you're a girl."

He must have really been panicking if he had missed something like that. Naturally, the fox didn't reply, and Kevin finished unwrapping the bandages. Taking out more cotton-balls and disinfectant he cleaned the fox's skin and fur of blood again.

Once all the blood was cleaned away, Kevin took a glance at the wound. Like last time it was closing up. In fact, it looked like the speed at which it was healing had increased. Where before it looked like the wound was closing in slow motion, now the skin was knitting together at an astonishing pace. The wound itself was almost healed over. The once jagged gash was now just a thin, red line. At this rate, Kevin doubted the fox would even have a scar.

With the fox seemingly out of danger, Kevin decided he needed to get out and do something to take his mind off all he had seen. A lot had happened today and he'd been hit with quite a few surprises. And in moments like this, there was really only one place he would go to clear his head.

His decision made, Kevin stood back up and walked out of the room. As he shut the door behind him, he didn't notice the fox raise her head and watch him leave.

Too bad for him.

Chapter 3: Love at First Sight?

Kevin's finger automatically squeezed the trigger to the red plastic gun he was using to shoot down the baddies on the screen, but neither his heart nor his mind were truly into it. The normally cathartic release that came from blowing the heads off of zombies in his favorite arcade game was just not keeping his mind off the injured fox.

There was just something off about that fox. Granted, the super healing abilities kind of made that obvious, but still, he couldn't help but feel there was even more to that fox than he had already seen. Some secret he had yet to uncover, something so incomprehensible that it could cause his entire view of the world and even reality itself to shift in a way that would change his life forever.

Or he could just be acting paranoid. That was also a possibility.

"Hey man," Kevin turned his head to see a pair of brown eyes staring at him with brows furrowed in barely concealed annoyance. "Pay attention. You've nearly had your head bitten off by a bunch of zombies in just the last minute, and I'm not going to save your sorry ass every time something tries to kill you."

Eric Corrompere was Kevin's best friend since childhood. They had met each other in elementary school and just sort of clicked. The two had been thick as thieves ever since. Or at least, they were, until Eric discovered the wonders of women, but that was a story for another time.

Eric had a head of short cut brown hair and dark eyes. He was very tall for a sophomore, standing nearly a head and a half taller than Kevin himself, and he was also very lanky. If Kevin was lean then Eric was a twig, with long, gangly arms and legs, and large feet. Like Kevin, Eric was very athletic and was on the Track and Field team with him.

He was also the biggest pervert Kevin had ever, and likely

would ever, meet, and he had no compunctions against proclaiming it to the world. There had been many times when Eric had freely told anyone willing listen that he was a proud Super Pervert. Yes, he was *that* kind of person.

Personally, Kevin just thought he was trying to emulate his favorite anime character, Jabidaia, the mentor of Natsumo from *Shinobi Natsumo*, by acting like a perverted idiot, but that was just a theory.

Eric's outgoing and perverse nature were probably the biggest difference between the two of them. Where Kevin was shy and could not talk to girls without his tongue getting tied and his stomach rebelling in the most unpleasant of ways, Eric would chase after girls like a dog chasing its tail, only he was ten times more lewd then dog could ever be.

And much like a dog can never seem to catch its tail, he had absolutely no success when it came to picking up girls, probably because most girls (and maybe even *all* girls) didn't like his open perverseness.

It didn't help his case that he had been caught trying to peek into the girls locker room several times since the start of the school year. Kevin was honestly surprised his friend had not gotten expelled for that. Then again, his dad was the Principle of their school so...

"Sorry," Kevin sighed, "I guess my mind's just not here today."

"Don't tell me your worrying about that fox?" Eric shook his head. "Honestly Kev, you're my best friend and everything, but your obsession with animals is not cool. This is why you can never get Lindsay to go out with you."

Kevin flushed. Lindsay Diane was the girl that he had been crushing on since middle school. They had been friends for a long time, but he had never been able to work up the courage to ask her out.

Of course, saying they were friends may be a bit of an overstatement these days. They used to be friends before, you know, Kevin realized that girls weren't just males without male genitalia. These days, he had trouble just talking in front of a girl without his stomach feeling like it was in free-fall much less asking the girl he had a major crush on out on a date.

"What do those two things have to do with each other?" Kevin did his best to cover his red face with a frown and tried to that pretend he was not blushing. It didn't work very well, so he decided to focus back on the game, thinking that maybe if he started killing more zombies his friend would drop the subject.

No such luck.

"Everything!" Eric very nearly shouted, which resulted in Kevin jumping back in surprise, the chord attaching the gun to the arcade game straining as it was pulled taut.

Coincidentally, this also killed Kevin's character, who ended up getting struck by a large, fat zombie wielding a chainsaw. Frowning as his character was quite literally split down the middle in a spray of violence and gore, Kevin slid his card through the small card slot in the arcade game and restarted his life to begin killing zombies anew.

Meanwhile, Eric continued, completely heedless that he had just gotten struck by a strange zombie with claws. The hypocrite. Hadn't he just been complaining about Kevin not paying attention a few seconds ago?

"Don't you see? You spend so much time obsessing over animals that you don't spend enough time working up the courage to ask Lindsay out."

"Those two things aren't mutually exclusive of each other," Kevin told his friend with a groan, even as he blew off a large zombie's head with a well placed kill shot. "Besides, it's not like I always obsess over animals. I haven't brought an animal to my apartment since 8th grade."

Though that might just be due to the fact that the last time he *had* brought an animal home he had gotten in a lot of trouble with the landlord because of the 'no pet' policy at their complex. Even after trying to explain that the coyote he found was not a pet and would be released after he fixed up its broken leg the man still wouldn't listen. Narrow minded idiot.

It only got worse when the man decided to call his mom and get her involved. He shuddered. Even over the phone that woman could be absolutely terrifying when she wanted to be.

"Then why can't you ever ask her out on a date?"

Kevin's face heated up again. In his embarrassment, he missed his characters head getting ripped off by a particularly vicious zombie. Blood and chunks of flesh sprayed all over the screen, but went ignored by Kevin who was now having other problems.

"I just..." Kevin's arms dropped to his side as the countdown to restart the game began. "What if she doesn't feel the same way? I don't want to make things awkward between us, or even worse, ruin what's left of our friendship over something like this."

"Oh geez," Eric groaned, "You're such a girl sometimes, Kevin." He ignored the glare his friend sent him. "You'll never know how she feels if you don't even ask."

"This coming from the guy who's been turned down by every single female he's ever asked out," Kevin shot back as the countdown ended and the large words Game Over in blood covered his screen. He didn't feel like playing anymore.

"Yeah, well, at least I have the guts to ask at all," Eric defended himself. "That's more than I can say for you."

Kevin had to admit Eric had a point there. No matter how many times he got shot down, the taller boy continued to hit on the girls at their school without shame. There was certainly something to be said for his friend's courage in the face of adversity if nothing else.

Or maybe it was just disillusionment. Kevin had never been able to figure out which.

"Whatever," Kevin grumbled as he holstered the gun back into its small groove. "I think I'm finished here." He stuffed his hands into his pockets and made to leave.

"Aw, come on," Eric grinned as he threw an arm around Kevin's neck and began pulling him to another game. "Don't feel too bad. I'm sure you'll work up the courage to ask Lindsay out… eventually… someday… maybe… in like, a thousand years."

"Really not helping me out here, Eric."

"Whatever. Let's just play some more games. That will cheer you up."

Kevin ended up spending the next hour or so with his best friend, playing all the arcade games they could. They mostly stuck with shooter games, which were what they enjoyed playing, but they occasionally played racing games as well.

Despite his hope that meeting up with Eric and playing a good, violent video game would help clear his head, it seemed to do just the opposite. Only now, instead of thinking about the fox he had found this morning, his mind was on how he still couldn't ask his crush to go out with him.

Heck, he still had trouble just talking to her, and this was in spite of having been her friend for going on four years now. How pathetic was that?

Very pathetic actually. It was probably the saddest thing ever for a man to be so shy around women, not to mention emasculating.

His thoughts troubled by his inability to talk to women—he blamed it on all the anime he watched where violent women were always beating on the main protagonist—Kevin rode his bike back home. He wanted to check on the fox anyway.

Entering through the front door and taking off his shoes, Kevin walked all the way to his room. He wanted to see how the fox's wound was healing. It should be mostly healed up by now.

There was a yip when he entered and Kevin was surprised to see the fox he had rescued was wide awake and staring right at him with twin, emerald eyes. It was a very unusual color for fox eyes. Kevin was sure most had yellow or dark brown eyes. As far as he was concerned, this was just another sign that there was something different about this fox.

"Hello there," Kevin greeted as he closed the door behind him and walked towards the bed. Just because there was something strange about the mammal didn't mean he was going to be distrustful of her. She was still a fox, and as an animal she inherently had a leg up on earning his trust.

After all, what could an animal do to him?

Well, if it was some super powered, mutant fox, probably a lot, but that was beside the point.

The fox's eyes followed him as he moved, her two tails swaying back and forth, up and down and from side to side in random, organic patterns that seemed to have no rhyme or reason to them. It was like her tails moved disassociated from her mind. How strange.

Kevin sat down at the edge of the bed.

"I didn't expect you to be up and about so soon."

He reached out with a hand, but paused, noticing the way the fox flinched at the action, as if expecting him to strike or something. Maybe it was just because she was a fox and they had an inherent disliking of humans, but Kevin thought there might be something more to her reaction than simple fear of humans.

"It's alright. I'm not going to hurt you," Kevin reassured the small kit as he finished his movement and his hand gently descended on her head. Her body stiffened for a moment, but as he began to caress and stroke her ears, her muscles relaxed and she began nuzzling her face into his hand.

A smile made its way onto Kevin's face at this. Deciding to be a fair bit bolder he scooped her up and placed her in his lap before he continued pampering her. After an initial moment of what could only be wariness from her, the fox relaxed and curled up in his lap.

She made for an adorable sight.

A moment later, while Kevin was cooing over how cute the fox was, a loud gurgling erupted from his stomach, making the young man blink. The fox shot up, her ears twitching as she too was startled by the loud noise next to her.

"I guess I'm a little hungry," Kevin said a tad sheepishly. "And I'm betting you are too, so why don't I make us something to eat?" The fox yipped, seemingly in agreement—which was impossible, of course, Kevin chided himself for the thought; foxes couldn't understand English—and Kevin scooped her up and made his way into the kitchen.

He set the fox down on the counter top. It would need to be wiped down for hair after this, but he really didn't mind all that much. It only took a second or two clean something like that.

"So let's see," Kevin frowned as he looked through the fridge to see what he should make for dinner. "I remember reading that foxes are omnivorous, so we'll definitely need some meat." He pulled out a package of steaks he had bought a few days ago. He hadn't expected to cook them so soon, but those were the breaks.

Setting the steak down on the counter, he looked over at the fox, who had been watching him the entire time. "Now the only question is should I cook a steak for you? Or do you eat it raw?" Well, she was a fox, so she probably ate it raw, but... "What the...?"

Kevin was given a slight surprise when the fox yipped and walked over to the small, portable grill situated right next to the stove top. She pointed at the grill with one paw, then at the two steaks, then back to the grill.

"So... you want me to cook it for you?"

He received a yip and a nod. Kevin paused.

"Can you understand me?"

Another yip. Another nod.

"Huh?" Kevin scratched the back of his head as he tried to come to terms with this new development. Maybe his theory about a government conspiracy wasn't that off the mark. Perhaps this fox had been gifted with a human or near human level intellect... or something, through genetic experimentation.

Then again, maybe not.

In either event, Kevin just decided to accept the fact that the fox could understand him and not question it. Some things were better left unquestioned. It would probably be safer for his sanity as well.

He continued working on dinner. Unlike most teenage males Kevin was actually a pretty decent cook. In keeping with the theme of most animes that center around a teenage protagonist, Kevin's mother was almost never home. Thus he had been forced to learn how to cook, lest he end up having to eat nothing but TV dinners every day. Granted, he could only cook simple meals, but it was enough to get by.

The two steaks were prepared with only a bit of seasonings: some salt, pepper and olive oil. Deciding to add at least a few greens, he steamed a couple of vegetables in the microwave. In a little over fifteen minutes, dinner was ready.

"Here we are." Kevin put the two steaks on separate plates (his had the one with the majority of vegetables on it) and set them down on the table. "Two medium rare steaks."

He turned to get the fox so he could bring her over to the table without injuring herself, but was surprised to find she had already hopped off the counter top and was now jumping onto the table via the chair.

"Well, looks like you don't need my help." The fox seemed to yip in agreement before digging into the food with much gusto. Kevin decided to follow suit.

As he ate, he watched the fox carefully as she tore into the juicy, red meat on her plate. Despite the fact that she had no hands and couldn't use any utensils, she ate with a surprising amount of poise. Not even a drop of blood or a strip of meat managed to make its way onto her fur coat or face.

He didn't know animals could eat with such... refinement? No. Maybe grace was a better word. In either event, watching the fox eat without making even a tiny mess was just another sign that this was not a normal fox.

Dinner was soon finished. Kevin took the dishes and rinsed them of blood before putting them in the dish washer. After wiping off the counter, he made his way to the couch, where he proceeded to sit down and turn on the TV. The small fox kit followed him, hopping onto the couch and curling up on his lap.

"What?" asked Kevin as the tiny critter looked up at him with large, emerald eyes. It was such an adorable look that he nearly cooed at the small kit. He didn't, but it was a near thing. "Do you want me to pet your ears some more?"

"Yip!"

"Kinda pushy, aren't you?" asked Kevin, though one of his hands did end up going to the fox's ear, where it began to pet and caress the tiny thing. The small, red furred creature gave a half-hearted yip, her eyes closing in what appeared to be pleasure.

That was how the next two hours were spent, him watching

TV as he idly rubbed the fox's ears and the fox making strange yet somehow happy sounding noises as her ears were rubbed. It was only after the clock showed 9:00 pm that Kevin decided it was time for bed.

"Come on," Kevin said, standing up. The fox hopped down to the floor and looked at him as he began walking away. After a moment, she followed the blond teenager into the bathroom.

Once he finished brushing and flossing and rinsing with mouthwash, Kevin walked into his room, changed into a pair of plain black boxers, climbed onto the bed, but didn't get under the covers. The fox followed him, hopping onto the bed as well, and Kevin decided it was time to check her bandages to see how her wound was doing.

"Alright, just lie down while I undo these bandages," Kevin instructed the tiny fox. She complied, laying down with her paws stretched out. Kevin proceeded to carefully take off the bandages. He wasn't very shocked to find that the wound was almost gone. There was just a very small, thin line that was healing even as he continued to look at it. He suspected it would be gone by tomorrow.

"It looks like you're not bleeding anymore," he murmured mostly to himself. "So I guess we don't have to put more bandages on you," he paused to look at the fox. "Unless you want me to?" The fox shook her head. "Guess not then."

Deftly scooping her into his arms, Kevin crawled further into bed and made himself comfortable. He set the fox down on his chest as he lay on his back. The tiny creature curled up on top of him, getting comfortable for the night.

"Good night." A soft yip that sounded surprisingly similar to 'night' came from the fox as Kevin's eyes began to grow heavy and he drifted off to sleep.

Had he stayed awake a little longer, he would have noticed the pair of emerald green orbs that remained awake for some time to come, staring at him with a look of adoration. Pray for him.

Chapter 4: My Little Kit... or Not

Kevin woke up the next morning to find a small weight on his chest. Blinking several times as his mind began the slow rebooting process, going from *'half dead'* to *'partially cognizant'*, Kevin looked down to see that the weight was actually the small fox he had rescued the other day. She was still asleep and had curled up into a tiny ball on his chest.

Now that he knew what the unusual weight was, he let his head drop back down onto the pillow with a sigh. A glance to his left revealed the still somewhat broken alarm clock on the nightstand. It read 5:45. That was a little early to be awake on a school day, but not late enough that he could afford to go back to sleep.

How troublesome.

It took him several minutes of lying there before deciding it was time to move. Or maybe that was just how long it took his mind to actually start working correctly. Either way, it was time to get up.

Cradling the fox against him so she wouldn't fall and awaken, he sat up, and put her on the pillow his head had just vacated. For just a second, Kevin thought he saw a very human-like frown come to the fox's face. It disappeared soon enough as the fox snuggled deeper into the memory foam pillow's warmth and Kevin played it off as a trick of the light. Foxes didn't have the facial muscles needed to frown like a human did, after all.

Minus waking up to a fox on his chest, Monday morning started the same as it always did. After taking a shower and getting dressed in a pair of blue jeans and a band T-shirt, he made it into the kitchen where began cooking a breakfast of eggs and bacon.

Standing in front of the stove, with two frying pans on two of the stove's cook-top, Kevin absently stirred the eggs in one and let the bacon cook in the other. Soon the sound of sizzling filled the room and the smell of cooked bacon wafted into the air.

A yip alerted him to the fact that he was no longer alone. Craning his neck as he continued to scramble his eggs, Kevin saw the fox was awake and sitting on the table again, staring at him with an awfully strange look. Stranger than last time she had been watching him at any rate. He couldn't quite put his finger on what that look was, but it was kind of disturbing.

Shaking his head, the young man greeted his foxy companion, no pun intended. "Good morning." Kevin wondered if anyone else spoke with animals so casually, or if he was just unusual. "You hungry?"

Definitely unusual.

"Yip!"

Kevin couldn't be sure, but he was positive she was saying 'yes'. The way her head bobbed up and down in the semblance of a nod helped. Just a little.

"Alright then. Just let me add a few more pieces of bacon for you."

"Yip, yip!"

Not long after, Kevin was seated at the table, eating from his plate, while the fox ate from the plate he had set for her. Once more, Kevin was able to see how strangely clean the fox was when she ate. It still kind of bothered him, seeing something like that, but he tried to put it out of his mind.

Breakfast was soon finished, the dishes were in the dish washer, his teeth were brushed, and Kevin was slinging his back pack over his shoulder as he prepared to leave for school.

There was just one problem.

"Yip! Yip, yip!"

The fox was following him.

"I'm sorry, but you can't go with me."

Was it strange that he felt guilty when the fox's head dropped to the floor in a very human gesture of sadness? Probably. At least, it would be if you weren't an animal lover like him.

"If you came to school with me everyone would know that there's a fox in my apartment and then the landlord would find out and you wouldn't be able to stay here anymore." There must be something seriously wrong with him if he was taking the time to explain something as complex as why he couldn't take her with him to school, whether or not she was a Super Fox with incredible intelligence. "There's a no pet policy in this complex, which means we're not actually allowed to have any animals in here. Not even gold fish."

Seeing the fox look up at him with those big, green eyes, staring at him imploringly had Kevin's inner fan-boy squealing.

Of course, he would never do something so unmanly as squeal out loud—yesterday's small incident where he had literally 'squee'd' notwithstanding—so he didn't. What he did do, however, was scoop up the fox and rub his nose against her snout. She seemed to like this because she started licking his face.

"Aw... You're just the cutest thing I've ever seen!" That wasn't a squeal, by the way. There was no 'squeeing' involved there. "Try not to be too sad, okay? It's not like I'm leaving for good. Just until after school. Luckily, I should be home pretty early today since we actually have a half day and I don't have practice."

He set the fox down and stood up. She still seemed depressed, but more from not getting anymore pampering than because he was leaving. Or at least, that was the feeling he got.

"So, you be good and don't let any of the neighbors or landlord see you." Kevin tried to look stern as he spoke, he really did, but she was just so darn cute that it was impossible. "Okay?"

"Yip!"

"Alright then, I'll see you when I get home."

***

Kevin arrived in his first class of the day and slowly sank into the chair. All around him people were chatting it up, talking about their weekends or the last sports game or latest fashion. In most cases, he might have joined in, but he did his best to ignore them this time. He wasn't in the mood for idle conversation.

"Hey, Kevin!"

Unless your name just so happened to be Lindsay Diane.

Kevin stiffened as he heard the familiar voice of his crush. He turned to see the girl in question, her blond pixie-cut bobbing as she walked up to him, and a smile on her cute face.

"L-L-L-L... Lindsay!"

"That's my name," Lindsay said, her smile turning into a teasing grin. "Think you could add an extra 'L' in there for me?"

Oh god! It was his crush! His crush was here, sitting next to him and talking to him and... oh, wait. They shared homeroom together. Of course she would be talking to him and sitting next to him! What should he do?! What should he say?!

Okay, Kevin. You can do this. Just don't panic and play it cool. You've got this.

"The sky is awfully black today!"

Lindsay paused halfway into her seat, blinking. "Uh... no, the sky is blue, actually."

Kevin flushed. "Right. O-o-o-of course! What I meant to say is the new black is orange!"

"Actually, I think it's red." Lindsay leaned in close to her friend, causing Kevin's face to catch fire in an almost literal sense. "Are you feeling alright, Kevin? You're looking a little redder than usual today."

Kevin didn't answer, because at that moment, Lindsay was leaning over him... and he could see down her shirt.

Lindsay—along with everyone else—were soon witnesses to Kevin's incredible capacity for holding gallons of blood when, without warning, blood shot from his nose like fire hydrant. The young man was thrown off his seat and into the far wall where he slammed into it with a harsh crack, then slowly proceeded to slide down.

Oddly enough, while the room was now painted red, Lindsay, who'd been standing right in front of her friend, remained pristine as ever. She stared at the now unconscious, bleeding from the nose Kevin, blinking.

"What just happened?"

***

Aside from his horribly shameful first class, school that day had been the same as it was everyday. Classes were boring, aside from a few that he liked.

Kevin went to Desert Cactus High School. It wasn't a very original name, but most high schools in Arizona seemed to be named after a cactus, a desert, a mountain, or all three, so it didn't bother him too much.

The school had over 1,000 students and consisted of large, blue and white buildings shaped as either a square or a rectangle. It had all the things a school of its size was expected to have: a library, over 150 classrooms, a large gym with a weight room, a theater, a cafeteria, a track field, a football field and an indoor pool. For a school, it was pretty impressive.

Because today was a half day, they didn't have lunch, so Kevin was able to leave right at one p.m..

And speaking of, just what was up with half days anyways? They were practically useless. You only go to a few of your classes and most of the time you are so busy waiting for the quick day to end that you don't pay attention in class. Kevin had never seen the point in half days.

A few of Kevin's friends asked him if he wanted to go to the arcade with them, which was really one of the only places they could go aside from the mall, which would be a boring place to spend time at.

Kevin declined.

Eric had teased him a bit after that, asking him if he was eager to go home and spend time with his fox lady, pun very much intended.

Kevin had smacked him in the back of the head.

It only took twenty minutes to get from school to home and visa versa on bike. That was another thing that was different about Kevin. Unlike most students under the age of sixteen, Kevin did not ride the bus. He disliked buses. Instead, he rode his bike just about everywhere.

Entering the apartment, Kevin expected to be greeted by a very excited fox kit. When he was not, a frown marred his face. Absently, he took off his shoes and made his way into the living room before calling out, "Hello! I'm home!"

The soft "pitter patter" of feet reached his ears. Kevin blinked. There was something off about the sound. He couldn't quite put his finger on it, but it wasn't what he expected a fox's walk to sound like.

Whatever the case was, he didn't have time to think any further on it because at that exact moment a figure appeared in the hallway leading to his room.

Kevin's eyes widened.

It wasn't a fox. It didn't have four legs. It wasn't even an animal.

It was a girl.

A very, very beautiful girl.

Screw beautiful. This girl had to be the most gorgeous example of a female that he had ever seen. And considering he had seen all the posters of half naked super models Eric had all over his walls, that was really saying something.

Her long, crimson tresses descended like a effervescent waterfall. Bangs framed a face that looked like it had been lovingly carved from alabaster by the hands of angels, with a small, button nose set between two large, innocent looking emerald colored eyes and a pair of perfectly shaped, ruby red, cupid bow lips. A single strand of hair fell over her left shoulder, following the contours of her collar bone to the swell of her left breast, before curving over the well-crafted bosom and ending as it reached her underbreast. The rest of her hair trailed all the way down her back to her butt. Her *bare* butt.

Which brought another point home. The girl before him was naked. As in, bare as the day she was born, completely exposed, all natural. Whatever you want to call it.

If Kevin's mind were not lost in limbo at the sight of this extraordinarily beautiful and naked girl, he would have had trouble determining where to look. At her angelic face, her slender neck and shoulders as they led into what Eric would call a grade-A chest, or that slim and athletically trimmed waist that gently sloped into a set of beautifully curved hips that had a very small patch of red hair just above the space between her legs. And speaking of legs, hers were incredible, mile long legs with beautifully crafted thighs and calves, flawless skin and sensuous curves, ended in a pair of small feet with cute little toes.

"Beloved," the girl breathed out in barely masked excitement. Her legs tensed, her toes curled and gripped the carpet and her knees bent as if she were prepared to jump into the air. It only lasted for a second before her body shivered from head to toe. After that, she took a deep breath and straightened up.

Then she smiled at him. It was the kind of smile that caused hearts to burst, and his heart was no different. It felt like it was going to explode out of his chest.

It also caused him to fall to the floor as his legs turned into jelly.

Hitting the ground with a dull thud, Kevin landed on his backside. It was a good thing he had made it onto the carpet instead of remaining on the tiled floor near the doorway or that would have hurt a lot more.

Another thing to be thankful for was that even though his mind was gone to places that no one in their right mind would ever want to go (the teenage mind is a horrible place), his body still had instinctual reactions. His hands were quick to move behind him, keeping him from falling over completely without his mind telling him to do so.

Whether this was so he would not smack his head on the floor or because his eyes wanted to keep gazing upon the vision of perfection in front of him was unknown, even to Kevin.

"Welcome home," her voice sounded like the gentle tinkling of wind chimes. It was lilting and beautiful and if Kevin were not already on the ground, that would have surely sent him down. "I missed you."

"Wha... Who... Eh...?"

Wow, monosyllables. As always, Kevin manages to speak with an eloquence that astounds all who hear him.

"Oh, that's right, you don't really know who I am since you haven't seen me like this before," the girl giggled. It was a beautiful sound and it sent all kinds of shivers down Kevin's spine. It was good thing then, that he wasn't really all there. Who knows what else that sound would have done to him if he were. "My name is Lilian Pnévma, but you may call me Lilly, or anything else you would prefer."

Despite her words, Kevin was not listening. Rather, the sole focus of his mind seemed to be going towards his vision, which would explain why he was staring at the girl with a stupid, open mouthed look on his face. We should probably just be glad he wasn't drooling like some kind of moron.

"However, I would be particularly pleased if you called me You Sexy Thing You."

With the light from the large window across the room creating beams of luminescence that illuminated her form, this girl, Lilian, seemed almost like an angel. Her long locks of gloriously red hair looked like it was on fire and there was a strange halo effect surrounding her, causing her perfectly unblemished and silky skin to gain an almost ethereal glow.

"My three sizes are 99-58-90. Oh! Wait," Lilian suddenly looked thoughtful as she tapped her lower lip with the tip of her index finger and scrunched her nose cutely. Kevin made a strangled sound at the utterly bewitching expression of adorable thoughtfulness on her face that went ignored by the girl doing the face making. "You Americans don't use the Metric System, do you? In which case, my three sizes would be 39-23-35."

Kevin didn't know how someone who couldn't be much older than him could have such an incredible hip to bust ratio. Of course, that was going off the assumption that he was actually paying attention to what she said, which he most assuredly was not. There were other, more distracting things keeping his mind occupied.

Like the fact that this girl was *still* naked.

"I don't really have much experience with this kind of thing, but then, given your age, I don't really think you have too much either." Her cute smile was back in place as she looked down at him. "I'm really looking forward to learning more about you as we deepen and explore our relationship together."

Really, how was it possible for someone, *anyone* to be this beautiful? Surely there was some kind of universal law that said everyone had some kind of imperfection. Even her feet seemed to be perfect. Perfect feet! What the heck was up with that!?

"I know we have just met recently, but if you wish to explore the more... physical aspects of our relationship, I would have no issues if we started right now." And with that, she clasped her hands behind her back, the act causing her to unconsciously push up her already magnificent bust.

Or maybe not unconsciously. This girl had to know what her body did to boys his age, right?

In either case, poor Kevin was unable to withstand anymore stimulation. He let out a strangled gurgle, his eyes rolled into the back of his head, and his arms gave out, causing him to fall onto his back. The last thing he saw before darkness claimed him was bright green irises surrounded by crimson strands of hair.

Chapter 5: A Kitsune's Mate

It was a strange feeling, being roused to consciousness after getting knocked out from over-stimulation, something Kevin could now officially attest to. His mind felt incredibly foggy, sort of like how he imagined those spoiled brats would feel when they were hazed out on drugs or something. Even the most basic thought felt beyond his reach.

It certainly wasn't the most pleasant of sensations. How those drug addicts dealt with it was beyond him.

He also had a splitting headache. It felt like Thor had taken his war-hammer, Mjölner, and bashed it against his head to help generate a thunder storm. Kevin could not help but wonder if he had smacked his head against the floor when he had passed out.

At the same time, he was surprisingly comfortable. The pillow his head was resting against was velvety soft and incredibly warm and felt oh so nice. There wasn't much that could beat the feeling of comfort and contentment that this strangely textured pillow gave him.

The fingers that were running through his hair also had a hand (pun not intended) in soothing his pounding headache. Kevin could not help but release a pleased sigh as a set of slightly longer than average nails gently scratched against his scalp. God, was there anything better... than... this...

...

...?

Hold up. Since when did pillows have fingers to run through his hair? For that matter, since when did pillows possess such warmth?

And now that he was thinking about it, pillows didn't feel all... strange like this. It didn't have the soft cloth texture of a pillow. So then what...?

Cracking his eyes open, Kevin found himself staring into bright green irises that were set into a face that was halfway hidden by a pair of well-developed breasts. A pair of well developed, *naked* breasts.

"Are you finally awake, Beloved?"

Eyes going wide, Kevin had a moment where he experienced the "WTF" kind of confusion anyone in his situation would suffer before he realized where he was. On a lap. The lap of the girl who had caused him to pass out in the first place. The lap of the girl who was still quite naked.

Well... at least now he knew why his, ahem, pillow, felt so odd. That had to count for something at least.

Kevin's already wide eyes widened even more as he found himself staring at a gently smiling face, judging from the soft and warm look in her eyes as she fondly gazed down at him. Her enchanting emerald eyes, which were alight with relief as she realized he was finally awake.

He couldn't see her lips, because at least half of her face was being blocked by the two large hills on her chest, but he could almost imagine the smile they were giving him at that moment.

Or at least, he would have been able to, if he were not dealing with other problems at the moment. Like those breasts, for example.

"I'm glad you're finally awake," her eyes held an obvious relief as she spoke. She ran her fingers through his hair again, but it didn't bring him any comfort this time. If anything, it made him feel like there was something kicking him from inside of his stomach, like some kind of monster was trying to break free from his gut after he ate some really bad soup. And yes, that was a *Spaceballs* reference. "I hope you're feeling better. I was really worried when you fainted on me."

It took Kevin exactly 1.2 seconds before the reality of his

situation came crashing down on him.

His reaction was not quite what most people would expect, but it was hilarious nevertheless.

"Hiiiiiiii!"

Releasing the most unmanly of squeals in the history of man, Kevin's head jerked up as he tried to get off Lilian's lap. It was a move committed out of instinct. It was also incredibly stupid.

Why was it so stupid? There were many reasons. The two biggest though was that, aside from the fact that it didn't actually get his head off Lilian's lap, it also brought both him and her a lot of pain.

Because the move was done out of reflex, Kevin had not taken into account the fact that Lilian's head was hovering just a little bit above his. So when he jerked his head up at such startling speeds that Lilian had no time to do anything other then widen her eyes, his forehead ended up smacking into the red head's chin, eliciting a cry of pain from the girl as her head was jerked backwards and upwards from the force of the unintentional strike.

Newtons Third Law of Motion states that when one body exerts a force on a second body, the second body simultaneously exerts a force of equal magnitude and opposite in direction to that of the first body. That is exactly what happened here. When Kevin's head hit Lilian's, her chin exerted the same amount of force that his head did, launching him back to his original position on her lap.

At least it did until the boy, in his pain, rolled off her lap and then off the bed entirely. He landed on the floor with a loud 'oof!' and brought his hands up to his head where it had met Lilian's chin.

He couldn't be sure because of the pain he was in, but Kevin was almost positive he was seeing stars.

No. Wait. Those were just spots where his vision had blurred out. Never mind.

"Ouch," Lilian moaned in pain as Kevin released his own pained groans on the floor below her. "You have a really hard head, Beloved. That hurt."

"I-I'm sorry," Kevin apologized automatically, completely missing the term of endearment that she had used for him. He had more important things on his mind. Like his headache for one. It had come back and brought friends. "I didn't mean to do that."

"It's okay," Lilian shook her head to clear it, then leaned over the side of the bed to look at Kevin. "Are you alright? You look like you took a hard fall."

"Yeah, I'm fine," Kevin sat up, still looking a bit dazed. "Thank you for your... Gurk!"

Yes. Kevin did just say 'gurk'.

The reason for this was, naturally, Lilian. The girl in question was still sitting there, looking at him with what could only be concern as she absently rubbed her now sore chin. There was a slight bruise on it, though it was disappearing at an astonishing rate.

She was also still naked. It was bad enough that she was female. That she had absolutely no clothes on was quite possibly the worst situation for a boy like Kevin to be in.

He could see every bountiful curve of her glorious body. No part of her was invisible to his eyes. Even the most sacred place a woman possessed was exposed to him as she let her legs rest over the side of the bed so she could look down at him.

Eric would have likely died of a heart attack if he had seen what Kevin was seeing.

Kevin felt like he was going to be sick. His stomach was doing flip flops and this was on top of all the butterflies he could feel, fluttering around in his gut. He could feel his heart hammering against his chest like a war drum or some kind of battering ram as it did its utmost to burst out from his rib cage. It wouldn't surprise him if it ended up exploding from all the pressure.

Worse still, he could feel all the blood in his body rushing towards two specific places. One of them was his face. The other shall not be mentioned for the sake of keeping this chapter to an M-rating.

"I'm glad you're alright," the girl said with a relieved sigh as she placed a hand against her chest, inadvertently drawing his eyes towards her large and perfectly shaped... um... assets. If Kevin's mouth had not been dry before, it was now. "I was so worried when you passed out."

"Gu... Huh... What..."

"I wasn't really sure what to do," Lilian continued, completely heedless of the way Kevin's eyes were beginning to bulge out of their sockets as he continued to stare at her nude frame. His face was beginning to turn blue as well, all except for the twin beacons of red on his cheeks. Breath Kevin, breath. "All I could think to do was put you in bed, but I wanted to do something like what you did for me when I was injured, except you didn't really have an injury that I could bandage."

"Wha... Wha... Wha..."

"Beloved?" Lilian looked down at Kevin in concern as his face began turning purple. Without really thinking about it, the beautiful girl climbed off the bed, got on the floor and crawled towards him on all fours.

Kevin thought he might die of sexy. Since the moment he had laid eyes on this girl (all of one or two hours ago before he passed out), he had known she was a beauty beyond most. Never was that beauty more obvious than now.

Crawling on all fours, she moved invariably closer with each 'step' she took. Placing one hand in front of the other in an almost painfully slow—at least to Kevin, feline motion that inevitably pushed her breasts together with each step. Behind the girl, her tail swayed hypnotically like an inverted pendulum, drawing the eye along the curve of her back to her small, shapely rear.

It was the most erotic act he had ever witnessed.

What was worse was that Lilian had no clue she was doing it.

And wait…. what was this about a tail?

Before Kevin had the chance to ponder the strange, furry object swaying behind her, Lilian was directly in front of him. The poor boy's entire body froze solid as the red haired beauty crawled onto his sprawled lap, straddling his legs with her gorgeous thighs as her hands went to the back of his neck.

With little warning, she pulled his head towards hers. For a second, his mind went blank.

It then went into a rapid series of thoughts that passed through his head at a rate so insane it was a wonder brain matter didn't start oozing out of his ears from overheating.

His thoughts were as follows: *'Ohmygod! Ohmygod! Ohmygod! She'sgoingtokissme! Ohmygod! Ohmygod! Ohmygod! Thoseboobs! Ohmygod! Ohmygod! Whatdoldo!? Whatdoldo!?'*

Kevin's mind was in a full-blown panic. His heart beat in his chest with rapid, staccato bursts. It felt like it was about to explode!

(Un?)fortunately, she didn't kiss him, but it's not like what she did was much better for his blood pressure. She pressed her forehead against his, bringing their faces so close that Kevin could make out every millimeter of her flawless, unblemished skin and lovely facial features.

This was the first time he had been in such an intimate position with any girl—Kevin was not going to count when his head had been lying on her lap, he had been unconscious for most of that anyways. Ever.

It was overstimulating.

"Are you alright?"

Wide blue eyes met concerned green. Lilian's breath washed over his mouth, her lips mere inches from his own. She was so close that her pleasant, natural scent was invading his nose, addling his mind. He was beginning to feel light headed again. And his stomach was churning.

Dear God! He really was going to die if this kept up!

"Wha… wha… wha…" somehow, miraculously, Kevin found the strength of will to speak, even though his mind and body were very close to shutting down again. "What the hell are you doing!?"

His shout startled Lilian enough that he was able to slip out from under her nude body and out of her grasp. He crawled backwards on hands and feet like some kind of crab, trying to put as much distance between him and this strange, naked girl as possible.

"What do you mean?" Lilian tilted her head and blinked several times. "I was just checking to see if you're alright."

"That's not what I meant!" Kevin practically shrieked as he tried to keep his cool. It wasn't working too well, especially when his eyes found her perfectly rounded breasts again. He was beginning to feel sick. If this kept up, he might end up losing what was left of his lunch.

Kevin jerked his head away so he wouldn't stare. A little too late for that, boy.

"It's not?" Lilian tilted her head. "Then what were you talking about?"

"Why are you naked!?"

Lilian tilted her head the other way, an adorable look of confusion on her face. Don't throw up, Kevin. Don't throw up.

"I don't have any clothes to wear." The way she said that made it sound like it should have been obvious.

"What do you mean you don't have any clothes!?" Kevin's voice was very high pitched. "You can't just go walking around naked! You must have something you can put on!?" His voice was pleading by the end.

"No," Lilian shook her head, "I lost my clothes a while ago. I lost them a few hours before you rescued me."

Naturally, Kevin, in his panic, embarrassment and the slew of other emotions he was feeling but couldn't place, completely missed her words about him rescuing her.

"Guh...." Kevin buried his face in his hands. "This cannot be happening," he mumbled. "There's no way there can be a naked girl in my room. This is just a dream. A really bad dream."

Lilian frowned at Kevin's mumbling. Her frown increased as she looked down at her nude frame. After a few seconds of silently contemplating her own body, she looked back up at Kevin.

"Does it bother you that I'm naked?" She sounded very disappointed. "Do you not find me appealing?"

"That's not the point!" Kevin wished he could crawl into a hole and die. Or wake up from this nightmare, for this could be nothing less. An incredibly erotic nightmare, but a nightmare nonetheless.

Rubbing his face with his hands in frustration, he tried to make his reasoning for her clear. "You shouldn't be walking around naked in front of others! It...—it isn't appropriate!"

"But, you're my mate," Lilian pointed out, as if these words solved everything. "It's perfectly acceptable if you see me like this."

"Mate?" Kevin blinked. What the hell did that mean? Was she talking about... surely she wasn't saying that he and her were...?

He blushed, unable to think about the implications of her statement.

Kevin was easily embarrassed like that.

"Yes," Lilian gave him a truly beautiful smile. Kevin felt his face heating up just from looking at it. "You took care of me when I was injured. You treated me with kindness and compassion instead of scorn like some of the other human boys who have seen me like that did." She placed a hand against her bare breast. Kevin's eyes were invariably drawn to it. He hadn't thought his face could get any redder then it was now. He had been wrong, apparently. "You don't know how much your kindness meant to me. Of the warmth I felt when you treated me so tenderly and lovingly. I haven't been able to get it out of my mind."

Kevin thought the girl was beautiful before, but when she began blushing, he thought he might actually die of moe. A girl with such a killer body should not be able to look so dang adorable.

"Is it any wonder that I've fallen in love you?"

For that single moment, Kevin's entire world came to a screeching halt. He stared at the girl with wide eyes. She did not just say what he thought she said.

"I'm sorry, but did you just say that you're in love with me?"

Surely she was going to say that she wasn't, that he had just been hearing things. Yes, he must have heard her wrong. That was it. He just had something crazy in his ears and had misheard what she said or misconstrued her words.

Lilian tilted her head to the side, wondering if he had really just asked her that, then nodded. "Yes."

Dammit.

"You don't even know me!" Kevin very nearly shouted. Lilian jumped in surprise. "How could you possibly love me when we've never even met until just a few hours ago?"

"What do you mean?" Lilian pressed a finger to her lips, her brows furrowed cutely. "Of course I love you."

"You can't fall in love with someone you don't even know!"

"Eh? Why not?" Lilian crossed her arms and pouted at him. "I've thought about this long and hard, you know." Yeah, because the little bit of time that she had known him was a really long time. Definitely long enough for her to make a decision like this. Yeah right. "I love you."

Kevin felt a headache coming on. Rubbing his forehead, he tried to think about what he should do about this strange, beautiful girl who had, for some reason he simply couldn't fathom, decided she was in love with him. There had to be something he could say that would convince her she was not in love with him. Right?

Good luck with that.

"Look, you can't just fall in love with someone you only just met a few hours ago," he started, only to inexplicably stop after making the mistake of looking at her again. Almost immediately, blood began rushing to his face.

He tried to look away, to look at anything other than the enchanting female, sitting on his carpet. It wouldn't do to find himself distracted by her beauty, or to pass out when he was trying to explain why she couldn't be in love with him. That would be bad. Really bad.

It was while he was trying not to look at the femme in front of him that he noticed it again. The furry red appendage with the white tip that he had seen only a minute before had curved around Lilian's body and was now resting across her lap, hiding the treasure between her legs. His curiosity got the better of him.

"What is that?"

"Hmm?" Lilian tilted her head in curiosity. "What is what?"

"That," Kevin pointed at the red... thing in her lap. He had seen it before, but it couldn't possibly be what he thought it was. No. That was just crazy. "What is that?"

Lilian looked down at where he was pointing. "Oh! You mean my tail?"

"Tail?" Kevin murmured. Well, it certainly looked like a tail. It was large and bushy and red and had a white tip. It looked like a larger version of one of the tails he had seen on that fox he rescued.

Speaking of which, just where was that fox anyways?

He's not very bright, this Kevin. Or maybe this is what they call denial?

Lilian looked up and smiled. "Would you like to see it?"

Before Kevin could tell her that, no, he did not want to see her tail (and boy was that a really bad pun), the girl was already moving.

Pushing herself back onto her hands and knees, the red haired female slowly turned around, revealing her bare backside to Kevin.

Kevin's eyes widened and his pupils dilated. Blood flowed into his cheeks and his breathing picked up as he found himself staring at more perfection. Starting from her slender shoulders, Kevin's eyes traveled down her frame, taking in the delicate curve of her back as it flowed into the small, shapely and perfectly formed rear end that would have made the likes of Eric salivate.

Did everything about this girl have to be so dang sexy?

As Kevin found himself trying to look away from the sight, his eyes finally found what they had been talking about. Her tail.

Jutting out from her tail bone just above where her firm looking, peach shaped butt began was a furry red tail with a white tip. Really, it was almost impossible to miss. Just how he had missed it was beyond him.

It's called shock. It's also called a Plot Device, but let's not get into that right now.

"A tail," Kevin found himself muttering as Lilian (thankfully) turned back around and sat back down on her thighs. Not that it did much good because there was just as much to look at on her front as there was her backside, but Kevin did his best to ignore all that. "You have a tail."

"And ears," Lilian said, smiling, "Don't forget about my ears."

"Ears?" Kevin found himself blinking as he stared at her head and saw what she was talking about. Sticking out of her head and parting her beautiful crimson tresses were two long, furry red animal ears with white tips. They were currently standing upright and perky on her head.

How the heck had he missed those?

Such is the power of a woman's innate sexiness. It possessed the ability to make men go blind to all but her body, with everything else relegated to the background. He would realize this, eventually.

"Those are fox ears," Kevin, being the animal lover that he was, recognized the ears for what they were despite the fact that they were sitting on the head of a girl around his age for some reason he still couldn't fathom. Cosplay maybe? "And that's a fox tail."

"Of course they are," Lilian nodded to his words. "I'm a Kitsune. It's only natural I would have fox ears and tails."

"Kitsune?" Kevin blinked. He knew that term, vaguely, but he still knew it. "You mean those supernatural creatures from Japanese mythology?" Kevin tried to recall what he knew about them. "Those are fox's that can shape-shift into humans and generally cause a lot of mischief, right?" If this girl was a Kitsune, it probably didn't bode well for him.

"I have no idea why people think we came from Japan." Lilian pouted, folding her arms under her bust which inevitably pushed up her breasts. Kevin gulped. "It's not like all Kitsune live in Japan. We're pretty much spread across the globe. My family is from Greece. Well," Lilian looked up in thought, "my mom actually came from England, but we've lived in Greece for as long as I can remember."

"Is... is that so?" Kevin tried to wrap his mind around what he was being told. Needless to say, it wasn't easy. "So... you're a Kitsune?"

Lilian nodded and smiled. "Yes."

"A real life Kitsune?"

"Of course silly," Lilian giggled. "What else would I be?"

"Oh... okay," Kevin nodded...

...And then he passed out... again... for the second time that day.

He wouldn't realize it until much later, or maybe he did and just didn't fully understand all the implications, but from that day onwards, his life would be forever changed.

Welcome to the wonderful world of Yōkai.

Chapter 6: Stolen First Kiss

Kevin's rise from half asleep to at least partially awake was a surprisingly slow process the next day. Granted, it normally took him a while to wake up, but today it was even slower than usual.

Of course, when one thought about it, maybe it really wasn't so surprising. After all, it wasn't everyday you learned that Kitsune actually existed and that the tiny fox kit you rescued a little over a day ago just happened to be one of them. That would catch anyone off guard.

One also had to take into account that said Kitsune wasn't just a Kitsune, but also an extraordinarily beautiful girl, and one who was apparently in love with him. If the fact that all those myths on Kitsune were real didn't cause enough shock to make someone pass out, then having a beautiful, naked female with foxy features claiming, for all intents and purposes, to be your soul mate, would. Especially if your name was Kevin Swift.

Yes, allowances had to be made for someone who'd had so many shocking revelations thrown at him within such a short time span.

Blinking several times as the sunlight filtered into his room through the window by his bed, Kevin tried to cut through the haze that had come over him and get his mind back into working order. It was a difficult process to be sure. While a part of the difficulty he had waking up this morning definitely had to do with the revelations that had been thrown at him last night, another part was due to the fulfilling warmth of his bed. It was a very comforting warmth that made him want to close his eyes and drift back off to sleep again.

But even with the veil of sleepiness that covered him, he could not help but wonder why this was. His bed had always been comfortable, yes, but not this comfortable. He had never felt the lulling sense of peace and contentment while sleeping in this bed that he did now. Not only were his eyes feeling droopy, but his body felt heavy, like it was being weighed down by something.

That might have had something to do with the pillow on top of him. It was so warm that Kevin couldn't help but want to snuggle into it and fall back asleep.

Deciding to do just that, Kevin tightened his hold around the body-length pillow and made to drift back off to sleep. Because more than half his mind was still caught in the land of dreams, he did not even bother to wonder why there was a body-length pillow on his bed when he had never had one before.

At least, not until the pillow moaned.

Kevin's eyes shot wide open. Like a bolt of lightning as it struck a large body of water, shock coursed through his nervous system and froze him in place. Wanting nothing more than to pretend he had not heard that, yet being unable to resist his own curiosity, Kevin found himself looking down.

Hair. The first thing he saw was hair. A lot of it. Long tresses of beautiful red hair splayed across his chest and the bed, looking like crimson flames as each strand caught the light of the morning sun that filtered into his room.

Creamy white skin was the next thing to catch his gaze. Making out the fair colored flesh of bare shoulders in between the gaps of hair was not very difficult. He could not see a face, which was currently nuzzling his chest, but he could most definitely feel the very feminine body that was pressing against his own.

Kevin could also feel warm breath hitting his chest. It caused shivers to run across his back and his skin to break out in goosebumps. Despite how pleasant the warm breath felt against his skin, his mind was more on the verge of panic than thinking about the pleasurable sensations.

In a situation like this, Kevin did the only thing he could think of.

He screamed. Loudly. Unleashing a shriek of surprise so loud that he likely woke up the entire apartment complex, the young high school student tried to scramble out of bed and away from the girl on top of him.

He really should have known better than to do that in a situation like this. Not only was she laying on top of him, but Lilian had a firm grasp around his torso, holding on like he was some kind of life-sized plushy. Even if he wanted to, he would have not been able to escape.

Not that this stopped him from trying. It just meant that instead of getting out from underneath the girl and off the bed, he ended up taking her with him when he fell.

"Oof!"

His back hitting the ground with a loud thump, all the air rushed out of his mouth. Lilian landed on his chest and stomach, further compounding the problem and increasing the amount of pain he was in as well as the speed with all the oxygen in his lungs was expelled.

Somehow, while Kevin ended up getting dazed from fall, Lilian was simply stirred enough to rise from her slumber. Kevin may have been envious that nothing really happened to her while he ended up suffering, but his mind was a bit too busy trying to figure out why spots were appearing in his vision.

And while Kevin was dealing with his spotty problem, the young Kitsune laying on top of him sat up, her thighs straddling Kevin's waist as she put one delicate and feminine hand on his chest to keep herself upright while the other moved to rub her eyes cutely.

"Uwah..." Lilian made strange but cute noises as she yawned widely enough that, were Kevin not currently trying to get his brain screwed on right after taking his fall, would have allowed him to see her elongated canines. As the girl began waking up, her foxy ears twitching slightly as the cool air from the fan hit her, her eyes looked down and immediately zeroed in on her mate.

"Morning, beloved." She gave him a sleepy smile. "Did you sleep well?"

Kevin blinked several times as the spots began slowly disappearing from his eyes. His lungs inhaled, sucking in some much needed oxygen, causing the rest of the spots to vanish. When he could finally see again, he was greeted with the sight of Lilian's face mere inches from his own.

"Gyah!"

Somehow, Kevin managed to scramble out from underneath Lilian's beautifully shaped thighs (Eric would be so disappointed), much to said girl's dissatisfaction (so was Lilian, apparently). She had been hoping he was finally over his surprise, or whatever he was dealing with by now so that they could get down to all the things that mates did, but it looked like that was still a ways off.

You are going to have to work much harder if you want to help Kevin get over himself, Lilian.

"Well, that's disappointing," Lilian said to no one in particular. Or at least, that's what appeared to be happening.

Sorry.

"It's okay. I know it's not your fault."

That's very kind of you to say. Thank you.

"You're welcome."

Kevin ignored the strange girl's rambling—just who was she talking to?—and pointed an accusing finger at her.

"You! What are you doing sleeping in my bed!?"

"What do you mean?" Lilian looked honestly confused by his question. And she was. As far as she could see, there was nothing wrong with what she had done. "Where else would I sleep?"

The question actually caught Kevin off guard for a second. It was a good question. Just where would she sleep?

It was as he thought about this that he remembered who he was talking to.

"How about in your own home?"

"Can't," Lilian shook her head. "My home is in Greece, and I have no way of getting there right now."

Kevin frowned. "What about your family? Your parents?"

"Well, my father's dead, I think," Lilian tapped her chin. "I never knew him, and mom doesn't talk about him that much."

"O-oh," Kevin looked away. Great, now he felt guilty for bringing up her parents. Way to make him feel like an insensitive jerk, Lilian. "Sorry."

"It's fine," Lilian smiled at him, not that he saw it, busy as he was trying to focus on anything but the beautiful naked girl sitting on the ground a few feet from him. "Like I said, I never knew him."

"So, um," Kevin scratched his chin. Wow, this was incredibly awkward. Couldn't this girl put some clothes on or something? At least then he might be able to look at her without his vision going dark. Oh, right. She had already told him she didn't actually have clothes to wear, hadn't she? Well shoot. "What about your mom?"

"Ah, well," Lilian blushed in embarrassment. "I don't actually know where she is right now. You see, I got separated from my family so..."

"So you're saying you don't have anywhere to go," Kevin sighed as he rubbed his face. He couldn't very well kick her out now, could he? Nope. Definitely not. It just wasn't in his nature to ignore someone when they were in trouble.

He was way too nice for his own good. Naturally. What Hero would be complete without having some kind of Hero complex or a 'saving people thing'? There wouldn't even be a Plot for this story to continue without that.

"Well, I guess you can stay here for now," Kevin ran a hand through his hair and sighed. "At least until you can get a hold of your family."

"Oh, thank you!"

"Gua!"

Once more, Kevin found himself lying on his back as Lilian bodily tackled him to the ground and began nuzzling her face against chest. Just how she could gain enough momentum to actually force him onto his back when she was sitting down was beyond him. She must have some impressive thigh muscles.

Not that he was paying attention to such things. Really. At the moment he had other issues that were more prominent. Like trying to keep all the blood rushing to his cheeks and... somewhere else that he did not want to think about right now.

***

"I knew I made the right choice when I chose you to be my mate!"

"Wha... what are you doing!? Get off!"

"Now why would I do that? I need to show you how grateful I am. I promise you'll have fun... ufufufu..."

"F-F-Fun!? I don't even want to know what you're idea of fun is! And what's with that laugh!?"

"Don't worry about that. For now, let us begin furthering our relationship."

"We don't have a relation — eep! What are you — eek! Oh God! Stop!"

"Ufufufu, let's just get rid of these."

The sound of ripping echoed throughout the room.

"My pants!"

"Ufufufu, you won't be needing them anymore." A pause. "Though I am curious to know how those got back on you. I could have sworn I stripped you after you passed out last night."

"You what!?"

"Well, whatever. Now, let us get down to deepening the physical aspect of our relationship."

"Oh God! Stay away! No! NO! NNOOOOoooo…..!"

***

Several minutes and a lot of embarrassment later, the young Main Protagonist of our story found himself taking the coldest shower of his life. Icy cold droplets of water cascaded down his back as he pressed his palms against the tiled wall, his breathing heavy and his eyes clenched shut.

While it helped cool his nearly overheating body, it did very little to settle his mortification. That last scene where he just barely managed to escape Lilian with his virginity intact had left some serious mental scars on his psyche. He wouldn't be surprised if he needed counseling after this.

Please stop exaggerating, Kevin. It wasn't that bad.

And speaking of Lilian, there had to be something seriously wrong with that girl. Regular girls didn't sleep with people they had just met, and they especially didn't sleep with people they had just met while in the nude. Nor did they do… what she had just tried to do to him. It was like the girl had absolutely no sense of restraint… or any taboos when it came to things like nudity and sexual relations.

That last one was particularly bad for Kevin, her lack of any taboos, that is.

As if the mere thought of her was enough to conjure her up, the door began shaking as someone tried to open it.

Kevin's head jerked towards the door as the shaking picked up intensity, his eyes widening in barely masked shock and a little bit of fear.

After a moment or two the shaking stopped, and a voice spoke up.

"Beloved?"

It was Lilian, obviously.

Kevin stiffened, if only for a moment before relaxing. He had locked the door. There was no way she could get in, right?

"Y-Yes?"

"I was just wondering if you wanted me to wash your back," her muffled voice said.

Let the blushing commence.

"Wa-wa-wash... Why would I need you to wash my back!?"

A pause.

"Because it's too hard for you to reach on your own?"

"That's not a good enough reason!"

"Anyways," she ignored him. "Do you think you could unlock the door. It will be hard for me to wash your back if I can't even get in."

"D-Don't bother! I'm almost done anyways!"

"Oh..." Lilian sounded disappointed. "I guess I'll just let you finish then."

"Thank you."

Kevin couldn't hear her receding footsteps over the spray of water, but he hoped she had really left. In his haste to get away from her, he had forgotten to grab a pair of clothes for himself, and he didn't want Lilian seeing him like this. Just thinking about what she might to do him if she saw him in the buff made his temperature rise as all kinds of feelings he preferred not to contemplate inundated him.

On a side note, was it just him? Or was steam actually beginning to rise despite the water being on its coldest setting?

Seeing how the shower did not seem to be helping him anymore, Kevin decided to get out, dry off, and get dressed. Thankfully, Lilian really had left and he didn't run into her on the way to his room. He managed to get there with his chastity intact.

After he found a clean pair of jeans and a plain black T-shirt, he headed into the kitchen to make something to eat. While he was moving down the hall, however, his nose picked up the delicious smell of what he could only guess was eggs and something else being cooked. Walking into the kitchen where the scent was coming from, the poor boy was greeted by a sight that pretty much negated the effects of the ice cold shower he had just finished taking.

Lilian was standing there, wearing one of his overly large t-shirts and nothing else. Her little toes wiggled cutely against the cool tile as she hummed a soft tune to herself. Slender calves and shapely thighs made themselves present as the shirt she had decided to wear just barely covered her shapely rear much less her legs.

It was a sight that Kevin doubted even Eric would ever be able to come up with in his wildest, most perverted dreams. Just looking at this stunning example of a female, standing there in his kitchen, wearing one of his shirts was nearly enough to nearly force his mind go catatonic again.

It didn't help that her tail was out and kept swaying back and forth like a pendulum, forcing the shirt to rise and show off more of her small, tight and shapely rear end than was already being revealed. Really, it was like the dang thing was purposefully doing that because it knew he was watching.

"How was your shower, beloved?" Kevin started with the realization that she was actually talking to him. His mind quickly tried to think of something, anything to say.

"Uh…. fine, I guess…"

Well, it wasn't the smoothest, most sophisticated of answers, especially when speaking to a girl like Lilian, but at least he was talking. It was certainly an improvement over his previously tongue tied state.

And at least he didn't pass out again. That would just be embarrassing. Not to mention hilarious.

"Breakfast is almost ready," she said with a smile as she turned back to the stove. "Why don't you sit down at the table and I'll bring it over soon."

It was only after she finished speaking that he realized the smell was actually because this girl was cooking. No. Not just cooking. She was cooking for him. Kevin didn't know whether he should feel embarrassed that some girl he had just met was making him breakfast, or warm and fuzzy for that very same reason. Really, this whole situation was just too confusing.

"Okay."

Unable to do much else, Kevin did exactly as Lilian asked and sat down at the small table next to the wall that separated the dining room from the kitchen. As he did, his eyes could not help but stare at the girl who was humming away while she cooked, using the fork to lift what looked like the edge of cooked eggs.

Was this really happening? Was there really a Kitsune — a creature he hadn't even believed existed until just last night, standing in his kitchen, cooking him breakfast, *while* wearing nothing more than one of his shirts? This had to be some kind of dream. That was it. None of this was real. He would just pinch himself and he would wake up and be back in his bed and none of this would have ever happened.

"Ouch!"

"Are you okay, beloved?" Lilian turned from her cooking to give him a concerned look.

"Ah... I'm fine," Kevin's ears turned pink as he rubbed the small nail marks on his arm. Lilian looked at him for a moment longer before turning away to finish cooking.

Kevin sighed. This definitely was not a dream. Which meant, of course, that everything happening to him was real. He had really found a small two tailed fox, brought her home and bandaged her injuries. That fox really was a Kitsune, a creature of ancient Japanese Myth, and she really had proclaimed her love for him the night before and was now making him breakfast. There was so much going on that shouldn't be possible that Kevin didn't know what to think.

It was probably better to just not think at all. Don't think about it, Kevin. Just don't think about it.

"Here you go."

Not thinking about his impossible situation was going to be impossible with Lilian here.

"Thank you," Kevin mumbled as a plate was put in front of him. For a good several seconds, he found himself staring at the food like it was some kind of foreign entity. How long had it actually been since he had not been forced to make his own breakfast (and lunch and dinner)? A year? Two? Something like that.

He had to admit, the breakfast looked really good. It was an omelet that had been folded around spinach and various chopped vegetables; carrots, broccoli, cauliflower and asparagus. A glance towards the sink confirmed that Lilian had chopped them just a little while ago. The cutting board was sitting on the drying cloth, having already been washed sometime while he been in the shower or getting dressed.

"Is something wrong with the food?"

"No," Kevin shook his head. "I was just thinking about something."

Not sure of what else he should do and not wanting to look like a jerk after this girl had gone through the trouble of making breakfast for him, Kevin grabbed a fork and cut a portion of the omelet so that he could stab it and stick it in his mouth. As he chewed the food, Lilian sat herself on the other side of the table, placed her elbows on the wood, propped her chin on the butt of her hands and watched him.

Heat began rising to Kevin's cheeks as he felt her eyes boring into him, piercing him, stripping him, *devouring* him. It was unsettling, extremely so. Kevin wanted to say something, if for no other reason than to make this girl stop staring at him with those bright green eyes that looked like they were about ready to take his chastity, but he couldn't. His vocal chords weren't working. Even if they were, he was not entirely sure what he would say.

Was this how all those girls Eric stared at felt? No wonder they disliked him so much.

"So how is it?" Kevin started at the sound of Lilian's voice. He looked up from his plate to see the red head smiling at him. For some reason, her expression reminded him of a child. It was very innocent despite the feelings her eyes gave him as they bore into his own. He could just picture her feet swinging childishly underneath the table as she watched something she felt was interesting.

"It's good," Kevin admitted after swallowing. "Really good, actually. Better than any breakfast I've ever made."

Kevin was a simple guy who preferred making simple foods. He didn't like the hassle that came from trying to make anything too complicated. It just took more time and effort than it was worth. His breakfast usually just consisted of plain old scrambled eggs and bacon. Sometimes if he wanted to eat something different, he would make pancakes, but that was about it.

"I'm glad to hear that," Lilian's shoulders relaxed significantly as she released a large gust of air. It was as if a weight had been lifted off her shoulders. "I don't cook omelet's very often, or at all really, though I was taught how. Usually, our maid is the one cooking for us."

"You have a maid?" So this girl was, like, super rich or something? Only the rich could afford a real life maid. Not even the spoiled brats in those large houses could afford their own maid. Someone to clean for them? Yes. But a full time maid that would wait on them hand and foot? No.

At least, not unless they wanted to get rid of those $120,000+ cars that cost an extra $10,000 to $15,000 a year to maintain.

"Well, I guess servant would be more appropriate," Lilian said thoughtfully as she looked up at the ceiling. "Kotohime pledged herself to our family sometime around 150 years ago." Hearing this caused Kevin to nearly choke on his food. "I don't know much about what happened during that time. I was just a vixen back then."

"Wait, wait, wait, wait!" Kevin looked at the girl in shock. "What do you mean 150 years ago? Do you mean to tell me that you have a maid who's over 150 years old?" That was freaking ancient! Not even Gandhi lived to be that old!

"Of course," Lilian looked very confused for a second before her eyes lit in understanding. "Ah, right. I forgot that you humans are very short lived." Her back straightened and she looked at him, a single finger pointed towards the ceiling as she raised her arm; she looked like a teacher who was about to go into a lecture. "To sum it up, Kitsune live a lot longer than humans do." She tilted her head to the left. "Kotohime has 3 tails, so she's older than 300, but younger than 400." She pressed a finger to her lips and tapped it. "I don't know exactly how old she is, though." She shrugged. "I never asked."

Kevin bit his lower lip and furrowed his brows in thought as he processed the information he was just given. "So Kitsune gain a tail every 100 years then?"

"Yes," Lilian nodded. "We first start off with just one tail, that's when we're still just plain old foxes. After our hundredth year we gain our second tail and a human form."

"Oh," Kevin blinked, "That makes sense, I guess." He frowned as he looked at the girl in front of him. "But what about you? Since you have a human form, that means you should have two tails, but I only see one." He was curious to know how old she was, but knew better than to ask. It was one of the bits of wisdom his mom had given him. Never ask a woman her age.

"I do," Lilian chirped. "Like most Kitsune, I usually only keep one of them out. We don't really like the feeling of our tails being completely hidden, because our tails is where the essence of our power are stored." She looked at him, a strange glint in her eyes. "Would you like me to bring out my second tail?"

"Ah, no," Kevin shook his head, "That's alriiiiiiighhttt! What the heck!?" Kevin's shocked squeak was precluded by the feeling of something wrapping around his legs. After banging his knees on the underside of the table when he jumped out of his seat, Kevin looked down, his eyes blinking several times as he tried to associate what he was seeing with reality.

There, wrapped around his legs, were two furry, bright red fox tails. They were surprisingly soft and warm, but he was more focused on the fact that there were two fox tails wrapped around his legs!

"Did I mention they could extend to over a meter in length?" Lilian asked innocently. Too innocently. Kevin narrowed his eyes. It looked like those stories about Kitsune being pranksters might hold some merit after all.

Trying to ignore the girl who had retracted her tails, Kevin ate in silence. It was hard with her watching him, but he made do and did his best to ignore her. When he finished, he cast a glace at the small clock on the stove, his eyes widening as he saw what time it was.

"Oh crap!" He swore as he bolted from his chair and made a mad dash towards his room. Acting with all the haste of someone who had a horde of Orcs on his tail (or some other manner of dangerous and ugly fantasy monster), Kevin shoved all of his binders and homework into his bag with little regard to whether any of it got crushed or not. He soon came barreling back out and hurried towards the door.

He skidded to a stop, however, when he saw Lilian standing in front of the door that would allow him to leave. She was looking at him, hands clasped together in front of her. Kevin nearly lost it when he saw how poorly the shirt actually hid her breasts as they were pressed together.

"Leaving?"

"Uh..." Only the knowledge that he was running late allowed his mind to properly reboot. "Yeah... I have school... so..."

"That's right, I forgot that you went to school," Lilian perked up, literally. Her slightly drooping fox ears actually quivered before standing straight up on her head. It was such a cute gesture that Kevin only managed to stop himself from squealing like some kind of yaoi fan-boy and reaching out to caress them by reminding himself that Lilian wasn't actually a fox, but a Kitsune, and that there was no telling what she would do if he caressed her ears. "I've never been to school before. My mother always home schooled us."

"Ah, I, I see," Kevin tried to steer this conversation back on course so he could finish it quickly. "Listen, I have to go or I'll be late... er! Later than I already am. You can stay here for as long as you want, I guess." It wasn't like he could in good conscious kick her out. Not unless he wanted to be guilt ridden for several months. "Just, um... try not to break anything. Oh! And don't go into my mom's bedroom."

"Don't worry about me, Beloved," Kevin's cheeks flushed at her apparent pet-name for him. A tad slow on the uptake, wasn't he? "I'll be fine. You go to school. I'll wait for you here." Saying this, the red haired beauty closed the distance between them, leaned up on her toes (she was several inches shorter than Kevin), and pressed her lips to his in a quick kiss.

Kevin's eyes widened as he felt her warm, soft and slightly moist lips glide over his own. Even though it was just a small peck, it was still enough that Kevin felt a jolt run through him, like lightning was coursing unhindered through his body at the contact. He could not help but compare Lilian's lips to the finest satin as they gently ghosted over his own in an ephemeral kiss.

Of course, this is Kevin we're talking about, so all these thoughts would not come to him until later. Much later. Right now, his mind had pretty much short circuited.

"Beloved?" Kevin blinked. Lilian stared at him in concern. "Are you okay?"

"Ah... Ah..." Kevin's mind recovered with admirable speed. Admirable for him, at least. "Yes..." he mumbled. "I'm fine. It's just..." he trailed off, feeling embarrassed as he murmured something out that Lilian could not hear.

"What was that, Beloved?"

"That was... my first kiss," Kevin mumbled lowly, his head turned down so he was looking at the ground instead of Lilian. It was infinitely more interesting than the gorgeous fox girl in front of him anyways.

Yeah, right.

Lilian smiled at him, her own cheeks tinging pink.

"That was my first kiss with a male too."

"I see," Kevin stared in surprise. "That was your first... wait," he blinked several times as his mind caught up with the rest of what she said. "With a male?"

...

Cue long awkward silence.

"Damn that Iris."

"Wow," Kevin whistled in a completely Out of Character kind of way. It's generally called an OC moment. "I just don't – wow. I don't even know what to say to that." Seriously, what does someone say to that?

"A-Anyways," the fox girl tried to get rid of her embarrassment by changing the subject. "Shouldn't you be going to school?"

"Right." Was it just him, or did this girl just sound almost like one of those stay at home wives he heard about on those fifties shows his mom used to love watching when she was at home?

Ugh, whatever. He didn't have time to deal with this. School had started five minutes ago and it would take him twenty to get there. He would deal with this strange fox girl, and everything his new situation entailed (and yes, that was a pun just now) later. Right now, it was time to head out.

Little did he know that there would be more problems than just an angry homeroom teacher to deal with when he finally arrived at school.

Chapter 7: A Not so Normal School Day

"You're late, Mr. Swift!"

Kevin barely managed to withhold a wince at the sharp tone in his homeroom teacher's voice. Ruby Vis was one of those hardcore teachers who was very... passionate? Yes, passionate. She was very passionate about her job. It was her art, and if math was her chisel than teaching was her hammer.

Which meant he and the other students were the marble upon which she would strike.

Ouch.

She was a very plain looking woman with mousy brown hair, dark eyes and pale skin. Whenever Kevin saw her, he could not help but be reminded of a vampire. The only reason he did not suspect her of actually being a vampire was her lack of sparkles. Despite this, her skin was certainly white enough to be a vampire's. It was so translucently pale that he often wondered if she ever got outside beyond walking to and from her car.

Probably not.

"Sorry, Ms. Vis," Kevin apologized quickly. "I had some... erm... trouble, waking up this morning." Internally, he winced at the terrible excuse. Dang his inability to tell a good lie! Maybe he should have said something about a black cat crossing his path forcing him to take the long way around?

Yeah, as if she would believe that.

"You missed my lecture," Ms. Vis continued as if she had not even heard him. Uh oh. That wasn't a good sign. Whenever a teacher pretended to not hear you, it usually meant they were going to punish you. That just sucked, especially since it hadn't been his fault he was late. He had been dealing with a close encounter of the sexy fox-girl kind.

Too bad he couldn't tell her that. What was he supposed to

say? "I woke up with a naked girl in my bed. Oh, and by the way, she's a Kitsune. You know, those supernatural creatures found in Japanese Mythology." Yeah, he could see that going over *really* well.

"Take your seat and ask your neighbor for the notes on *my* lecture that *you* missed." This time, Kevin did wince, especially on those emphasized words. She was definitely peeved at him. "You'll need it if you want to complete your assignment for today."

Kevin almost couldn't contain his surprise. He was getting off without being punished? Or was she just saving her punishment for another time? Either way, it was probably best not to look a gift horse in the mouth.

Trying his best not to make it look like he was in a rush, Kevin walked to his desk. He didn't want to ruin this moment by seeming hurried. That would just make this whole situation that much worse. She might smell blood in the water, so to speak, and decide he really should be punished.

As he sat down at the desk assigned to him, his neighbor turned in her seat and gave him an amused smile. "It's not like you to be so late, Kevin." She looked like she was taking way to much enjoyment from his unfortunate situation. Not that he noticed. He was having other problems at the moment. "Having some problems at home?"

Kevin's breath caught in his throat as Lindsay spoke to him. He and Lindsay didn't have many classes together, except homeroom and their last class of the day. This was one of the only times he actually got to be with her. He both loved it and hated it. Loved it because he could sit next to her. Hated it because he could never think of anything to say, and every time he made an attempt, he would usually end up not saying anything at all and would just stare at her with a stupid-looking, open-mouthed expression instead.

Nothing said idiot better than looking like you were trying to do a fish out of water impression in front of your crush.

Lindsay was a very petite girl, nowhere near as curvy as some of the other female's in their school, and not even close to Lilian's generous proportions, but she had her own strong points. While small, Lindsay possessed a very lean, athletic body from all the sports she played. Her legs and arms were toned, her stomach was taut. The girl didn't have an inch of fat on her thanks to how active she was. That was actually one of the things Kevin liked most about her.

Her love of sports, not her body.

Not that her body was bad or ugly. He thought she had an amazing body. It was just that he was way too shy to actually think about Lindsay's body that way. At least not without his face turning all kinds of red.

"Hello? Earth to Kevin? Anybody in there?"

Kevin blinked several times as a hand was waved in front of his face. It took him a moment to realize that he had been staring... again.

He jerked his head back as if slapped. Already his cheeks were beginning to heat up as he once more embarrassed himself in front of his crush. He could only imagine how red his face was.

Lindsay was still staring at him. Quick, Kevin! Think of something to say!

"Uh... um... hu... hi...?"

Smooth Kevin, very smooth.

"Hey," Lindsay snickered at him, amused. "Finally back here on Earth with us?" Kevin blushed at her comment, but didn't say anything. "So... any reason why you were so late?"

"Um..." Late? Why was he late? Oh! Right. "Ah... I just had some... problems with this... erm... injured fox I found yesterday."

"A fox?" Lindsay perked up. "You brought a fox home? Isn't it against the rules to have animals in your apartment?"

"Well, yeah," Kevin squirmed uncomfortably as he was reminded of that fact. Not that it mattered. No one would think Lilian was a fox so long as she remained in her human form. And on that note, he really hoped she had the good sense to hide those tails of hers. It wouldn't do if someone, like, say, the landlord, came over and saw her with *those* added appendages out. "That's why I was late. I had to make sure no one would be able to see her from outside of the apartment."

"I gotcha," Lindsay nodded her head. "I remember you always did love animals back when we were younger."

Kevin ducked his head down to hide his red cheeks while the girl sitting next to him grinned.

"Anyways, here." She held out her spiral notebook. "Those are the notes from today. Just give that back when you're done copying them."

Carefully reaching out with his hand, his heart pounding against his chest, Kevin touched the notebook Lindsay was offering him. He grabbed it almost reverently, ignoring the millions of butterflies that had welled up in his stomach. They had nothing to do with the binder she gave him, or the skin on skin contact he felt when his hand touched hers. Really.

"Thanks," Kevin's barely audible voice mumbled out. "You're a life saver."

"I know." Lindsay's small, cocky smirk somehow managed to enhance how attractive she was. Kevin nearly swooned, but being a man (real men didn't swoon!), he held himself back. Barely.

The rest of class was mostly silent. Only the sound of pencil scratching on paper and the occasional cough broke the monotonous stillness that permeated the room. Behind her desk, Ms. Vis sat, watching them all like a hawk, making sure they did their work in complete silence. Anyone caught talking or passing notes was given a swift warning not to do so again on pain of detention and those with phones out had them taken away until class ended.

Kevin dutifully copied down all the notes Lindsay had written down in her notebook. The girl had very neat, very precise handwriting, so it was really easy to copy. She was an excellent note taker.

As he finished copying down the notes and then started working on the assignment that Ms. Vis had assigned to them, his mind traveled back to the fox-girl currently rooming in his apartment. He wondered what she was doing right now.

He also hoped to God that she wasn't causing any trouble. The last thing he wanted was to come home and find some kind of disaster in the works.

The bell soon rang, signaling an end to class. As everyone began leaving, Ms. Vis reminded them that any work they had not completed in class was homework and due tomorrow. Those who did not complete their assignments and turn them in on time would get a failing grade for said assignment. Kevin could have sworn she was looking at him when she said this, but he played it off as his imagination. He had never failed to turn in an assignment on time and wasn't about to start now, thank you very much.

Kevin's class after his morning math class—why they made math the first class in the morning was beyond him, most of his peers were still half asleep at that time—was French.

A lot of people wondered why he bothered taking French when they didn't live anywhere near France. Eric in particular thought it was stupid, since they lived just a few hours drive from Mexico, but Kevin had his reasons for taking French instead of Spanish.

To put it simply, he already knew a good deal of French. Since his mom spent a lot of time in France for her job, she had been forced to pick up the language, and since she learned French, Kevin did as well by association. That meant he could coast along on his laurels in that class and still maintain a high grade.

Lazy? Some people would say that, but Kevin liked to think of it as an intelligent decision with the purpose of decreasing his workload so he could put more effort into his other classes. Why go through all the trouble and time of learning another language for high school credit when he could take a class where he already knew the language, gain the credits *and* not spend several hours each week doing the work?

Because very few people took French, the class was quite small. Where a normal class would consist of anywhere from twenty to twenty-five people and sometimes even thirty and over, this class only contained a grand total of twelve. That made it very easy for Kevin to memorize the names of all the people in his class. It helped that he'd had to partner up with all of them at least once last year.

While he wouldn't consider any of the people in his class friends, he did get along with all of them to some degree or another. Well, except for the girls, but that is so obvious by this point in the story it really shouldn't need mentioning.

His teacher for the class was a rather airy woman by the name Madam Bonnet, which was ironic because the teacher in question was always wearing a bonnet. Always. He had never seen her take it off, not even once.

Madam Bonnet was a middle aged woman with black hair that had shots of gray in it and bluish gray eyes. She was tall and willowy, with the personality of someone whose mind was always very far away. Even the way her eyes were constantly shifting seemed to denote that she wasn't really all there. Kevin and the other students all thought she was a very odd woman.

Still, she made French class interesting. Madam Bonnet had

an unusual method of teaching and, more often than not, her method involved the students in her class embarrassing themselves by getting in front of everyone and making a presentation of some kind. Sometimes she would bring in cooking supplies and have them make foods found in France, then give both a lecture and assign a written report on the food they made. Other times she would have them do skits from various French plays. One time she even made someone transpose and sing a song. Now that had just been embarrassing. Kevin had felt bad for the girl who had been forced to do that.

Whatever it was she had them do, they always had to speak in French. No English at all. As in, none whatsoever. If they made even one comment in English, she would deduct points from their overall grade.

On this particular day, she had them work in pairs and told them to write a poem about a specific area in France. It could be a province, a city, a historically significant building or a national landmark. Kevin had been paired up with a rather skinny kid with glasses and shaggy black hair named Nathan Luculen. He was a very intelligent kid, one of those students who had a GPA that was over 4.0. He was taking all honors and AP classes and would likely go on to become a nuclear physicist, a neuro surgeon or some equally impressive and rewarding career.

Kevin wouldn't say he was friends with the other boy, but they got along well enough. It probably helped that he wasn't the type of person to judge another because of their deficiencies or strange personality quirks (and really, with his girl problem, Kevin had no right to judge others for their oddities), unlike a good deal of athletes who, for some reason or another, enjoyed picking on those who were less athletically inclined than themselves, including Nathan who had no athletic abilities whatsoever.

The region of France they had chosen was Nora-Pas-De-Calais, an area of France that was bordered by the English Channel. The only trouble they really had was coming up with the right words to describe the region in a way that sounded poetic. Neither of them were the artsy type. Nathan was studious and kind of nerdy and Kevin, while fairly intelligent and good at French, was a jock, not a poet. He had no artistic abilities to speak of. Still, they did manage to scrounge something together that Madame Bonnet approved, and really, that was all that mattered in the end.

After French, Kevin had Physics followed by Social Science. He wasn't the best in either class, but he still maintained above average grades in both. He had managed to maintain an "A" average in Physics while he only had a "B" in Social Science.

The only reason he didn't have an "A" in that class was because of a test he had not done as well on due to having not studied as much as he should have in favor of track practice. Still, even with that small black mark, he was one of the better students in class.

Neither class was all that appealing to him, but they would look good on his transcript when he applied for a college. Most people would probably think it highly unusual to find a kid his age who was actually thinking ahead, but that's just what happens when someone grows up to be pretty much independent of their parent due to how often she was gone. Granted, it wasn't like he was actually looking into colleges at the moment, but he was at least thinking about his future, which was more than most high school sophomores could say.

As the bell rang in Social Science class, Kevin could barely keep the sigh of relief from escaping him as he hauled butt out of there. Social Science was boring enough as it was, but his teacher, one Professor Nibui, an old Japanese man who spoke in a thick accent that made understanding him difficult, only added to how dull the class was. It was like the man had never heard of the word "fun" before in his life. He was pretty much the antithesis of all things lively.

He could put the dead to sleep.

Then again, most teachers were like that, so it wasn't like he was alone.

Hmm. Thinking about it, maybe he should ask his Social Science professor if he knew anything about Japanese Mythology, and Kitsune in particular. He was Japanese, right? So he had to know something. And it would definitely be good to know more about his apartment's new... tenant. The only reason Kevin even knew what a Kitsune was in the first place was because of all the anime he watched.

Anime, the breaker of all boundaries and social clicks.

Deciding to think on the merits of speaking with Professor Nibui later, Kevin made his way to his next class, gym, which he shared with Eric and a few of the acquaintances he knew on the Track team. It was, quite expectantly, his favorite class of the day. There was nothing like working up a good sweat by throwing dodge balls, shooting hoops or exercising in the weight room to clear the mind, never mind the fact that he couldn't shoot a basketball to save his life.

It was the principle of the act that mattered.

Turning a corner as he made his way to the locker rooms, Kevin suddenly found himself falling to the ground as something hard and unyielding smashed into him with enough force to make his body spin like a top. A hiss of pain escaped his lips as he rubbed his sore shoulder where he had been hit. Dear sweet God, what the heck ran into him!? A brick wall!?

"You'd better watch where you're walking, shitstain!"

Blinking as the rough, snarling voice reached his ears, Kevin found himself staring at the pair of black sneakers that were in his view. He followed the shoes up to a pair of the most disgustingly hairy legs he had ever seen, quickly bypassing them to see a pair of black shorts, a white T-shirt that was stretched across a beefy chest and finally to the vicious looking, bulldog-like face of none other than Chris Fleischer.

Kevin paled. Chris Fleischer was a Junior who just so happened to be the vice-captain of the school's wrestling team. He likely would have been captain, but had been cited for poor sportsmanship during last years tournament. Built like a brick shit house and with a smell to match, he was the boy that everyone else, even Seniors avoided at all costs.

And he, Kevin, had just run into him.

Not good. This was *so* not good! Chris was the kind of person who enjoyed beating on those smaller than him for no other reason than because he could! Even looking at him the wrong way could lead to a smack down of epic proportions!

In short, Kevin was screwed.

"I-I'm sorry," Kevin tried to apologize as he made to stand up. Maybe if he prostrated himself and begged for forgiveness, he would be spared. It was a long shot, but it was all he had. He didn't want to get beaten to a pulp like the last person who pissed this guy off.

Chris decided to help him up by grabbing the front of his shirt and hauling him off his feet so they were at eye level with each other. Kevin's feet hung limply in the air and his hands went to the thick, hairy wrist that was clutching the neckline of his shirt tightly.

Frightened blue irises stared into angry black. The older boy was so close Kevin could smell his putrid breath as it was panted into his face. He felt his throat constrict as his instincts told him there was something dangerous about the older boy and that if he didn't run away right now, he might never get another chance.

"I don't wanna hear your sorry excuses, pussy!" Chris snarled at him like a rabid dog. "You'd better watch yourself from now on or I'll... I'll..." Kevin blinked when the boy trailed off. He blinked again when the older boy started sniffing the air around him. What the heck? "That smell..."

"Kevin!"

If he had not been trying very hard to keep from acting in a manner that would be considered unmanly (in other words, he was trying to keep from relieving his bladder), Kevin would have cried in sweet relief as Eric and a few other students came into view. He was saved! Not even Chris would be stupid enough to do anything when there was a crowd full of witnesses! Right?

"Tch," Chris' hand released it's grip on Kevin's shirt. Because of how high up he was being held (Chris was over six feet tall, really tall for a Junior and way taller than Kevin), the younger boy fell to the ground and landed on his backside, hard.

The sophomore track and field runner winced a little as pain lanced up his tail bone and worked its way up like electricity going through a wire, but he was too thankful at no longer being subject to the Junior's glare (as well as his horrid smelling breath) to complain about his sore bottom.

"You'd better watch who you hang out with, shitstain, or I'm really gonna fuck you up the next time we meet."

With that last vague threat hanging ominously in the air, Chris stalked off, but not before tossing a glare at all of the people who had found them before the situation could get out of hand. Many took a step back at that glare, and even more flinched.

The group parted like the red sea as Chris made his way through them, shoulder shoving a good number of students out of the way when they didn't move fast enough, including Eric, who complained loudly at being pushed around.

Fortunately, Kevin's friend didn't have to worry about Chris trying to harm him, since his dad was the Principle. He could complain all he wanted.

"What the hell was that about?" asked Eric as he moved over to help Kevin out.

"How should I know?" Kevin groused as he let his best friend help him to his feet. He dusted himself off, then let out the breath he had been holding in relief. That had been too close. "Thanks."

"Not a problem," Eric grinned before shaking his head. "Seriously though, what the hell? I know Chris is a jerk ass and everything, but I didn't think he would mess with someone who's on a school sports team. It's one thing to mess with nerds and those loner kids, no one cares about them, but he could get himself expelled if it got out hat he was messing with one of the track team's star runners."

It was not surprising that Eric knew how the school worked, with his father being the Principal and all. What *was* surprising was to hear him actually mention it. He didn't really like anything that had to do with rules and regulations or even school in general. It probably had something to do with the fact that Eric kept getting into trouble with his dad when the girls caught him trying to install cameras in their locker room.

Or when he got caught trying to peep on them through the ceiling.

Or when he hid himself in one of the girls lockers.

Or that one time he tried dressing up like a girl and changing with them.

Eric was a very depraved person.

Kevin didn't really like how his friend spoke of the kids that Chris normally bullied, but couldn't disagree with his words either. Chris normally picked on the kids who either wouldn't say anything about his bullying anyways, or the ones that no one would believe even if they did say something. It was one thing to beat on those kids. It was quite another to beat on someone who was not only a good student, but also on one of the school's sports teams.

The school loved their sports teams. They were the pride of any school.

"I'm not the star of anything," Kevin frowned. Eric scoffed.

"My sexy, perverted ass you're not. Who was it that managed to break the record for the fastest 100 meter dash recorded in the history of this school? Because it sure as hell wasn't David Longsan."

"That doesn't mean anything," Kevin argued as they entered the gym locker room and walked over to their lockers. After twisting the dial through the combination and opening the locker, he began pulling out his gym clothes. "I've only gotten that time once, and you're forgetting that Chase almost managed to match my time. Besides, I haven't hit that time since my first try-out last year."

Eric sighed exasperatedly as he followed suit. "I don't know if you're just being modest or if you actually believe the crap coming out of your mouth." He shook his head, disgruntled. "What's worse is that you don't even use your position as the star of the 100 and 200 meter dash to gain any privileges with the ladies. If I was a star runner like you, you can be sure I would've used my stardom to bag myself a hottie like Caitlin Fairchild first chance I got."

Kevin rolled his eyes and contained his desire to release a long suffering sigh as Eric went into a rant about the hot, senior captain of the cheerleading squad and all of the things he would like to do to her. Some of those things made Kevin's face feel like it had been stuck in a furnace. He didn't even know if some of the acts his best friend was talking about were humanly possible.

And he really didn't need to know about his friends fantasy involving rubbing oil, chocolate sauce and several sets of whips and chains

No, really. Don't ask. You don't want to know either.

As he did his best to block out Eric's lecherous ranting, his thoughts turned to his confrontation with Chris.

Of course, calling it a confrontation would imply that Kevin actually stood up for himself. In truth, he had been too frightened to do anything. The older boy scared him witless.

Thinking back on his almost-beat-down at the hands of the wrestling vice-captain, Kevin remembered the boy's words. He had told Kevin to "watch who he hung out with." What did he mean by that?

Shrugging his curiosity off for now, Kevin finished getting dressed and followed his friend out of the room. It was probably just the older boy's way of trying to frighten him or something, though it was a strange way of doing so. Regardless, class was starting and he didn't want to think about his near death experience when he felt he should be enjoying his time working up a good sweat.

Kevin exaggerates a lot.

Chapter 8: An Embarrassing Night

After a long day of school followed by an equally long practice for track, Kevin found himself riding his bike home. The sun hadn't quite begun to set, but it was starting to go down. It wouldn't be long now before the sky started to lose its color.

As Kevin pedaled his bike along the darkening street his mind turned to a subject that he had been dreading to think about, namely, what he would find when he finally got back to his apartment. He wasn't sure what to expect when he reached his home, but he hoped it would be a nice, clean place, and not a disaster in the making. He didn't want to find his apartment looking like a Level Five Hurricane had run through it.

He also prayed that the girl was still fully clothed—at least insomuch as could be expected, considering she only had his shirts to wear. The last thing he needed was to come home and find a naked fox-girl prancing around his apartment. Definitely not.

Not that he had much hope. In all the manga he'd read that started similarly to this story the Main Hero always came home to find the Main Heroine running around in the buff, often times in the wake of some household disaster like the dish washer going on a rampage and spewing water everywhere, or the microwave having exploded after being used to cook a giant marshmallow, or a household appliance coming to life and attacking the Main Heroine and tearing her clothes off.

Thinking about all of the disasters that could have befallen his apartment and knowing that, with his luck, such a thing happening was not out of the realm of possibility truly depressed him. The only thing Kevin could do in this instance was pray that those manga were all wrong.

When you're relying on a manga to determine your course in life, there's already a problem.

Stopping to check his mailbox, Kevin found several letters and what looked like a publication of some kind. He grabbed them and decided to look through them a little later while he was watching TV or something. There wouldn't be any bills or anything of that sort in there His mom paid all of her bills online, so he wouldn't have to worry about that.

It was nearing 6:00 when he finally arrived at his apartment. Reaching the stairs Kevin lifted his bike up the steps. He was tired and the act of hauling it upstairs was a lot harder than usual. Coach Deretaine had really pushed them hard today. The aches on his muscles had aches of their own.

That was, like, twice the standard acheage. He hadn't felt this sore since the time his coach for gym had first started making them workout in the weight room. That had been brutal.

After he managed to make it upstairs, Kevin chained his bike to the railing and locked it up. Technically speaking, he wasn't really supposed to have his bike chained to the apartment railing, but no one had said anything yet, so he figured it was okay. After his bike was secured, he unlocked the door and entered with only a small amount of trepidation.

Taking off his shoes and stepping into the apartment, the first thing Kevin noticed was that nothing seemed to be out of place. There was no naked fox girl prancing around. No disaster in the making. No post apocalyptic zombies rising from the dead wanting to drink his semen...

Don't ask. No, really. Don't ask. It's better that you don't know.

The second thing he noticed was the most delectable scent wafting through the air.

Taking a deep breath, Kevin tried to determine what he was smelling. Food, definitely. And well made food if the scent was anything to go by. Kevin considered himself a decent cook, but whatever was being cooked in his apartment at least smelled like it kicked his food to the curb. He couldn't identify what was being cooked, but he didn't really care. It smelled *that* good.

Following the scent, Kevin made his way into the kitchen and found Lilian cooking dinner. He was surprised, but at the same time not. Hadn't she just made him breakfast this morning? It didn't seem out of place that she would try making him dinner as well. That, and seeing how she was the only person who had been inside this apartment since he left, it would only make sense that she was the one cooking.

What excellent skills in deduction. Kevin should think about being a detective.

Please note the sarcasm.

For several seconds, Kevin watched as the girl went about her business, humming to herself as she washed the cutting board, knife and bowls she had used to create whatever dish was currently cooking in the oven. Like the last time he had seen her, she was wearing his T-shirt and nothing else. One of her tails was also out and waving around behind her.

A part of him felt he should be glad she was at least somewhat, kind of, sort of, but not really, decent. He couldn't be, however, because that dang tail of hers was constantly lifting the shirt enough that her backside was completely exposed to his eyes every several seconds. No, he really couldn't find it in him to feel truly grateful about her state of dress.

Deciding he had watched her enough, and feeling pretty embarrassed about having spent so much time staring at her backside, Kevin decided to get her attention.

"Uh... hey... um... Lilian?" That was her name, right? Last night he had been so busy freaking out over the fact there was a beautiful, naked, fox-girl in his apartment that he hadn't really paid any attention when she introduced herself.

"Ah!" Lilian spun around in what Kevin could only guess was surprise. Guess because the moment her eyes landed on him any surprise they might have held left as her emerald green irises lit up brightly enough to power a city block for several months. "Beloved!"

Kevin's eyes widened as the girl almost literally disappeared in a burst of speed, her body a mere blur as she darted straight for him. He had read enough manga to know exactly what would come next. Yet like a train wreck, Kevin was unable to do anything in time to stop it from happening.

Credit must be given to him, however, as he at least tried.

"W-wait! What are you—oof!—mmph!"

That was him trying, just in case you didn't realize that.

It happened so fast that while some part of Kevin knew what was going on, he still found himself confused. In only a split second he was lying on his back, Lilian was straddling his waist and her hands were clenching his shirt. Her lips were pressed firmly against his in a kiss that was usually only seen in movies... or hentai.

It took him a few more seconds to understand his new situation.

Three.

Two.

One.

Kevin's eyes began to practically bulge from their sockets as his mind caught up to what his body was experiencing. Lilian was kissing him! Oh God! She was kissing him! And... and...

...Dear, sweat, merciful lord she was *really* kissing him. He could feel her soft, moist lips moving over his own, creating a delicious feeling that was unlike anything he had ever felt before.

Adding to this mind numbing sensation, Lilian's pink, glistening tongue was pushing its way inside of his mouth. It bumped and squirmed and wiggled, always moving inevitably deeper into his mouth, like she was trying to caress his tonsils with the tip of her tongue.

He tried to say something, anything , but there were two things that prevented this from happening.

The first might have had something to do with the fact that Lilian's *tongue* was in his *mouth*. It's kind of hard to talk when someone is shoving their tongue into the far reaches of the hole you use to speak.

The second? The term is referred to as "brain overload." To put it simply, his mind had shut down in order to prevent his brain from melting out of his ears… or something, though perhaps not quite as graphic—this wasn't anime after all.

If you want a better analogy, think of his brain as a computer that began overheating and needed to shut down in order to prevent the circuitry from melting and you will have an idea of what happened to him.

In either event, this left him completely defenseless against Lilian as she assaulted his mouth with skills she must have learned from this Iris person who had shared her first—and presumably every other—kiss. The girl in question seemed to take great pleasure in exploring as much of his mouth as her tongue could reach. She was everywhere; licking the roof of his mouth, the inner sides of his cheeks, playing with his tongue and pushing her own as deeply into his mouth as it could possibly go. Lilian was bringing a whole new meaning to the term "tonsil hockey."

It was probably a good thing that his mind wasn't all there at the moment. Otherwise the shock from this kiss might have actually killed him.

The amount of time that passed as Lilian took advantage of Kevin's catatonic state shall not be told. It was indeterminable. No one would ever know how long she spent exploring the inner reaches of his mouth. By the time she broke away because she had finally run out of oxygen (just how long can this girl hold her breath for anyway?), Kevin was pretty much a pile of goo.

As Lilian lay above him, her body pushing down on his and her face hovering mere inches from his own, Kevin found his mind trying, and mostly failing, to reboot after shutting down from the sensations that had bombarded him.

He had heard quite a bit about kissing. A lot of the guys he knew talked about it as if it was the greatest thing since, well, ever. A good number of his peers often bragged about how amazing a kisser their girlfriends were and how far they were willing to go. They would literally go on for hours, and all of it was very descriptive, very graphic. Some of the things Kevin had heard about kissing were enough to make him blush from the roots of his hair down to his chest.

Which honestly wasn't that difficult given that this was Kevin, but still...

Anyway, the point was, Kevin knew about kissing in theory, but this was the first time he had ever experienced a kiss like this for himself.

If his brain was working properly, he would have freely admitted that all the hype was correct, accurate down to a "T." It truly did feel amazing. Indescribable even. The feel of Lilian's soft, lush lips pressing down on his own, the way her tongue moved and rubbed against the inside of his mouth, caressing his own tongue and creating all kinds of deliriously pleasurable sensations. There were simply no words to properly describe how wondrous it felt.

But since his brain was not properly engaged at the moment, all the aforementioned thoughts were things he would be thinking about well after the fact. Right now he was a little too busy dealing with the wonderful sensation that was Lilian's tongue in his mouth.

"Welcome home, Beloved," Lilian smiled at him. Her fair

cheeks were flushed a pale pink that seemed to enhance her already inhumanly gorgeous face.

Though thinking about it, it might be more accurate to say Lilian's previous activity, seeing how Kevin had been, for all intents and purposes, brain dead, during their kiss.

"Huh... uh... wha..."

Unable to properly engage his brain, all Kevin could do was utter random monosyllables. His mind felt like it was on some kind of high, like a druggy whacked out on dope—only instead of dope he was dealing with a searing kiss containing enough passion that his ancestors were probably blushing.

However, one must give the boy credit where it was due: at least he didn't pass out.

While Kevin's mind wandered through some kind of mental wonderland, Lilian was experiencing bliss. There was a look of such rapture on her face that you'd think she'd just experienced a mind blowing orgasm. Never in her life had she felt such pleasure, not even when she and Iris had been... um, practicing! Yes, practicing! Not even when they had been practicing their kissing technique with each other had she felt such incredible pleasure, and Iris was admittedly a much better kisser than Kevin.

Which is kind of to be expected since Kevin hadn't actually reciprocating her kiss, but let's just let Lilian pretend that he did.

As she thought about the difference between kissing her beloved and kissing Iris, she wondered if the reason it felt better was because he was her mate? If that was the case, then she could finally understand why some of her aunts and her servant spoke of kissing their previous mates so fondly. Was there anything better than kissing her mate?

Well, there was sex, and the aforementioned mind blowing orgasm that could only come from sex, but it was clear they would not be doing the horizontal mambo anytime soon.

That was okay though. Lilian was patient. She could wait. Besides, it is only the eighth chapter. She had a good number of chapters to go before the story ends, and that wasn't even including the next installment of the series or the various expansion packs. Lilian was sure there would be plenty more time for her to get in her mate's pants.

She sure is confident, this Lilian.

Sighing in content Lilian leaned back down, her veil of red hair falling over the two of them like a beautiful, fiery curtain. The thousands of strands shone like a brilliant flame as the lights hit them. Her incredibly long tresses pooled about the two of them as her face leaned ever closer to Kevin.

For a second it looked like she was going to kiss him again, but instead she just rested her forehead against his, seemingly taking just as much pleasure from the simple skin on skin contact as she had from raping Kevin's mouth.

"I missed you," Lilian stated, pouting a bit. Kevin didn't say anything. Or, to be more accurate, he couldn't say anything. His mind was still lost in limbo. "It was *so* boring here without you, Beloved." Her face then broke into the loveliest of smiles. She was clearly ignoring the fact that Kevin wasn't even paying attention, or she was just that oblivious. "I'm really glad you're back. I've cooked dinner for you." Her face took on a seductive, narrow eyed expression that would have had most men in the palm of her hands. Not Kevin, though. No. He *still* wasn't all there in the head. "Though if you want to skip dinner and go straight to desert, I certainly wouldn't mind... ufufufu..."

At this point Kevin's mental faculties had been revived enough that he could comprehend her words. He was also more than capable of feeling her body bearing down on his.

Naturally, he blushed from the roots of his hair down to his chest.

"Wh-what—desert?! What are you saying?!"

"You know what I'm saying, Beloved. Why don't we just skip dinner and get right down to business?"

"H-h-how about not!"

"Mou... don't be like that. Come on, Beloved, let's let our bodies join together in a passionate embrace!"

"There will be no passionate embracing here!"

After a small scuffle that ended with Lilian trying to tear off Kevin's pants and Kevin fighting with whatever waning strength he had to keep his pants on, a loud "Beep, beep! Beep, beep!" was heard from the kitchen.

"What's that noise?"

"Oh! The food is ready!"

Lilian reluctantly got off him and hurriedly made her way to the stove, where she shut off the timer and opened the oven. Steam billowed out as the red haired beauty put on a pair of black cooking mitts and pulled the tray of whatever she had baked out of the oven and set it on the stove top.

Meanwhile, Kevin managed to work his pants back on and stood warily to his feet.

"Beloved," Lilian caught his attention. Kevin blushed. He wondered if he would ever get used to her calling him such an intimate name. Probably not, but you never know. "Why don't you sit down at the table while I set out the food?"

Kevin almost did exactly what she told him, but caught himself at the last second. With a small shake of his head and a deep breath to gather what meager amount of courage he possessed when faced with circumstances such as this, he moved further into the kitchen and stopped Lilian from grabbing the tray of food.

"Beloved?" Lilian's tone was questioning as she spoke.

"Why..." Kevin's voice cracked, but he quickly cleared his throat with a cough and tried again. "Why don't you sit down while I set the table." Lilian blinked and actually looked like she was about to protest when he spoke again. "I mean... it looks like you worked really hard to make this and, uh, well, I guess I just don't feel right making you do all the work so... um... uh... what I mean is... you've already made dinner, so it would only be right if I... you know..."

Those who knew the problems Kevin had when in the presence of the fairer sex would have been surprised by just how much he had been able to get out before he started stumbling over his words. Eric would have needed a quadruple bypass if he had been here to see this.

Even Kevin was surprised by his own boldness, such as it was. Though, his came more from the fact that he was being polite to the girl who had barged into his life without any regard to his thoughts and feelings than because he was actually capable of speaking to her. Seriously, this girl had practically destroyed any sense of normality his life possessed, yet here he was, treating her kindly and offering to do things for her. Anyone else would have kicked the girl out by now.

It must have been because of all the lessons his mom had instilled in him about how it was important to always be a gentleman. That was what happened when you were raised by a single mother. With no father figure in his life, the only person he had to listen to was her. Thus, everything she said was taken as the gospel truth and applied to his life without hesitation. Her words and lessons were pretty much ingrained into his psyche.

Lilian stared at Kevin with The Look. It was a look that he had never quite seen before, but some other males may have when they did something surprisingly sweet for their girlfriend/lover/spouse/significant other. Kevin, who had never had a girlfriend before and thus never been subject to The Look found himself struck speechless... and red. He had never felt so flustered in his life.

No. Wait. He did. Whenever he was in Lilian's presence, he felt this way. Never mind.

He should just be thankful it wasn't THE LOOK™, which was frightening enough to send any man running for the hills.

Speechlessness turned into a burning sense of self-consciousness when Lilian smiled at him, leaned up, and gave him a lingering kiss on the cheek.

While his face felt like it was being burnt by a flame thrower, she gave him an adoring look and said a soft, "thank you," in his ear before moving towards the table and sitting down.

Kevin found himself standing there, his face burning as if someone had stuck it in the very oven that had just been used by Lilian to cook dinner. It felt so hot he would not be surprised if someone told him he had steam pouring out of his ears.

He really needed to work on this blushing problem of his. It wouldn't do if he blushed every time Lilian did something like this, especially since it was going to be happening quite a lot in this story.

Trying to shake himself from his stupor, Kevin quickly made to grab the tray of what looked like some kind of chicken dish with potatoes and various vegetables. While he didn't know the name of the dish, he did recognize it from his cookbook. It was one of the meals he had never made before, mostly because it took too much time to cook for his tastes.

He picked it up and walked over to the table where Lilian was waiting with a small smile, her tail curled around the chair with surprising dexterity. After setting the food down and serving a plate for both himself and Lilian, the high school sophomore sat down opposite the fox girl.

For the first several minutes neither of them spoke. Lilian seemed to be waiting for him to say something and Kevin simply didn't know what to say. This was not a position he had ever been in before. It felt almost like he and Lilian were on a date.

Not that it was! A date, that is. It was just him and the gorgeous girl he had taken home with him having dinner together.

That... sounded a lot worse than it really was, didn't it?

Anyway, his lack of experience in these kinds of situations, combined with his general inability to form coherent sentences around members of the female persuasion most of the time made it impossible for him to actually start a conversation.

Good thing he was the only one who had that problem.

"I hope you like the food," Kevin was startled when Lilian spoke up. He looked up to see the girl staring at him with the same look she always gave him. It was a look that would have made him blush... except he was already blushing so it didn't do much at the moment. "I found it in that cook book of yours so it's new for me. I don't know how good it is."

Not sure how to respond to the girl, Kevin cut a slice of the chicken, stuck it in his mouth and began to chew. So long as he was eating, he wouldn't have to talk, right?

"So how is it?"

So much for that thought.

Swallowing, Kevin said, "It's pretty good." And it was, the chicken was a tad over cooked, but the only reason he could tell was because Kevin was a Master when it came to cooking meat. It was really the only talent he had when it came to cooking. He had at least a +32 skill set when it came to cooking meat (at least it would be +32 if this were one of those MMO video games like WOW or something). The rest of his cooking was okay at best, but certainly nothing to brag over.

And it wasn't like having chicken that was overcooked by a minute or two detracted from the meal. Everything else was pretty much perfect. The spices were blended to perfection; the vegetables were steamed just right; the potatoes had been baked flawlessly and had just the right amount of seasoning.

"Really?" Lilian sighed in relief as she began cutting up her own food. "I'm glad to hear that. I was kind of worried. Even though this is supposed to be really easy to make, I wasn't sure how good it would be. It's my first time cooking dinner on my own, you see."

"Really?"

"Mhmm." Lilian stuck the slice of chicken she had speared with her fork into her mouth. She chewed thoughtfully, swallowed, then continued where she left off. "I usually had help from Kotohime. This is my first time cooking without her telling me what to do."

"Well, don't worry too much," Kevin mumbled just before he took another bite of food. "It's good. You're a much better cook than I am." Truthfully, Kevin was kind of jealous. This was technically the first meal she had ever cooked on her own and it was already better than anything he had ever made and he had been cooking for years.

Really, the only consolation he had was that he was better at determining the amount of time needed to grill the chicken, and that wasn't much of a consolation.

"Thank you." Lilian smiled brightly at him, making the boy almost choke on the piece of chicken he had swallowed. He managed to avoid doing so, but it was a close thing.

Feeling bashful, Kevin decided to do his best to ignore Lilian and eat the food on his plate. This didn't seem to bother the redhead, who simply began eating as well.

She was still staring at him though.

It made him feel really awkward.

"So how was school?" she asked after several moments when the only sound was the "chink, chink" of eating utensils clinking against plates.

"Eh? It was alright, I guess," Kevin mumbled after a moment or two. "Nothing really interesting happened."

He decided not to mention Chris. No need to talk about that incident when he wasn't even sure what it was all about.

"What's it like?"

"What? School?"

"Yeah."

"It's... alright, I guess. There's really not much to tell." He shrugged. "It's school, we go there, learn stuff, hang out with friends, then go home. It's kind of boring actually." Kevin looked at the red haired fox girl a bit oddly. "You sound as if you've never been to school before."

"I haven't," Lilian answered. "I was home schooled all my life. In fact, before meeting you, I never really had the chance to meet many humans."

"Seriously?" asked Kevin, forgetting for a moment that the person before him was an attractive female as a look of thoughtful curiosity overcame his features.

Come to think of it, he was pretty sure he remembered her telling him something about her being home schooled earlier today.

She had, actually. Kevin had just spent so much time freaking out that his mind had simply skimmed over

When Lilian nodded her head, Kevin leaned back in his chair. "Wow." Deciding to indulge his curiosity some more and ask a question about something that had been bothering him, he said, "So what are you doing all the way out here, anyways? Were you and your family on vacation or something?"

"Ah!" Lilian gasped, causing Kevin to jerk in surprise. He looked at the girl, who had a light flush of pink on her cheeks that seemed to bring out the softness of her angelic, princess-esque features.

Naturally, Kevin began blushing too.

"Well... you see..." Lilian started to answer his question, only to stop, her face turning an even darker shade of red. The girl quickly shrank in on herself, the lower half of her face becoming hidden within her shirt... his shirt. "It was... well..."

As Lilian continuously failed to answer his question and stumbled over her words, Kevin began to frown. It shouldn't have be that hard to answer, should it? It was a simple question. Had something embarrassing happened for her to end up in this area without her family?

Then again, given how bloody she was, maybe her family had been attacked by some other group of supernatural creatures. It was perfectly possible. If Kitsune existed, then surely there were other mythological beings out there as well.

Or maybe they had been ambushed by a military unit that dealt with the supernatural and wanted to perform inhumane experiments on her and her family in order to make an army of super powered humans and she was just worried about telling him, a human, about what happened in case he decided to betray her trust and reveal to said group of para-military scientists that he knew where she was.

Regardless of Kevin's ridiculous conspiracy theories, neither of those scenarios seemed plausible at the moment, nor would they explain why Lilian was blushing like some kind of anime schoolgirl.

After several seconds of stumbling and stuttering, Lilian attempted to move off the subject of how she had arrived in Arizona without her family by saying, "So have you tried the potatoes?"

It wasn't a very subtle way of changing topics—it wasn't subtle at all, but Kevin decided that if she didn't want to answer, he wouldn't force her to tell him anything.

He really should have.

After dinner, Kevin decided to wash the dishes. Not necessarily because he wanted to be polite, but more because he simply felt weird about having a girl who was only a temporary (he hoped) resident in his apartment do all the chores.

Lilian tried to tell him she could do it, but he was insistent. In the end, she hadn't been able to out-stubborn him. Strangely enough, the thought of using her sex appeal, which would have worked on him like a charm, didn't occur to her.

When he finished cleaning the table and washing the dishes, Kevin found himself sitting on the couch, watching a soccer game between Brazil and India. No, that wasn't quite true. It would be much more accurate to say he was *trying* to watch the soccer game, but most of his attention was on the girl who had taken to cuddling directly into his side.

When dinner had concluded he had told Lilian to go sit on the couch, which she had. As soon as he joined her and turned on the TV, she scooted over and leaned into him until their forms had practically melded together. Now Kevin was trying to distract himself from the feel of her amazing body as the two of them sat together like a young couple in love.

As you can probably tell, he wasn't having much luck.

Some people would probably wonder why Kevin didn't just tell her to stop if she was making him uncomfortable. It could be because he was very weak-willed when it came to denying women anything, or maybe it was because he had been rendered speechless by the girl snuggling with him, as well as the fact that she was snuggling with him in the first place.

Besides, it wasn't like he was really suffering. He wasn't gay, just shy. And no man, shy or not, wouldn't enjoy having such a beautiful female cuddled up to them. Period.

Let it be known now that All Men are Perverts, even when they can only be considered Accidental Pornomancers and not the true Deus Sex Machina version of that particular trope.

And so he sat there, stiff as a board (in more ways than one), trying to keep himself from passing out. It was only when the clock chimed to let him know it was past nine p.m. that Kevin realized there was another problem, one he hadn't thought about until that moment.

Sleeping arrangements: he needed to find a place for Lilian to sleep. He had given her permission to stay until she could get in touch with her family and he wasn't going to be a jerk and kick her out, but there were only two beds and he didn't feel comfortable letting her sleep in his mom's room.

"So… I guess you can sleep in here," Kevin told her as they found themselves standing in his bedroom. He had just finished his nightly ritual: brushing his teeth and getting dressed in a pair of pajama bottoms (he normally wore boxer shorts, but didn't feel comfortable walking around in boxers while Lilian was there for obvious reasons) and was now ready to go to bed.

On a side note, he was very uncomfortable with the way Lilian kept staring at his bare chest like she was imagining something tasty. It was extremely disconcerting. The way she was licking her lips didn't help.

Maybe he should put a shirt on as well. Just in case.

"I'll sleep on the couch."

"Huh?" Lilian frowned at him, her countenance expressing confusion. Her head tilted ever so slightly to the left and her foxy ears twitched. Kevin was torn between wanting to look away to hide his renewed red face and wanting caress her ears.

As expected of an animal lover, even in the face of

embarrassment, he couldn't help but be fascinated with her foxy features. And yes, that was a pun.

"Why would you want to sleep on the couch?"

Kevin sent her a surprisingly blank look. "Where else would I sleep?"

"With me."

"S-somehow, I feel I should have expected that answer." He really walked into that one. "B-but we can't... uh... y-you know... we can't do... *that*."

The look on Lilian's face told Kevin that she had no clue what he was talking about. Her words only confirmed what he had already guessed. "Can't do what?"

"We can't...." Kevin's cheeks felt inflamed, "you know...."

"No, I don't know." Lilian frowned at him, clearly bothered that he wasn't just getting on with telling her what he was talking about. She wanted to sleep with her mate and wasn't willing to wait much longer. "What can't we do?"

She was really going to make him say it, wasn't she?

"We can't... can't...." Kevin looked around warily, his head turning left and right, as if expecting someone to be listening in. When he saw that there was no one aside from him and the girl before him, he leaned towards Lilian and cupped his hand to his mouth, then whispered, "We can't sl... sle...slee...sleeeeooo..."

"Sleep together?" Lilian raised a single, delicate eyebrow.

"Yeah, that."

Lilian just continued to stare at him. She couldn't quite comprehend where he was going with this. "Why not?"

"Why not?" Kevin parroted, gawking at her. "Because it's... it's wrong, that's why. It's inappropriate for a girl and guy to sleep together."

"You're silly," Lilian smiled as she grabbed his hand and tried to pull him towards the bed. "Of course it's okay for us to sleep together. You're my mate. And besides," Lilian's smile widened as she looked at him from over her shoulder. "I believe it is time we finally got down to committing passionate acts of eroticism... ufufufu..."

Kevin's reaction to those last four words was very impressive. First, his eyes widened almost comically, to the point where it looked like his eyeballs might just roll out of their sockets. Next, his jaw dropped into an open mouthed gape. And finally, he blushed from the roots of his hair all the way down to his chest.

A second later, Kevin passed out. Again.

He's been doing that a lot since Lilian came into his life. Such was the price of becoming involved with a Kitsune.

***

Kevin woke up to the sun burning into his retina through the large window in the living room. Releasing a low groan, the young boy closed his eyes and decided that the day could begin a little later. Like when the sun wasn't trying it's damnest to blind him.

After waking up from his shocking, or not so shocking, moment of unconsciousness, Kevin had told the girl, in no uncertain terms, that they wouldn't be sleeping together. Lilian had pouted and tried to tell him that it was perfectly acceptable for them to sleep with each other and explore the more physical aspects of their relationship (she'd even had that creepy 'ufufufu' laugh. Seriously, what was up with that?), but Kevin had been stubborn in his refusal, reiterating his reasons and claiming they didn't have a relationship to explore.

Eric would have been very disappointed in him for not taking advantage of the opportunity given to him.

A pitiful moan escaped his lips as he opened his eyes again. Oh how he wished that stupid window had not been set on the east side of the apartment. Whoever had come up with the idea of making stupidly large windows that spanned entire rooms to let mass amounts of sunlight in needed to be shot.

Well, maybe not shot, but they should definitely be punched in the face for coming up with such a horrendous architectural design. No one wanted to wake up to blinding sunlight streaming in their eyes. Kevin sure didn't.

Blinking his eyes several times, Kevin's vision soon cleared. When they did, he was met with red.

Massive amounts of red.

His bleary eyes looked at the color in confusion. Because he was still so tired he couldn't quite tell what he was looking at. It just looked like a large, blurry blob of red that had no definitive shape.

Shifting a bit, the young blond male made himself more comfortable as he tried to figure out why his vision was being more or less blocked by so much red.

A soft moan made him freeze. His eyes widened as shock coursed through his body like a bolt of lightning. There was no way he could forget that voice, not after last night.

Oh no. No, no, no, no, no! There was no way she could be in here! She was sleeping in his bed, wasn't she? She wouldn't give up a comfortable bed just to sleep with him, would she?

Looking down, Kevin's delusion was shattered when he saw Lilian sleeping peacefully, her head on his chest and her hands resting against his torso. Her two fox tails were out and lying limply behind her and one of her long, beautiful legs was exposed as it had fallen off the edge of the couch, the top of her foot and toes on the floor.

Her shirt had bunched up above her lower back, meaning her small, perfectly shaped, tight derriere was completely visible to Kevin's not-so-virginal-anymore-but-still-very-innocent eyes.

Worse still, sometime during the night he must have gotten a really bad case of wandering hands because both appendages were currently holding a handful of said deliciously shaped buttocks. Almost out of some kind of genetically bred instinct, Kevin's hands squeezed the fleshy and well-toned rear end, ellicting a much lustier moan than the last one that had issued forth from Lilian's lips.

His eyes widened further as his mind began to truly comprehend and realize his situation.

Lilian was sleeping on him.

Her shirt had exposed her rear end to him.

His hands were currently on said rear end.

Oh, and she wasn't wearing any panties.

Naturally, he did the only thing he could think of.

He screamed.

***

In another apartment and several seconds before Kevin woke up to find Lilian using him as a pillow, another couple was currently resting in the apartment directly beneath them.

Mr. and Mrs. Smith were your stereotypical middle aged couple. Mr. Smith worked an average job with average pay and Mrs. Smith was a stay at home wife who cooked, cleaned and did the laundry. Think Lucy Ricardo from that old TV series *I Love Lucy* and you've pretty much got it.

They didn't have any children, though not for lack of trying. Nor did they know whose fault it was that they couldn't procreate as they hadn't gone to a doctor to find out. Mrs. Smith didn't want her husband to feel inadequate by finding out he was impotent and Mr. Smith didn't want his wife to be heartbroken by discovering she was sterile. Now that was true love.

Currently, the two were asleep in their bed, resting peacefully, but that would change very soon.

"GYYAAAAHHHHH!"

Shooting straight up in bed, the two looked around frantically as a shrill scream that seemed to hold the absolute embodiment of terror pierced the air. Never in their lives had they heard someone sound so horrified before. It was bone chilling.

In another dimension, like, maybe in some kind of alternate reality, this would have been the end of it right here. Mr. and Mrs. Smith would have gone back to sleep being none the wiser as to what was happening above them. Unfortunately for them, this was not another dimension or an alternate reality.

"LILIAN! WHAT THE HECK ARE YOU DOING ON MY COUCH!?"

Mr. and Mrs. Smith blinked. There was a slight pause. The two thought they heard someone speaking, but the noise was too low and garbled for them to hear.

"I don't care if I'm warmer than the bed! I gave you that bed for a reason!"

More blinking ensued.

"NO, I WON'T JOIN YOU ON THE BED!" A pause. "And what do you mean "Why not?" You should know just why not!" Another pause. "Don't answer my question with another question!"

Massive blinking.

"What do you think is going on up there, dear?" asked Mrs. Smith.

"NO YOU CANNOT JOIN ME IN THE SHOWER!"

There were several loud thumps, followed by several more equally loud thumps, which was also followed by what sounded like someone pounding on a door. After a few seconds of this, the pounding seemed to stop.

While Mrs. Smith's face blushed a bright red, Mr. Smith grunted. "I have no clue." He laid back down and rolled onto his side. "And I don't wanna know either. It's too early for this crap. I'm going back to sleep."

Mrs. Smith stayed up for a while longer as her husband began to snore away. After several moments in which nothing happened, she also laid back down and decided to get some more shut eye. The horrifying scream and strange conversation that followed it were soon forgotten as she found herself in the land of Morpheus.

Life for Mr. and Mrs. Smith continued on normally.

Chapter 9: The Life of a Not so Normal Teenager

For the next week, life for Kevin continued normally.

Or at least as normally as possible when you had a fox girl who claimed you were her mate, called you Beloved instead of your actual name and tried to jump your bones every chance she got.

When put like that, his life didn't sound all that normal, did it?

That being said, he had at least managed to work out a daily routine that, while not ideal, kept him from losing what was left of his sanity. This "routine" went something like this: wake up, find Lilian asleep with him on the couch, share a "moment" with Lilian some time after he woke up in which he would become embarrassed because she was trying to sex him up, and she would pout because she hadn't succeeded. He would then go to school, stay after school for track practice three days out of the week, come back home to work on homework and have dinner, go to bed, and repeat the whole thing over again. That was the basics of what his life now entailed.

Sounds almost like the life of a regular high school student.

...

Pfft! Yeah right.

Sometimes Lilian would be waiting with food on the table when he got home, like on the days where he came home after track practice. He had to admit those times were nice. Lilian was an extraordinary cook. Even meals she had never made before often turned out better than anything he made, regardless of how long he had been cooking said dish compared to her.

It was a real blow to his pride as a chef, or at least someone who had been cooking for a number of years.

Life was just so unfair sometimes.

Other times, he would arrive early enough that after he finished his homework, he would be able to make dinner. He wasn't as good of a cook as Lilian, and didn't think he ever would be, but this didn't bother her one bit. Lilian loved it whenever he made something for her and had no trouble... expressing? Yeah, let's go with that. She had no trouble expressing her gratitude towards him.

Kevin couldn't help but feel a little hot under the collar when he thought about some of the things she had done to show her gratitude.

It shouldn't come as a surprise that all of those instances involved her trying to give him more physical affection than he could stand, often times while she was naked.

Considering she only wore one article of clothing anyways, that really didn't mean much.

Several particularly sexy situations stuck out in his mind more than others. One instance had really imprinted itself in his psyche. It had been a truly scarring experience. He didn't know people could bend like that.

Regardless of any of that, he had to admit that living with someone else, and a girl at that, was an interesting experience. Potentially lethal (Lilian was Dangerous with a capital D) and incredibly embarrassing, but interesting nonetheless.

He didn't think he would ever get used to it though.

After dinner, once again depending on the day, he would either get started on his homework or, if he was already finished, sit on the couch with Lilian and watch TV. Or play video games. Kevin had learned from Lilian that she had never played video games, which was a crime because video games were awesome. Apparently, her mom didn't approve of her children corroding their brain via video games, television or any other type of brain corroding media, or at least, that was the vibe he was getting from Lilian.

Talk about harsh.

On a side note, Kevin had blushed heavily when he noticed just how cute Lilian looked when concentrating on whatever video game they were playing. Whether it was killing zombies in Resident Evil or tapping away on the guitar controller for Guitar Overlord XII, she would always have this look of intense concentration where her delicate eyebrows would furrow cutely, and her small tongue would poke out from between her lips as she stared at the screen with a look of such utter focus that one would almost think she was watching Kevin while he slept.

And that sounded kind of creepy. Scratch that, it sounded *really* creepy. Good thing Kevin didn't know she did that. Watching him while he slept, that is.

Of course, just because he thought she was cute didn't actually mean anything, Kevin reassured himself every time Lilian did something that made his face heat up in a good way. You know, like an "aw, that's absolutely adorable!" kind of way as opposed to the "oh my god! I can't believe she just did that! I'm so embarrassed!" kind of way. And yes, there is a difference.

...Anyways, just because he thought she was attractive didn't mean he liked her like, well, like *that*. He was still in love with Lindsay, as he kept telling himself every time Lilian would catch him off guard with a kiss (you think he would be used to those after a week of being on the receiving end of them, but no).

Or when she would crawl onto the couch and sleep with him after he had fallen asleep even though she had a perfectly good bed.

Or when he would wake up the next morning to find her sleeping with him on the couch and them both in a very compromising position.

Yes, none of that stuff did anything to change his love for the girl he had been crushing on for the past three years.

Because having a girl that was the epitome of female perfection show how devoted she was to him would never change his mind. This wasn't some kind of anime where the beauty of the heroine is directly proportional to how quickly the main protagonist falls in love with them. If Kevin wanted to see that kind of crap happen, then he would go watch *Rosario+Vampire*.

Well, if nothing else, having a super hot fox-girl crawling onto his couch (and him) and using him as a life sized teddy bear gave him a great appreciation for the female figure.

As Eric would say, the girl was stacked.

This morning had been no different from all the other mornings he had woken up since Lilian barged into his life, even though it was a Saturday and there was no school. He had woken up after falling asleep on his couch. Like always, Lilian was lying on top of him, her head turned so that her cheek was resting against his chest, her breasts smashing into his torso and her legs a tangled mess with his own.

She still wasn't wearing panties, a fact that made itself known as she unconsciously rubbed herself against his left thigh, leaving behind a wet trail of something he'd prefer not to think about.

Needless to say, compromising did not begin to describe the situation properly.

As it had been five days since the first night Lilian had snuck onto the couch with him, he did not react by screaming his head off like all the other times this had happened.

He did, however, flush a deep shade of lobster red as he felt the girls bosom squishing against his chest. She still wasn't wearing a bra—not that she had one to use in the first place—so he could feel the stiff twin peaks on her chest rubbing against his skin through her shirt. Distracting also did not describe the situation properly.

Eventually, after laying there for upwards of five minutes like some kind of red faced idiot, Kevin managed to gain some semblance of self control.

Really, all that means is he managed to keep from passing out. In any case, with him now awake and no longer incapable of acting, he rolled the red haired beauty onto her side and got out from underneath her so he could take a shower.

It should be noted that this was much more difficult than it sounded. The reason being that Lilian seemed to be capable of sensing when his presence, or maybe the warmth of his body, was attempting to leave her. Each time he tried to get out from underneath her, the girl's hold on him would tighten. Often times she would actually wrap both her arms and legs around him in order to keep him from moving, making escaping her grasp a real challenge.

This morning was no different. Removing the girl's limbs from around his body took nearly ten minutes. Even her tail had decided to get in on the action.

Once in the bathroom and stripped down, Kevin put himself under the ice cold spray of the shower in an effort to bring the temperature of his overheating body back to manageable levels. Seriously, just staying in such close proximity to that girl made his entire body feel like it was being roasted over a fire.

As he stood there under the shower head, his eyes closed and his body shivering from the cold, the sound of the door clicking open went completely unnoticed.

While the sound of the door opening and closing went unnoticed, the shower curtain being pulled aside did not.

Startled, Kevin turned around, more out of instinct than any real desire to see who had intruded on his shower. It wasn't that hard to figure out who he would find standing behind him. There was only one other person in the apartment aside from himself.

Having turned a full 180 degrees, Kevin laid eyes upon the

person who was now in his presence.

His eyes widened. His jaw dropped. A shiver went all the way from the crown of his head down to his toes and his heart stopped beating for a full second before it sped up until it felt like a hummingbird was trying to fly out of his chest.

Lilian was standing before him, completely naked as she looked him over with a bright smile and flushed cheeks.

An odd strangled sound issued forth from Kevin's throat. If it had to be described, the sound would be something like "murgle." Naturally, Lilian ignored the noise he was making in favor of examining her mate in all his naked glory.

In his shock and blank-minded state he had not covered himself.

"Morning, Beloved," she looked him up and down once, then licked her lips in a way that was as blatant as it was suggestive. "You're looking delicious this morning. Seeing you like this makes me want to eat you... ufufufu..."

Her words managed to bring some coherency to our Hapless Hero's mind. His reaction was about what has come to be expected from him.

"W-Wh-What the heck are you doing in here!?" His voice was very high pitched as he spoke. More like shrieked. Not that he could necessarily be blamed, even if he *should* have expected this to happen at some point.

"I came to see if you wanted me to wash your back," Lilian was still staring at him. Her smile widened as she looked down again. "Though I could also help you wash... other hard to reach areas if you wanted... ufufufu..."

When he noticed just where her eyes were looking, he gave a mouse-like squeak and moved his hands to cover his crotch. Lilian pouted at him, but he ignored it.

"Out!"

"Aww, come on, Beloved."

Lilian's eyes grew phenomenally wider than usual as she looked at him. They became quite dewy as well. To top it off, her lower lip began quivering. The combination of wide, teary eyes and quivering lips created an irresistibly adorable look that would put any man regardless of sexual preference down for the count. In short, she had just unleashed the ultimate technique.

"Please..."

"Guh!"

Kevin struggled not to give into the dreaded Puppy Dog Eyes. Or would they be Foxy Kit Eyes? He supposed it didn't matter. No matter what this fearsome technique was called, it was a struggle to keep his resolve from breaking at the sight of something so *moe*.

The fox ears drooping on her head did not help one bit. Nor did the fact that she was naked.

"I-I won't be swayed..."

In an attempt not to let her expression or nudity get to him, Kevin ended up covering his eyes with his hands (and thus forgetting to keep other things covered).

This effort to not look at the girl before him was ruined before it even began because Kevin, bless his soul, despite being a shy and easily embarrassed young man, was also a teenage male. Some things never change when it comes to the male gender

All Men are Perverts is a trope that can be applied to all men, which meant it applied to Kevin just as surely as it did for someone like, say, Eric. It is this thorough and well-explained reasoning that expounds upon why the young man's efforts were doomed right from the very start.

What did he do that made his efforts end up being in vain?

He did what any male in his position would do.

"You're peeking~" Lilian sang out in a teasing and pleased voice.

"Wha—!?" Kevin quickly covered his eyes more fully. "N-No I wasn't!"

"Oh?" Lilian quirked one of her delicate eyebrows. Her lips curved into a smile. Not that Kevin could see it anymore. "Then what were you doing?"

"N-Nothing."

Liar.

"Hmm... well, whatever. If you don't want to admit you were peeking at me that's fine."

"Ugh!"

That was Kevin receiving a metaphorical punch to the gut.

"Just knowing that you were looking at me is enough to make me feel special."

"Urk!"

This girl was quite merciless.

"I-I wasn't... I mean, I didn't..." Kevin tried to explain himself, not that he would be able to because, really, he would be lying and everyone knew how good he was at that. And it wasn't like it mattered anyways. Lilian wasn't listening anymore.

"Sure, sure, I believe you." She obviously didn't. "Anyways, are you sure you don't want me to wash your back? I promise you'll enjoy it, ufufufu."

Lilian took a step into the shower. Kevin twitched as he peeked through his hands again when he heard her feet make a 'pitter, patter' sound against the wet tile.

A second later he squawked in surprise and began backing up

while Lilian advanced on him. Soon, he found himself pressed against the tiled wall with nowhere to go as Lilian continued to walk more fully into shower and stopped once she was directly under the spray of water.

"I didn't get to help you wash up these last few days because you always woke up and finished showering before I could join you." Naturally, because he had planned it like that ever since she first tried to join him. "So I was hoping I could wash your back today."

His arms dropping to his side like a pair of fifty pound weights had been strapped to them, Kevin's pupils dilated as he took in the sight before him. And what a sight. Standing under the spray of the shower head, Lilian looked even more bewitching than she normally did.

That was saying a lot, considering Kevin had already freely admitted, if only to himself, that she was the most gorgeous example of a female he had ever seen.

Her long, lustrous red hair was matted down on her head and plastered to her skin. Her bangs stuck along her cheeks and forehead, surrounding and somehow making her emerald irises even more enchanting than they usually were. Several of the longer strands were sticking to her body in strategic locations that almost seemed like they had been placed there for the sole purpose of drawing his eyes to the beautiful curves she possessed.

Kevin subconsciously gulped as he saw one particularly long strand flowing down her neck, moving across her collar bone before roving over the upper swell of the ample curve of her bosom as it traveled a dangerous path straight down the center of her incredibly well formed breast, just barely managing to conceal her nipple from view. Another was flowing along the outer swell of her right breast, following that perfect curve before sticking along the side of her slim waist.

There were many other strands that drew attention to more of Lilian's perfect body. Kevin found it hard to keep his eyes from trying to follow all of them.

And that was to say nothing for the water that traveled down her glorious figure. Tiny droplets from the spray above that soaked her body and trailed wet paths across her perfect, unblemished skin. Kevin's eyes caught one adventurous droplet as it left a trail down her slender neck, traveled along the dips and curves and contours of her upper body as it moved towards her chest, where it proceeded to roam along the swell of her breast before disappearing between her cleavage and reappearing along her taut, flat stomach several seconds later. After dipping into and out of her belly button, it disappeared within the trimmed patch of red hair just above her, well, let's just call it her girl spot.

Looking back up, Kevin's eyes were inexplicably captured by the hypnotic green irises of the girl who had claimed he was her mate. She was smiling at him, seemingly pleased about something, though he could not fathom what. Actually, he couldn't fathom much of anything right now. His mind had temporarily left him.

It may have had something to do with all the blood flowing from his head to somewhere else.

"Well?" Lilian asked, forcing Kevin to snap out of his daze. He took one look at her mischievous and seductive expression, then flushed bright red.

"N-No thank you," Kevin's breathing was heavy as he tried to retain his hold on his consciousness. His vision was beginning to darken, but he valiantly fought against it. *Do not pass out, Kevin. Passing out in the shower is bad.*

"In that case," Lilian began again, turning around and exposing her backside to him. It was currently hidden by the waterfall of long, thigh length red hair, but that would change soon.

Grabbing her hair, Lilian moved the silken strands over her shoulder, exposing her entire backside to him. She then craned her neck to look at him out of the corner of her eye. "Perhaps you would like to wash my back?" A seductive smile crossed her lips as she wiggled her tight, toned tush at him. "Or maybe you'd like to wash something else?"

This time with an unfettered view of her backside, Kevin found himself once more trailing the girls flawless form. His eyes took in her soft, feminine shoulders and traveled along the delicate arch of her back before stopping at the tight, peach-shaped butt that seemed to jump out at him as dozens of water droplets traveled over and around it. The single tail she had out was even lifted into the air so that it would not spoil his view of those perfectly rounded twin cheeks.

Kevin's breathing picked up. The feeling of light-headedness intensified and his vision started to blur.

This was not the first or even the fifth time that he had seen Lilian naked. Kevin had become far too familiar with some of Lilian's more prolific habits, such as her dislike of wearing clothes when reading. He had caught her a number of times, laying on her stomach, bare as the day she was born, her feet kicking in the air as she read whatever book she found (she seemed to be mostly interested in his manga).

The girl seemed to have no sense of modesty. So yes, he had caught sight of her naked plenty of times this past week.

But this? This was different. Those other times she had been nude, yes, but it was more like she simply enjoyed being in a more natural state of dress. Or undress, as it were. He could deal with that, albeit, his face would burn like nothing else, but he could still deal with it.

What he could not deal with was this deliberate act of eroticism. Never in his life had he dealt with or even *seen* something like this. It was like something out of one of those pornos Eric had hidden under his bed.

In other words, it was far too much sexy for him to take.

Had Eric or any other male been in Kevin's place, they would have surely lost any and all sense of self restraint. A good thing it was Kevin and not those other males then. While they would have probably ravished Lilian right then and there, Kevin did the exact same thing he had done when the fox-girl had first introduced herself.

He passed out.

**

Somewhere around an hour later, Kevin found himself sitting at the table, eating a small breakfast of scrambled eggs and bacon with a glass of milk. It was a nice breakfast. Lilian had put spinach and chopped onions, as well as a mix of spices beyond salt and pepper, in his eggs to enhance the overall flavor.

Despite how good it was, he could hardly taste it. Which was strange since he was focusing on his meal with far more intensity than most people would ever give their food.

Even his movements seemed to denote that in spite of the amount of focus he was giving his breakfast, he really wasn't all there. They were mechanical, automatic. If a robot could eat, it would likely be eating with the same mechanized precision that Kevin was currently using.

Why was he focusing so much on his eating to the exclusion of everything else? What could cause such a reaction out of our Main Protagonist?

The reason was as simple as it was obvious: Lilian. The girl in question was sitting where she always sat, on the opposite side of the table. Having finished her own meal, the red head had taken up her favorite past time of watching him.

It was disconcerting to the extreme. Enough to make anyone

self-conscious, even those who had so much confidence in themselves that they were straddling the line of arrogance and narcissism.

Naturally, Kevin was trying to find something, *anything*, that could help keep him from looking in her direction. Hence, the focusing on his eating, not the food itself, but rather the movements that were involved in the act. It was his belief that if he focused exclusively on what he was doing, he would be able to ignore the fox girl's flagrant staring.

It wasn't working out very well. He could literally feel her eyes boring through his skull. It caused his own to look over at her every now and then. When this happened, she could catch his eye and smile. This would cause him to blush and look away, unable to maintain eye contact for any longer than that as his mind replayed the shower scene of a few minutes ago.

A part of him, a very large, significant part, was still having trouble comprehending that scenario. He just couldn't understand what had possessed her to do that. Did she really think sneaking into his bathroom while he was taking a shower and doing... what she did was a good idea?

Who the heck was he kidding? Of course she thought it was a good idea. As far as Lilian was concerned, he was her mate. Any chance of them doing... something that he had absolutely no intention of even thinking about, much less doing, was a good idea to her.

Speaking of which, he still wasn't really sure what being her mate entailed. He understood what the term meant in the animal kingdom, but he couldn't see how they could mean the exact same thing in this instance, considering Lilian was most certainly not an animal. Was it like some kind of Kitsune marriage or something?

Ugh, now there was something he didn't want to think about. He was only fifteen. The idea of being married at his age was not appealing.

And besides, he was in love with Lindsay. Yeah, Lilian was gorgeous. Way prettier than Lindsay or any other girl could ever hope to be, but looks weren't everything. He liked — loved! Lindsay for who she was, not how she looked.

Of course, Lilian had her good points too. She was actually a very sweet girl (when she wasn't pulling a sexy act on him), and nice, and she really did seem dedicated to him and—

—No! Don't think about her, Kevin. Remember Lindsay, the girl you're in love with. She had plenty of good qualities. She was athletic and outgoing. She wasn't like those really fake girls who complained about everything and were really rude. Lindsay had substance.

Lilian had substance too, but it was a whole different kind of substance. It was the kind he was not willing to get into, lest he end up having some kind of anime moment and be blown back by a nosebleed or something equally impossible for a regular human to actually do.

Given all that had happened so far, he wouldn't be surprised if impossible actions like that were not only possible, but extremely probable.

Against his will, his eyes returned once more to the girl sitting across from him. Lilian was already watching him so she saw when he looked her way. The moment their eyes connected, a smile that lit up the entire room came across her face.

Kevin felt his own face become hot. In an effort not to get too embarrassed, he looked down.

This turned out to be a mistake. The moment he looked down, his eyes came in line with something that was even more distracting than Lilian's beautiful face.

Two guesses as to what that was.

"Do you like them?"

"Wha...?" Kevin's head snapped up so quickly that a loud crack came with the action. Containing a wince, he stared at Lilian, who was smiling broadly at him.

"My boobs," she said, and once more Kevin got to witness just how shameless this girl was as she grabbed her own breasts and began squeezing them together. "Do you like them?"

"Guh!" Screw the furnace. Kevin was pretty sure his face had just gone nuclear! "O-O-Of course not! Wh-wh-why would you ask something like that!?"

"Well," Lilian stretched out the word as she looked down at herself. Kevin followed her gaze and "eeped!", yes "eeped!" when he saw the red head hefting the two, perfectly shaped globes in her hands. Despite being clothed, he could easily see her nipples outlined by the shirt as her breasts were pressed together. "You've been staring at them a lot. I just thought you might like them."

She looked up and once more locked eyes with him.

"It's not like I mind if you look, you know." Her cheeks tinted pink as she looked down. It was such a rare moment of demure from the normally bubbly and shameless girl that Kevin's mouth went dry and his face, impossible as it may seem, became even hotter. "I want you to look at me. It makes me feel special."

Well crap. What was he supposed to say to that?

"L-Look," Kevin stuttered, "It's not that you're not pretty or anything, cuz you are." The smile that lit Lilian's face made him feel very ashamed for some reason. "But I wasn't looking at, well, I wasn't looking at... those."

Lilian seemed very disappointed to know that he wasn't looking at her breasts. Her head dropped down to look at the table, long bangs falling over her face to further shadow her eyes from view as a frown marred those beautiful lips.

To go along with this crestfallen look, Lilian's shoulders slumped to further give the impression of someone who was down in the dumps. Even her ears began drooping in what could only be described as depression.

Kevin felt like a heel, but at the same time he just didn't understand. Why did this girl enjoy it when he ogled her? Didn't girls not like it when you stared at their... uh... feminine parts so blatantly? Eric had gotten slapped more than once—try a couple dozen—because a girl caught him staring at her chest.

Then again, Eric was a well known pervert, with multiple peeking infractions.

Nothing said "I have no respect for women" better then spying on girls via hiding in one of the unused lockers and peeping them while they changed. Just how his friend had managed to get out of that particular scandal with only two weeks worth of suspension was beyond him.

Ah, the benefits of having a Principle as a father.

Tangent on Eric's perversion aside, that still didn't answer his question. That being why she was so okay with him staring at her like she was a piece of meat. There had to be more to it than her simply not possessing any nudity taboos. Was this another Kitsune thing? Or was it just a Lilian thing? Did she not mind him staring at her because she thought Kevin was her mate? Or was there some other reason?

Kevin didn't know. Just thinking about it gave him a headache.

"So, if you weren't looking at my boobs, what were you looking at?" Oh God, even her voice sounded downtrodden. Was it really that big of a deal? Maybe he should have just been honest with her?

No. There was no way he could do that. Not after he had already told her that he had not been staring at her breasts. He would have to come up with an excuse to get out of this.

In other words he needed to lie.

Too bad he sucked at lying.

Think quick, Kevin.

"I was looking at... your clothes."

"My clothes?"

Lilian looked down at the large band T-shirt she was wearing. It was one of Kevin's shirts that she had taken to wearing around the house because he had asked her to.

Personally, Lilian would have been perfectly content to walk around naked all day, but for some reason her mate preferred her to be dressed in something. She wasn't quite sure what to think about that, whether she should be insulted or not, but had deferred to him as he was her mate and this was his apartment.

She looked back up a second later.

"What about them?"

"Well..."

Kevin scratched at his cheek as he tried to figure out where he could take this. Dang. This whole 'being dishonest' thing was a lot harder than it looked. How did Eric manage to come up with such awesome lies?

"I was thinking that we should get you some of your own clothes to wear."

Hey, that actually sounded like a pretty good idea. She didn't have any clothes of her own, right? Of course not, she had told him so during their conversation the morning after their first meeting.

The more he thought about it, the better an idea it seemed. Maybe having her own clothes would even make her stop trying to prance around naked all the time.

And maybe pigs would start flying, hell would freeze over and the dead would rise to devour the flesh of the living.

"I mean, you can't go anywhere wearing one of my shirts and nothing else." He was being literal with that.

"I guess not," Lilian frowned, her nose wrinkling cutely. "You humans have very strange taboos when it comes to public decency."

"I don't think they're that strange," Kevin said just a tad dryly. "Besides," he continued to try and drive his point home, "You wouldn't want just anyone to see you running around in your…" he paused, trying to think of a delicate way of saying what he wanted to say, "…birthday suit, would you?"

Lilian didn't even take a second to think about the question before shaking her head. "No. The only person I want looking at me when I'm naked is you."

Having not expected such a response, Kevin choked on some of the eggs he was eating.

"Beloved!"

Lilian rushed out of her seat, moved behind her mate and began gently rubbing his back as he started pounding a fist against his chest in an effort to dislodge the bits of egg that went down his windpipe.

"Are you alright, Beloved?" she asked as Kevin began taking grateful breaths of air after nearly asphyxiating on his food. That would not have been a very pleasant way to die.

"I'm fine," Kevin coughed a few more times before looking up at the girl. "Thank you."

"You're welcome." The smile she gave him had Kevin turning away to hide the redness of his cheeks. Lilian cast him a curious glance as he looked away, but decided not to question him and sat back down in her seat.

"So, anyways..." after several minutes of awkward (to him at least) silence, Kevin tried to get back on track. "I was thinking that since today is Saturday, we could go and get you some clothes of your own after breakfast."

"Okay," Lilian said, smiling at the blond haired sophomore. "Thank you."

"Ah...ahem," Kevin coughed into his hand to hide the squeak he emitted. "You're welcome."

Chapter 10: Skirts, Skorts and Lingerie

Kevin was sure that everyone pointing and whispering at him and Lilian as they walked through the mall were making fun of him.

How did he know this? Technically speaking, he didn't, but that wasn't going to stop his mind from coming to such a conclusion. He could just tell.

They were probably making fun of how red his face was. It was red enough that he could outred a red star.

That was a *seriously* red face.

After washing the dishes, Kevin had decided he would take Lilian shopping at the nearest mall, which was only several minutes away from his mom's apartment by bike. Convenient right?

Naturally, they had run into their first problem before they even left. Lilian didn't have any clothes to wear. How was she supposed to even go outside if she had nothing to wear?

They had managed to solve this problem easily enough. While his mom was a size or two larger than Lilian, as well as being a good half a foot taller, they fit her well enough that so long as she used a belt to keep her skirt up, they wouldn't need to worry about her outfit falling off.

They had chosen a fashionable skirt that went down to Lilian's knees and was being held up by a belt, a pink spaghetti strap blouse that complimented her crimson locks of hair very well and a pair of sandals. They actually didn't look too bad, even if the straps of her shirt had tried to slide off her slender shoulders several times within the past few seconds alone.

On a side note, Lilian had categorically refused to wear any of his mom's panties. Not that they would have fit anyways. She was slimmer than his mom.

Thankfully, she had agreed to at least wear a bra. Surprisingly, Lilian and his mom had the same bust size, which was more information than he ever wanted to know about the woman who gave birth to him. Seriously, who wants to know their mother has the same sized tits as the girl claiming to be in love with them? On the other hand, it was interesting to note that because Lilian was slimmer than his mom and shorter than her as well, her breasts actually appeared to be much bigger than they really were.

After he had finished making this observation, Lilian had questioned why his face was so red, which just made him blush more.

Now they were walking down one of the large walkways inside of the nearest mall, Lilian was holding his arm tightly, and consequently smashing said arm between said breasts. Which, by the way, was the reason Kevin's face had retained its redness ever since they had arrived. In all honesty, it was surprising that the boy had not passed out from over stimulation yet.

Perhaps he was gaining some kind of resistance? Or maybe it was just a convenient Plot Device? Who knows.

Lining either side of the large walkway were numerous shops that sold everything from toys and books to sports gear and shoes, to clothing and sunglasses. It was a very large mall, with somewhere around a hundred stores so there was a lot of variety.

Milling around the store, walking and chatting with their friends or just going it alone, were all kinds of people. Kevin could see everything from businessmen talking on their cellphones to goths that looked very similar to new aged Vampires with their dark clothes, heavy amounts of eye shadow, mascara and the ridiculous amount of sparkles that made them look like they had been shot several hundred times with a glitter canon. The mall was a place where all kinds of people could go to relax and enjoy some down time.

"You seem awfully excited," Kevin tried to make conversation so he could ignore the stares and his own burning face. Both were hard to ignore, especially since half the reason for his face was due to the stares.

It should be noted that a number of those staring were men, and the ones not actually glaring at Kevin were staring at Lilian, not him. He just didn't know that because he had his own problems to deal with.

Meanwhile, the women those men were with were glaring at their boyfriends/lovers/significant others for their staring... that, or they were glaring at Lilian for being the cause of their boyfriends/lovers/significant others staring. It was almost like they were blaming her for being hotter than they were.

Strange right?

A good few of the men that were blatantly ogling Lilian ended up receiving a smack to the back of the head when they were caught staring at certain parts of the red head's anatomy that they really shouldn't be staring at.

Still keeping herself latched onto his arm as they walked side by side, Lilian stopped her enthusiastic gawking of the mall and turned her head to look at him.

"I've never been to such a big shopping center before," Lilian informed him, her voice sounded just as excited as the light of wonder in her eyes looked. Kevin was surprised. What girl had never been to a mall before? Girls were supposed to love malls! "The town I grew up in was very small. I think there were only a couple hundred people living there all together. We didn't have a mall, just a grocery store, a clothing store, and a couple of places to eat."

"I see," Kevin mumbled as he tried to shift out of Lilian's grip. No luck. The girl was stronger than she looked, and she was latched onto him like some kind of leech. "You mentioned you were from Greece." Lilian absently nodded as she went back to looking around the mall with an almost childlike eagerness. "How come you're so good at speaking English? I would have thought you'd at least have an accent or something. If you hadn't told me you were from Greece, I would have never believed you were Greek."

"Technically, I'm not Greek. I think I told you my mom is English. We just moved to Greece before I gained my second tail, so I don't remember much of my time in England."

Chagrined, Kevin said, "Ah, right. Sorry."

"It's fine." When Lilian smiled at him, he flushed red and looked away. "The reason we can understand each other and I don't have an accent is because I'm a Kitsune." When he looked back to give her with an expression that quite clearly said "I'm confused" she elaborated by saying, "Kitsune are blessed by Lord Inari with the ability to understand any language spoken to us so that we can better integrate ourselves into human society no matter what country we live in. This ability works both ways, so the people we are talking to understand us no matter what language we're speaking."

She grinned at him, and for the first time since meeting her, Kevin got a glance at her sharper than average canines.

"For example, I bet you think I'm speaking English, right?"

"Well… yeah…"

"Thought so." Lilian nodded her head. "The truth is, right now, I'm speaking Greek. You just hear it as English because that's your native language. If your native language was German, you'd hear me speaking German. Same with Japanese, Mandarin or any other language you could think of."

"That's pretty convenient."

"The Author felt it would have been a waste of his word count to create a chapter centered around us trying to figure out what the other was saying because of something like a language barrier."

Even though such a scene would have been awesome.

"It would have definitely been funny," Lilian agreed.

"Who are you talking to?" Kevin asked suspiciously.

"No one."

"No one?" Kevin eyed the girl with a look that clearly said "I don't believe you." There was something very odd about this girl... fox... fox-girl. Whatever she was.

"No one," Lilian nodded her head in affirmation. Kevin decided to drop the issue. A part of him was sure he didn't want to know.

"So Kitsune have the ability to break all language barriers," Kevin got back to the topic at hand. It was interesting. And it kept him from thinking about other things. Things that could easily be considered morally reprehensible or at least morally ambiguous, which was always a plus.

"Not just Kitsune." Lilian shook her head. "All Yōkai have this ability. The only difference between our ability and theirs is that ours comes from our patron god, Lord Inari, while other Yōkai gain their abilities from their respective patron gods."

"Huh?" Kevin blinked in surprise. "So wait, there are other supernatural creatures out there besides Kitsune?" He ignored the gods part, as in plural, more than one. Kevin was not what you would call a devout Christian or anything, but the idea of there actually being multiple gods was just too much for him to take in at the moment.

"Of course," Lilian said as if the answer to that question should have been obvious, even though, you know, it wasn't. At least not to a human who has just been introduced to the world of Yōkai. "Aside from Kitsune, there are Kappas, Nekomata, Oni, Ookami, Yuki-onna... Inu." Her nose wrinkled slightly, as if she had smelled something foul. "There are a large number of Yōkai in this world. So many that even though our matriarch has been teaching me as much as she can about the various races, I still don't know all of them."

"Huh," Kevin scratched the back of his head with his free hand. "You learn something new everyday, I guess." Having satiated his curiosity for now, Kevin decided to get back to the reason they had come here in the first place. "Anyways, we should probably check out one of these stores..." He looked around at the different clothing shops with a frown. " Although, I'm not sure which shop we should go to first—Woah!"

And just like that, Kevin's and Lilian's shopping excursion began in earnest as Lilian, her enthusiasm at the thought of shopping in a real mall overpowering her, began dragging the poor, shy boy by the arm.

They walked from store to store, looking at everything. Lilian was all smiles as they moved about the mall: it seemed that even fox-girls had the fascination with shopping that normal girls have.

The first shop Lilian dragged Kevin into was The Gap, which just happened to be the closest clothing store near them. Kevin had shopped there on occasion. The jeans he was currently wearing were actually from there.

It was at this store that Kevin got his first experience in shopping with a woman that was not his mom.

The first thing he discovered about shopping with a girl was that it was just as bad as every guy who ever complained about shopping with their girlfriend said it was. Of course, seeing as this was Kevin, his reasons for not liking the idea of shopping with a female were completely different than most of the other guys. Other men just didn't like being used as a pack mule to carry around all the clothing their girlfriend's bought. Kevin honestly didn't mind that part. It was certain... other parts about shopping with a female that caused him trouble.

The second thing he discovered about shopping with Lilian, and part of the reason he was not enjoying the experience one bit, was due to Lilian's sense of fashion. It wasn't that she had a bad fashion sense. Quite the contrary. It was just that the clothes she enjoyed wearing were the kinds of clothing that made Kevin's face and body feel all kinds of hot.

There was also the suspicious tightening of his pants that came from looking at Lilian's clothing choice, but he didn't want to think about that.

That's right, Kevin. Just try to ignore it. Clear your mind, calm your raging hormonal body and find peace and zen... or something.

One of the things Kevin noted about the type of clothing Lilian loved to wear was that pants were not on the list. The girl didn't seem to enjoy wearing pants at all. The one time Kevin had suggested a pair of pants for her to wear, she had given him a *look*. It wasn't quite THE LOOK™, but close enough that his mouth had snapped shut and he felt an inexplicable urge to cower in fear. Needless to say, he didn't suggest she get another pair of pants for the rest of their shopping trip.

Lilian, it seemed, enjoyed wearing either very short, tight, hip hugging shorts that allowed him to see every curve of her lovely rear and incredible looking legs, or very short skirts that gave the perfect panty shot when she twirled around in them or bent over.

And on that note, it was during one of those times where she had done just that, which made Kevin realize the girl *still* wasn't wearing any panties. For a second, he could have sworn his heart had actually stopped.

For tops, Lilian enjoyed sleeveless shirts that exposed a good deal of her midriff. Some of the shirts she had chosen had been pretty scandalous, and more than a few made Kevin feel light-headed enough that he was sure it was only a matter of time before he fainted. That he didn't become an insensate body devoid of all life showed how much fortitude he had gained since Lilian entered his life. He had most definitely gained at least +20 bonus points in desensitization.

Matters were only made worse for Kevin because Lilian not only enjoyed very revealing clothing, she had also decided to give him something of a fashion show. Each store they went to, she grabbed all the outfits she thought were cute, made him wait while she went to change, then paraded about in clothing that would have overprotective fathers everywhere up in arms.

It probably doesn't need to be mentioned, but Kevin's megaton blush was not going to be ending anytime soon.

It was Lilian's need to show off the outfits she wanted to try on that had Kevin standing in front of a changing room in a Fashion21 store two hours into their shopping excursion. He was waiting for Lilian to come out in one of the several outfits she had taken from the racks.

They had already gone to two different stores. Sitting at his side were three bags worth of clothing that Kevin had paid for with the credit card his mom had given him for emergencies. He didn't know what exactly would constitute an emergency, but felt that having a half-naked fox-girl running around the apartment in nothing but one of his larger t-shirts definitely qualify.

While he waited, Kevin nervously tapped his foot on the ground. He was trying to ignore some of the middle-aged women and older teenagers that looked like college girls as they pointed and giggled at him. They had been doing that ever since he got there.

Come to think of it, just about every girl he and Lilian had passed did pretty much the same thing: point, whisper and giggle. At least, they did that when they weren't busy smacking their significant others for staring at Lilian's backside or chest.

He wondered: were they making fun of him because he was in a women's clothing store? Or maybe they just thought it was funny that he was allowing himself to get dragged around by a girl. He didn't know. He wanted to say he didn't care, but that would be a lie.

As more giggling erupted from a gaggle of girls to his left, Kevin tried, and failed, to contain his impatience and mortification. Just how long did it take for girls to get dressed? It felt like he had been standing here for hours!

The sound of swishing curtains and clinking metal alerted him to the fact that Lilian was finished. "What do you think, Beloved?"

Kevin looked up, about to give her a piece of his mind for making him wait so long with all those girls staring at him…

…When he was struck speechless. Lilian was standing there, wearing one of the outfits she had chosen, and she looked good. Really, *really* good.

As Eric would say, she looked delectable.

Actually, he would probably say something along the lines of how he wanted to shove his face between her "bazongas" and start motor-boating her or something, but that's beside the point.

Starting from the torso, Lilian was wearing a crop top featuring a southwestern inspired pattern with mostly earth tone colors. The creamy, fair skin of her shoulders and toned, flat stomach were exposed to his gaze and the fabric of the top stretched tautly across her well-developed bust.

If that wasn't enough, as Kevin's eyes traveled across the exposed expanse of her flat tummy, they landed on what she was wearing around her hips: a black, crochet tiered layer skort.

It was probably a good thing the skort came with an inbuilt pair of shorts, otherwise Kevin likely would have lost consciousness right then and there. As things stood, the skort was not only wrapped around her so tightly that it allowed him to see her shapely hips and firm butt perfectly, it was short enough that almost all of her long, curvaceous legs were exposed.

Before he could even think of stopping himself, Kevin found his irises wandering down the expanse of those beautiful legs. Toned thighs and shapely calves the likes of which super-models spent the totality of their lives trying to attain were revealed to him in their entirety. His roaming only ended when his eyes landed on what she was wearing for shoes; a pair of cream colored, leather gladiator sandals that featured two ankle straps with buckle closures.

As he found himself staring at the open toed sandals, her toes, which had been painted dark red to match her hair (when did she do that?), wiggled cutely.

Kevin blinked, then shook his head. There must seriously be something wrong with him if he was thinking about how cute someone's feet were. He hoped he wasn't turning into one of those feet people or something. That would just be weird.

"So," Lilian smile widened when she saw her Beloved staring at her. It was nice to see that she could affect her mate like this. No girl didn't like being appreciated by their boyfriends. Even if he wasn't actually her boyfriend. That was a small detail barely worth mentioning. "What do you think?"

Kevin worked his mouth as he tried to speak with no success. His throat seemed to have constricted, leaving his vocal chords incapable of producing any form of sound.

It was only after several seconds of staring that he managed, in a very strained voice, to say, "You look... nice?"

"Why did you sound so unsure when you said that?" Lilian pouted, crossing her arms under her bosom and pouting at him. Kevin would have gulped at the act, but he was having trouble just breathing. Was she doing this on purpose? "Do you think this outfit looks bad on me?"

"No! Of course I do!" Kevin quickly tried to reassure the girl. "I mean I don't! I mean, it looks really good... on... you..." Kevin knew he was not making any sense. He'd better wrap this up before he made himself out to be even more of a fool than he had already shown. "I mean, It's just... I'm not really used to doing this kind of thing... giving my opinion on clothes and... stuff."

"Really?" Kevin nodded. "I suppose that's okay then." She paused to look at him. "So, just to be sure, you like my outfit, right?" Another nod. Lilian smiled brightly. "In that case, I think I'll get this one too. I just want to try a few more outfits on," she winked at him, "Then I've got a present for you. Okay?"

"Ah...um...okay." Kevin absently wondered what kind of present she had for him and whether or not it would end with his death. Given how Dangerous this girl was one couldn't deny there was a very distinct possibility of that happening.

Lilian tried on several more outfits, each and every one of them just as revealing and appealing as the last. Kevin couldn't be too sure, but he thought he was actually getting kind of used to her clothing of choice. As time went on he had stopped blushing (mostly), and even managed to give a more comprehensive opinion of what she was wearing. It probably helped that he was used to Lilian wandering around the apartment in much less.

Much, *much* less.

It was almost enough to make one wonder why this was so difficult for him in the first place.

When she had tried on the last outfit and he had given her a satisfactory response, they walked off towards the cashier with several new sets of clothes and ended up waiting in line.

While they stood there, Lilian had wrapped her arms around Kevin's left arm and placed her head on his shoulder. She looked so content that he just couldn't bring himself to tell her off. Or maybe he couldn't tell her off because his voice box wasn't working due to her proximity. Who can say?

After nearly ten minutes, it was finally their turn. At the cash register there was a young woman who looked to be in her mid twenties. She took one look at them and smiled.

"You two make such a cute couple," she stated wistfully. Naturally, Kevin's face looked even more awkward as it began to take on a shade of red that would make tomatoes jealous. Lilian, on the other hand, smiled brightly and held his arm even more possessively.

The total cost for the clothes came to $143.82, which was about what they had spent the other two clothing stores. It was expensive, especially compared to what his clothes normally cost, but then, he never before had to buy an entire wardrobe. Allowances had to be made. And since he was using his emergency credit card, which had a $1,000 limit, the cost didn't really bother him. His mom would understand once she realized why he was spending so much on clothing... women's clothing...

He was doomed.

With Lilian now having her own wardrobe, and one large enough that she wouldn't have to wear his clothes anymore, Kevin was ready to leave. Unfortunately for him, Lilian had one more place she wanted them to go to.

"I still have to get your present," were her words as she began dragging him off again. "I saw this nice, little store while we were walking that has something I think you'll like."

It was her tone more than her words that put Kevin on guard, but as she was not doing anything that could be construed as suspicious, there was little he could do other then let her drag him around. It probably helped that she was a lot stronger than she looked.

In very short order, they arrived at the "nice, little store" that Lilian had found. The moment they did, Kevin suddenly found the strength to halt them both in their tracks, strength fueled by dread.

"Is something wrong, Beloved?" asked Lilian, turning her head to look into his wide, incredulous eyes.

"I can't go in there!" a panicked Kevin nearly shouted, his voice squeaking like a scared little mouse. The sound of his shout attracted a number of stares from passerby, but he was hardly noticed. His focus was on *the store in front of him*.

"Why not?" Lilian asked plaintively.

"What do you mean why not!?" Kevin's voice cracked dangerously. He looked like he was on the verge of having a panic attack as he stared at the girl with a wild look in his eyes. "Do you know what store that is!?"

"Of course I do," Lilian huffed and crossed her arms under her chest, which had its usual effect, which many passing males noticed.

Several of these males were then thrown backwards as a jetstream of blood spurted out their noses. Yes, it was a Nosebleed, a very popular trope in Japanese media. Healthy young men who have no sexual outlet will often suffer nosebleeds upon seeing the naked female body, or even just a pair of well-filled panties. This is also known as anime law number 40; the Law of Nasal Sanguination, which has been theorized to be a result of the larger eyes often found in anime and manga taking up too much space and causing males to have smaller sinuses and thinner sinus tissue.

Of course, all this is just theory and really has nothing to do with the story. Please continue reading.

"Then you should know why I can't go in there," Kevin argued back, looking scared. His eyes darted towards the store, the source of his fear, then back to Lilian.

"You'll be fine." Lilian almost rolled her eyes at her Beloved. She loved her mate dearly, but he could be such a prude. "It's just a lingerie store." And with that, she dragged him inside.

The place that Lilian called "just a lingerie store" was actually

Victoria's Secret, a place that sold some of the deadliest (for anyone named Kevin Swift) clothing in the entire world. Bras, panties, thongs and all manner of sexy that was specifically designed to arouse the male gender.

For a person like Kevin Swift, it was like stepping into his worst nightmare. There was so much pink, and the images of women wearing nothing more than a bra and panties was far too much for the boy poor to take and he was going to pass out if this-kept-up-because-there-was-just-way-too-much-sexy-and-he-was-beginning-to-feel-light-headed-and—

"Come on," Lilian yanked on his arm, jerking Kevin out of his stupor and dragging him to the back of the store. Along the way, he saw several women who worked at the store looking at the two of them. Many were giggling as they saw him being manhandled by a girl several inches shorter than him. Obviously, they were taking pleasure in his discomfort.

Dang, women could be sadistic when they wanted to be.

"Here we are," Lilian declared brightly, causing Kevin to refocus his attention.

His eyes promptly widened.

"Why are we over here!?"

"For your present, of course. I thought I told you that."

"B-b-but this is the lingerie section!"

Indeed it was. Surrounding them on all sides were racks of clothing that could only be described as 'sexy sleepwear'. Nightgowns, baby-dolls, chemises. You name it, it was here.

"Well, yeah," Lilian said in a "duh" kind of tone, "I was hoping to get something sexy that I can wear for you since you've been so good to me." She gave him a strange look. "Are you feeling alright, Beloved?"

Kevin felt his brain begin overloading. His pupil's dilated as they landed on all manner of delightfully sinful clothing that his mind could not help but imagine the girl standing next to him in. His ridiculously over reactive imagination was not helping him one iota.

"Gu... couldn't you... I mean, I really don't think that..." Kevin pinched the back of his hand really hard as he felt all the blood he possessed start rising to his face, threatening to bring him to the brink of unconsciousness again. The pain helped bring clarity, albeit, just barely enough to keep him conscious. "I really don't need you doing this for me. I mean, I only helped you because it was the right thing to do." And it was the safest thing to do as far as he was concerned. "I don't need any reward."

Lilian smiled at him. A delicate hand came up and her fingers gently brushed against his cheek.

Kevin froze, right before a shudder passed through his entire body, threatening to topple him. He really didn't know how long he would be able to hold on if she kept this up.

"And that is exactly why you deserve a reward." She withdrew the hand and turned back around to look at the racks of clothing. Could this stuff really be considered clothing? "Now, be a good boy and let me do this for you. I guarantee you'll love it, ufufufu."

It was in that moment that Kevin knew he was doomed.

Soon Kevin found himself awkwardly standing next to another changing stall, doing his utmost to ignore the giggling women looking at him.

As you can probably guess, he was not having much success.

Waking up this morning, he never imagined he would be standing in a lingerie store, much less standing in a lingerie store waiting for a girl to parade around in front of him while wearing said lingerie. It was embarrassing, humiliating, and he really didn't want to be here.

And to think, all this because he didn't want to tell Lilian that he had been staring at her boobs.

He would have been better off just confessing the truth.

"Beloved..."

Kevin's back stiffened at the sound of the voice behind him. He didn't want to turn around. He really didn't. At the same time, his body seemed to be betray him and he ended up turning around to face Lilian anyway.

He felt like someone had just jabbed him in the gut with a taser set on high. Lilian was in front of him and she was electrifying. She was wearing something that put a whole new meaning to the words "bringing sexy back." He wasn't exactly sure what the outfit was called, but it looked some kind of spaghetti strap shirt made out of a motley see-through material that showed off almost the entirety of her upper body. Only her breasts were not visible, covered as they were by a built-in black bra with polka dots a shade darker than the base color of the outfit. Attached to the shirt by a pair of straps were sheer stockings made from the same material of the shirt. Covering her crotch was nothing more than a small, black triangle that was being held together by a pair of very thin strings.

For some reason, looking at Lilian as she wore the partially see-through material was even more erotic than seeing her completely nude. It was like the act of showing just enough to tantalize and tease, but leaving all those who saw her wanting more, made up for the lack of actually seeing anything.

Kevin found his eyes trying to decide where they should look and his face feeling like it was being cooked in an oven. Lilian gave him a demure look, her head tilted down so that her bangs were hovering over her face, not quite masking her eyes and giving them an aura of allure and mystery. A very light dusting of pink on her cheeks enhanced her features, and the way she bit her pouty, lower lip was more than enough to beguile Kevin's senses, befuddling his mind and almost sending the poor lad over the edge.

"What do you think, Beloved?" she asked, giving him an innocent smile that looked completely at odds with her sexy outfit, almost like she didn't even realize that wearing sexy lingerie was a sinful activity and just assumed everyone else wore stuff like that, too.

And then the two-tails began spinning around for him and giving him an unfettered view of her tight, twin cheeks, which were completely bereft of any kind of covering. Kevin felt as if he had been hit by a truck going seventy-five on the freeway. "Do you like it?"

"Guh... uh... uuuu..."

That was Kevin, who wasn't dealing with his new situational altercation very well.

"Beloved?" Lilian asked before panicking as Kevin's eyes rolled up into the back of his head and he ended up passing out. "Beloved!"

Chapter 11: The Start of a Terrible Day

Monday couldn't come soon enough for Kevin. Normally, he disliked Mondays because it meant he was going back to school—and what regular high school faring male didn't dislike going to school?—but this weekend had been a nightmare. At least, as far as he was concerned. Lilian, on the other hand, had been positively beaming ever since Saturday morning before the start of that disaster of a shopping trip.

Scratch that, she had been pretty much ecstatic the entirety of last week whenever he was around. He didn't think he had ever seen her not acting like her usual, peppy self.

Lilian had somehow managed to get him out of Victoria's Secret after he had fainted there, and back home without incident. He didn't ask her how she had accomplished this rather impressive feat. In truth, he had no desire to know how she had done it, fearing that the knowledge would lead to him questioning his perceptions on the very fabrics upon which reality, the multiverse, and whatever other anime references to the complex, multidimensional universe that he could think of.

Several hours after he had fainted, Kevin had awakened on his bed, Lilian's lap being used as his pillow, and her fingers gently running through his hair. That had actually felt kind of nice, if a bit embarrassing. What hadn't been nice was what had happened after she realized he was awake.

The moment she noticed that her "Beloved" was once again in the land of the conscious, the girl had pulled him into a monstrous hug, the end result of which had been her smashing his face in her divine cleavage.

Basically, she had smothered him with her boobs. And while that probably sounds like every teenage male's fantasy, it's not as pleasant as most would think. The problem was that with his face shoved straight into her breasts, Kevin found himself unable to breath.

Death by boob asphyxiation. What a way to go.

In either event, having his face shoved into the bosom of the red-haired beauty had not only caused Kevin's face to turn blue from a lack of oxygen, but also forced him to remember what happened just hours prior at the lingerie store. The combination of not getting enough oxygen to his brain and said brain going into overdrive as it conjured up images of what shall forever be known as "The Lingerie Disaster" caused him to end up unconscious... again. It wasn't until he woke up for the third (he had passed out at least once more after getting asphyxiated by Lilian's cleavage) time that he actually managed to keep himself from falling into that blissful darkness where no fox-girls could shower him with their, ahem, affection.

Kevin had been very disappointed. A part of him actually wished he *had* passed out again, if only to avoid Lilian.

While that was bad, it was not the worst thing that had happened that weekend. Sunday morning, Kevin had nearly been late to his newspaper route. The reason for that, of course, was Lilian. No matter how many times he told the girl to sleep in the bed he had provided for her—aka, his bed, she had categorically refused and kept sneaking onto the couch with him each night after he went to sleep. It was getting to the point where he was beginning to wonder why he didn't just start sleeping in his own bed again. At least then he would be more comfortable, relatively speaking.

Regardless of whether he actually wanted her sleeping with him or not, because of the comforting and lulling warmth she gave off while she slept, Kevin had been so content that he nearly slept through his morning newspaper run. He barely managed to get to the Newspaper Distribution Center to deliver the newspapers on time.

It was a very good thing he had not been late for that, as he did not want to know what his boss would have done had he not delivered the newspapers.

Kevin sometimes had nightmares about Davin Monstrang killing him Sumo-style.

Squish.

While that was bad it had only been one of the problems he had faced that day. Sundays were normally the days he would meet up with Eric and a few of their other friends and go to the arcade. This day would have been no different, except for the fact that he had one major issue that he didn't know how to deal with.

Lilian. Yes, her again. There was absolutely no way he could take her with him. If he showed up with a girl on his arm, especially one as beautiful as her, his friends, and Eric in particular, would have questions for him. Questions he could not answer. It wasn't like he could tell them that when he had found her, she had been nothing more than a tiny fox kit with two tails who had incidentally turned out to be a Kitsune and that he was allowing her to stay with him because she had nowhere else to go.

That would not go over well, even on the off chance that they *did* believe him. It might even be worse if they believed him. His friends might call the government and they would capture Lilian and take her to be experimented on at some super-secret government research facility. He didn't want that. As much as Lilian annoyed him, he wasn't so callous and cruel as to wish something so heinous upon her.

There was also Lilian herself to consider. From what he had seen so far the girl did not know the meaning of the word tact. She had blatantly declared him to be her mate, and had already stated multiple times that she wished to explore the more physical aspects of their relationship, which was still nonexistent as far as he was concerned. She pranced around completely nude, or barring that, wore one of his T-shirts and nothing else.

And when he said nothing else, he meant *nothing else*. Lilian seemed to have some kind of grudge against panties. Even now when she had several sets, she was reluctant to actually wear them.

To top all this off, she also wasn't afraid to drag him into a lingerie store in front of a lot of people and pose for him wearing some of the deadliest, most sinful sleepwear he had ever laid eyes on.

Who knows what a girl like that would say to his friends. He sure didn't, but he had no doubt that whatever she said would not be good for his continued health, for which he was starting to fear.

It was all the fainting, you see. That couldn't be good for him.

So he had two options: try to trick Lilian into letting him go to the arcade without her or not go at all.

Kevin had never been a very good liar. In fact, he was downright terrible at it. There was no way he would have been able to fool Lilian, and truthfully, he would have felt guilty for lying to her even if he had. He was just soft like that.

Not that it would matter even if he did manage to give her a convincing lie. Kevin had little doubt that if he said he needed to run an errand or something, she would want to go. The girl seemed to consider any time not spent with him as wasted time.

So he had decided not to go. When Eric called to ask where he was, he made the excuse of having stomach cramps. After some mild teasing his friend had let him off the hook with the promise they would hang out the next weekend.

Lilian had been curious about who had called, but he had managed to deflect her towards his Xbox 360. That was all it took to get the girl to stop asking questions. She really enjoyed it when they played video games together. Although, that may have been because she simply enjoyed spending time with him regardless of what they were doing.

That girl was an amazing zombie killer.

So Sunday was spent all day at home with Lilian. It wasn't all bad. The twin-tailed Kitsune was actually kind of fun to be around when she wasn't trying to get into his pants — which unfortunately happened more often than not. When they played video games together, they actually got along very well. Which may have had something to do with Lilian being too busy shooting down baddies, slicing them up with a sword or racing down various courses filled with obstacles and trying to make him lose by throwing banana peels to make any attempts at sexing him up.

All that being said, Sunday had officially come and gone and a new week of school would be starting. It was now Monday, meaning children and teenagers would soon be waking up and getting ready to head out to their respective centers of education.

Oh joy.

A stifled yawn sounded through the room as our Main Protagonist woke up that morning. Kevin blinked in an attempt to get the sleep out of them. When that didn't work he raised a hand and began absently rubbing them as they adjusted to the light, or lack thereof. It was still a bit dark out, the sun having barely risen enough to cast a few light purples and oranges across the sky.

Glancing around the room, the sophomore saw that he had forgotten to put away his Xbox 360 the night before. It wasn't often that he played it. Kevin preferred going out with friends as opposed to playing video games at home. He was a social gamer and had only gotten the game set for when he invited people over.

Craning his neck to look at the clock revealed that it was still quite early. Really early actually, like, 5:30 in the morning kind of early. School didn't start until 7:00. It only took thirty minutes to ride his bike to school, meaning he had a little over an hour before he actually had to leave. That meant he had around half an hour to do nothing.

The feeling of a body shuffling on top of him caused a barely concealed groan of discontent to pass through his mouth. It also caused another reaction, one that all men who are in the peak of their hormonal, teenage lives suffer through when they first wake up. This (un?)pleasant problem, otherwise known as morning wood, was only compounded by the body belonging to the gorgeous girl on top of him.

The blond-haired high schooler looked down at the girl who was yet again using his body as her pillow. He could not see much of her because, even though she was on top of him, the blanket that they were both buried under covered much of her body. The rest of her body was hidden by her long, luxurious curtain of red hair. He couldn't even see her face because she had tucked her head under his chin.

Just because he could not see her, did not mean he could not feel her. Her body was pressed against his so tightly it was unlikely there was even enough room to slip a sheet of paper between them. Her silky soft legs had become a tangled mess with his own. Even her arms had taken to wrapping themselves around his middle, her hands buried under his back. It was actually a wonder he could even sleep as those fingers dug into his skin.

Then again, those hands were very soft. He probably wouldn't have even noticed them if it weren't for the fact that A) they were actually softer than the seat cushions he was laying on and B) the index finger of Lilian's left hand had taken to rubbing circles on his lower back. A subconscious gesture perhaps?

Why couldn't he just get the girl to stay in her own (his) bed? Well, this was Kevin Swift. And Lilian. That girl was the worst kind of opponent for a person like him. Even if she wasn't sneaky enough to slip onto his couch while he slept, all she would have to do is give him *The Foxy-Kit Eyes* (patent pending) and that would be it—Kevin would be done for.

As Kevin lay there he wondered what he had done to deserve this kind of torture. He was a good student. He was responsible, and he had never been mean to anyone, not even those kids at school that everyone else made fun of and picked on. So why was he being punished like this? Had he been some kind of lecherous pervert in his last life and this was his penance?

Kevin looked back at the clock on the wall and groaned again when he saw how little time had elapsed between the first time he looked at it and now. It was only 5:40am. Only ten minutes had passed.

Realizing he would not be going back to sleep (not so long as Lilian was still using him as her cuddle buddy) anytime soon, he decided it would be best to slip out of the girl's grasp and head into the bathroom so he could at least take a shower and get the last vestiges of sleep out of his system.

With that thought in mind, he tried to free himself from her arms and untangle their legs. It was something he had a good deal of practice with these days. A whole weeks worth of practice in fact, so it should have been easy.

It wasn't. Not this time at least. Perhaps it was because Lilian had cottoned on to how he escaped her hold every time for the past few mornings, but this morning, the moment she felt his arms trying to remove hers from around his torso, her grip on him tightened to the point that it was actually kind of painful.

No, seriously. Kevin thought he actually heard his ribs creaking under the strain of her grip. That was never a good sign.

Grunting in discomfort, Kevin put more strength into his attempt to get this girl's arms off him. Yet the moment he strengthened his efforts, Lilian matched it with an equal amount of strength. To make things even more difficult for him, her legs also came into play and hooked themselves around his hips, making escaping her grasp seem even more unlikely.

Kevin's face was also turning red enough that someone would probably mistake him for a stove and try to cook eggs on it. The reason? With Lilian's legs locked around his hips, he could feel her groin rubbing against his own. To make matters worse, he was also sporting that pesky problem all teenager males who are undergoing that little thing called puberty have. Yes, it was *that* kind of problem.

The way Lilian moaned and began sleepily kissing his chest when her hot center ground against him, as if her body knew what was happening and was subconsciously responding to him, really didn't help. It really, *really* didn't help.

"Mmm..." Lilian moaned in her sleep.

Scratch that. It really, really, *really* didn't help.

"Ufufu, you're so naughty, Beloved."

He was doomed.

After fifteen minutes of struggling with all his flagging might to get out of the apparently randy fox-girl's amorous grip... and failing so miserably that it made all the effort he put into it seem utterly pointless, Kevin realized how hopeless his situation was. It was with a heavy heart and a face that told any theoretical witnesses how close he was to blacking out that he realized he would actually need to wake the girl up if he wanted to escape her lustful ministrations. Not exactly something he had wanted to do, but he wanted her to rape him in her sleep even less.

"L-Lilian," he stuttered out. When nothing happened except that she moaned happily and bit his nipple hard enough to make him wince, he began to shake her shoulders. "D-dang it, Lilian, wake up. Wake! Up!"

The beautiful red head lying on top of him stirred... and stopped biting his nipple, which he was eternally grateful because it really hurt. Lifting her head, she looked up at him, blinking several times as her eyes focused on his face.

"Morning, Beloved," she greeted with a sleepy smile.

"Lilian," Kevin hissed, his face a furious shade of red. "What are you doing on my couch?"

Even though it was clear her mind wasn't really all there, enough of it was working that her face was able to aptly express her confusion. "What do you..." her mouth opened wide as she let out a yawn, "... mean, Beloved? I always sleep on the couch with you."

"That's not the point!"

"Ufufufu." Lilian's laughter had his whole body shuddering. No. Wait. That was actually from the way her breasts were rubbing against him as she laughed.

A smile crossed her face.

"I know what you need," she whispered before leaning up to close the distance between their respective faces. "A good morning kiss."

She closed the rest of the distance, her lips pursed in the most seductive of ways as she leaned in to kiss her Beloved. Her eyes slowly closed before she pressed her silken lips against her mate. A content moan made its way out of her mouth. Was there anything better then kissing her mate?

It was only several seconds into their kiss that Lilian seemed to realize something was wrong. The skin her lips were pressing against was far too dry to be lips. It also didn't have the same feel as lips. She should know, having kissed her Beloved several times in this story already. And let's not forget Iris.

Her eyes fluttered open to discover that she was not actually kissing his lips, but a hand. Her beloved's hand, to be exact. It was some surprisingly quick thinking on Kevin's part. The Secret Hand Blocking Technique. A powerful ability in any Hapless Heroes arsenal. Who knew he had it in him?

"Wha...?"

"Look," Kevin tried to sound stern despite still looking like an overcooked lobster. "I need to take a shower. Could you please get off me?"

"Um... sure." Lilian looked a little out of sorts. Perhaps she had not been expecting him to put up any kind of resistance to her kisses. Still, she got off him and that's all he cared about. "Would you like me to wash your back?"

"I'm perfectly capable of washing myself," Kevin grunted as he got off the couch. He didn't give her a chance to respond as he headed into the bathroom, quickly closing the door behind him and locking it shut. He didn't want the girl walking in on him while he was taking a shower.

After a nice, cold shower, Kevin got dressed in a pair of khaki shorts that went down past his knees, and a black T-shirt with an awesome drawing of a pirate drinking rum and the words "Drink like a pirate!" underneath it. It was one of his newer shirts that his mom had bought him during the summer when they had gone to the Caribbean on vacation the past summer. He thought it was an awesome shirt, even though he didn't drink alcohol.

Breakfast was already on the table when he arrived in the kitchen. He scratched the back of his head when he saw that Lilian was not there to complete the picture. She was almost always waiting there for him. So where had she gone?

"Beloved!"

Eyes widening, Kevin ducked just in time to see Lilian go flying over him, her arms outstretched like some kind of linebacker hell bent on tackling him. The girl squawked in surprise when, instead of tackling her mate from behind, she ended up rolling along the tiled floor. It ended with her laying on her back, her legs propped up against the fridge, blinking as she stared at the boy who was returning her look with a wide eyed look of his own.

"What the heck was that all about!?"

"Mou..." Lilian pouted as she looked at Kevin from her upside down position. "You weren't supposed to duck like that, Beloved."

Kevin twitched. Did she just ignore him?

"What else did you think I would do? Stand there and let you tackle me?"

"Yes."

More twitching.

"Why do you think I would do that?"

"Because that's what always happens in Kenchi Miyumi," Lilian stated in a very sage-like manner despite looking at him upside down. "Ryomo always does The Glomp to Kenchi, and he always just takes it and then they both get sent to the ground. That's how it goes."

The Glomp: Grab, Latch On, Maintain Pressure. A powerful technique in the hands of an experienced user. It's a good thing for Kevin that Lilian is still just a novice. She needs more time to refine her technique.

"Don't worry. I'll keep practicing. My technique will get better. I promise."

That's good to hear. Looking forward to it.

Kevin didn't know who Lilian was talking to, but he was getting annoyed.

"This isn't an anime, you know? You can't keep doing things like this."

"Actually, I got the idea from reading manga."

"This isn't a manga either!"

"B-but this story is supposed to be based on Shōnen manga..."

"Ugh..." Kevin pressed a hand to his face. He was beginning to get a headache. "Whatever. It's way too early to deal with this, and I'm getting hungry."

With that he sat down at the table and began to eat. Or he

tried to eat. It was pretty difficult with the way Lilian stared at him with that dreamy look on her face.

"Could you stop that?" Kevin finally asked after trying to deal with her staring for another ten seconds. His patience in this matter was actually pretty impressive, especially when one considered how long he had been dealing with this before this morning.

One week. He had put up with her staring for an entire week. He could probably get in the Guinness' Book Of World Records for the longest time dealing with Lilian without blowing his top. Too bad the thought of sending in a submission never crossed his mind.

Lilian tilted her head to the side, her eyes blinking and her lips turning into a curious frown. Her confusion was evident. "Stop what?"

"That. You keep staring at me. It's making me uncomfortable."

"Ufufufu. There's no need to be embarrassed. I simply like watching my Beloved enjoy the meals I prepare."

"And why do you keep calling me Beloved?"

"Because you're my Beloved. Why else would I call you Beloved, Beloved?"

"Can't you just call me by my name?" grunted Kevin.

Lilian ignored that last bit. Naturally. She had a very bad case of selective hearing.

Several minutes after breakfast ended, Kevin stood in the doorway, his back pack slung over his back. Lilian was standing with him, her foxy ears drooping. As always, she was very sad to see him leave.

"You have school again today, don't you?"

"Yep," Kevin tightened the straps on his bag. He didn't want it getting jostled on his back when he rode to school. Nothing sucked more than having his homework getting knocked into his pens and finding them covered in ink when he took them out. "I've got school for the next five days." At least it wouldn't be all bad. He'd get to see the friends he didn't get to see this weekend because of Lilian. And being at school meant he would not be near said aforementioned Kitsune, which was the biggest bonus of all.

"We really need to do something about this." That was Lilian. "I don't want to wait here everyday for you to come home." She looked truly depressed. "It gets lonely without you."

"Not much I can do about that," Kevin shrugged. "I have to go school, and since you don't go to my school..." he trailed off and shook his head. "Anyways, I'll see you when I get home."

"W-wait!" Lilian's panicked voice sounded out as he rushed out the door, unlocked the padlock to his bike, and began flying down the stairs. "You forgot to give me a kiss goodbye!"

No he didn't. He just didn't want to give her a kiss goodbye.

Kevin took off down the road, leaving Lilian standing by the doorway. He put on as much speed as possible until he had exited the complex. Only when he had reached the main thoroughfare did he slow down and begin riding at a more leisurely pace.

Frowning as the buildings, trees and cactus passed him by, Kevin turned over the problem that was Lilian. He wasn't sure what to do about her. This morning he'd managed to avoid her advances, but only just. In the future, he would need to think up a more comprehensive means of dealing with her amorous intentions towards him.

And just what was up with her lustful advances anyways? She came barging into his life, completely turning it upside down within a week and she expected him to simply accept her advances because *she* had decided that he was her mate? What about what he wanted? Didn't he get any say in deciding whether he even wanted to be her mate? Did she even care what he thought?

Probably not. Kevin doubted Lilian had even thought about his feelings on the matter. The girl was determined to live in her own little fantasy world from what he had seen.

It wasn't long after Kevin arrived at school and locked up his bike that he found himself sitting in his first class of the day: math with Ms. Vis.

Cue pitiful groan. Why oh why was math his first class of the day?

"Morning, Kevin." Lindsay, who was already seated when he arrived, greeted him with a smile. She was one of those students who was always early to class. The girl was just punctual like that.

"Morning," Kevin mumbled in return as he sat down. Unzipping his back pack and taking out his notebook and pencil, he prepared for class. He didn't notice, but unlike most of the other times Lindsay spoke with him, he did not turn into a blushing, stuttering mess.

It just goes to show you how preoccupied his mind was. Not surprising really, given all the crap he's had to put up with this past week.

While he might not have noticed how little he reacted to Lindsay's presence, someone else did.

"Are you okay?" asked Lindsay, leaning over slightly so she could whisper to him while Ms. Vis was taking roll call.

"I'm fine." Kevin tiredly ran a hand through his hair. "I just didn't get much sleep this last weekend." Or the entirety of last week, but there was no need to tell Lindsay that.

"You weren't up late doing something you shouldn't have, were you?" asked Lindsay, a mischievous grin on her face.

Kevin began to choke and sputter as he tried to keep his mind from going down the gutter. Whether she knew it or not (she didn't, by the way; there was no sexual connotation to anything she had just said), Lindsay's words invoked a lot of images of a certain foxy female clad in various pieces of sexy lingerie.

"Mr. Swift," Ms. Vis glared at him, "Is there a problem?"

"No." Kevin smacked a fist into his chest a few times as he continued coughing. "Some air just went down the wrong tube. Sorry."

Ms. Vis raised an eyebrow. "Try not to disrupt my class again. If you do, I may decide to give you detention."

"Understood." As Ms. Vis went back to taking roll, Kevin tossed Lindsay a bit of a glare. The aforementioned girl blinked in surprise, having never been on the receiving end of that look from him before. "For your information I was not up to anything. I was just... busy."

"Sorry, sorry." Lindsay looked only slightly abashed. "I was just teasing you. I didn't mean to make you angry."

"No, it's fine," Kevin slumped in his seat. He must be more irascible than he thought if he was snapping at the girl he'd been crushing on for years. Dang, Lilian had really done a number on him. "I just had a very trying weekend and would rather not think about it, that's all. I didn't mean to snap at you. Sorry."

"That's okay," Lindsay said cheekily. "I'll forgive you, just this once." Her words had Kevin chuckling. At least they did until Ms. Vis decided to put him in the spotlight again.

"Something amusing that you would like to share with us, Mr. Swift?" asked Ms. Vis.

"No ma'am," Kevin said quickly. "I apologize. I was just thinking about something that happened this weekend."

Ms. Vis narrowed her eyes, but thankfully she decided not to pursue the issue any further. Once role call had finished the strict math teacher went straight into her lecture. They were covering the Pythagoras Theorem today.

It was certainly not a lesson he wanted to start learning when he was still trying to get his head on straight, but there was very little he could do about that. So he tried to pay attention to the stern woman's lecture, taking notes as dutifully as possible. He wasn't the best note taker—he wrote very slowly because his hand writing was so sloppy—but he at least managed to jot down the main points of her lecture. Hopefully, it would be enough to satisfy her.

Halfway through the lecture, however, Ms. Vis was interrupted by a knock at the door. With a very conspicuous frown on her face and a crease on her forehead at having her lecture so inexplicably halted, she marched over to the door and opened it up.

She blinked. "Yes?"

Kevin, along with the rest of the class, craned his neck to look in the direction of the door. He heard some excited whispering from those closest to the door, but he couldn't hear what they were saying. What was going on?

Ms. Vis was handed a note, which she quickly read, her frown growing even more prominent. After a moment, she handed the note back to whoever was on the other end of the door and rubbed her forehead. She looked exasperated. "Very well, come in."

Kevin watched with growing trepidation as someone stepped into the room, following Ms. Vis to the front of the class. The person in question was a girl around his age. Her beautiful tresses of red hair fluttered behind her as she walked. Her hips seemed to swing with a sensual elegance that drew more than a few eyes. At least it drew the eyes that weren't staring at her chest, which bounced and jiggled enticingly with each step she took.

Regardless of where they looked, every single male in the classroom was staring at her like she was a piece of meat, blatantly stripping her with their eyes.

She was wearing a white Sunset Cliffs tank top with embroidered patterns at the hem, a gathered neckline with subtle ruffles, double straps and dark wash, and low rise shorts with floral embroidery at the bottom. On her feet were the pair of gladiator sandals that she seemed to have taken a liking to.

None of that was what caused Kevin to feel a sense of dread well up in the pit of his stomach, that had his heart feeling like it had stopped cold, and his mind grind to a screeching halt. No. The reason he felt like he wanted to crawl into a hole and die was because he knew the person now standing in front of the classroom, gathering the attention of every single person there.

It was Lilian.

Chapter 12: The New Student

"Class," Ms. Vis tried to bring the attention of her students back to her. She didn't do a very good job. Most of the class was still gawking at the perfect example of feminine beauty they had ever seen standing right next to her.

"Dude, dude! Check out the ass on that chick!"

"Fuck the ass! Check out those tits!"

"I'd totally tap that."

"Hell yeah."

Right. So, maybe they weren't gawking so much as they were making lewd comments about the gorgeous red head. It seemed Eric wasn't the only perverted male in school. He was just the most blatant and daring one.

"Look at that slut. Who does she think she is, dressing up like that?"

"Hmph. That's what happens when you've got breasts like hers. Look at those things. They're practically popping out of her clothes."

"I hate girls with large breasts. They always think they're so much better than everyone else."

"Couldn't agree with you more."

Or in the case of the girls, judging Lilian because of her clothing and looks.

Ms. Vis' lips thinned into a tight line as no one listened to her. Barely masking what had to be some serious displeasure at being ignored, she continued with a raised voice. "We have a new student who just transferred here."

She looked at Lilian, glaring at the girl as if it was her fault none of the students were paying attention to their math teacher. Which it was, but it's not like she was doing it on purpose. Place the blame where it belongs, Teach, the teenage boys who couldn't keep their hormones in check and the girls who had a serious case of breast envy.

"Why don't you introduce yourself," Ms. Vis suggested, her cold glare increasing in intensity as she was forced to give the floor to Lilian, who stepped forward, her hands clasped together in front of her. Kevin wondered if the girl even realized that the action had pushed her breasts together, making her already impressive assets severely strain the fabric of her shirt. And if she did, did she know what effect it had on the boys in their class?

Somehow, he doubted it. The girl seemed oblivious to almost all male attention with the exception of his own. He remembered that when they were shopping at the mall, she hadn't looked at any of the men there, even when they had been walking right through her field of vision. It was more than just ignoring their presence for his own. As far as she had been concerned, they weren't even there.

"Hello!" Lilian greeted everyone with a truly beautiful smile. It was the kind of smile that made men melt. It was also the kind of smile that made every girl seethe in jealousy. "My name is Lilian Pnévma. I hope we can all get along with each other." Her eyes scanned the crowd, searching, before they landed on him. Kevin paled when her eyes light up like a mega watt bulb as she waved at him. "Beloved! Look! I decided to join your school!"

All noise ceased. Even the crickets had stopped chirping. Kevin sunk into his chair as the eyes of every single person in class turned to him, their expressions incredulous, accusing, or both.

Realizing that the cat was officially out of the bag and that trying to deny knowing her would only make things worse, Kevin sighed and gave the girl a wan smile.

"Hello, Lilian."

"Mou, Beloved. I thought I told you to call me You Sexy Thing You."

A good number of jaws, meaning the jaw of everyone in the classroom, dropped. Kevin tried, and failed, to not blush. "Not happening."

"Anyways, isn't it amazing that we're in the same class together?"

Was she ignoring him again?

"I suppose that would depend on who's asking."

"I'm really looking forward to spending more time with you."

Yep. She was definitely ignoring him.

"Urk!"

A shiver went down his back. Was it just him, or had the temperature suddenly taken a nose dive?

It wasn't just him. Surrounding Kevin were a bunch of hormonal, teenage males, all of whom were glaring at him with DOOM in their eyes. If they had heat vision or the ability to shoot high intensity laser beams from their eyes, he would have undoubtedly been dead by now.

It was a good thing none of these people were named Cyclops or Superman.

"Mr. Swift, Ms. Pnévma," Ms. Vis gave the two a stern glare, "stop disrupting class. Ms. Pnévma, go find a empty seat and ask your neighbor for the notes on today's lecture that *you* missed."

"Okay!" Lilian replied, cheerful as ever. At least she seemed to ignore Ms. Vis' disdainful tone as surely as she ignored anything Kevin said that she didn't like. Not that Kevin thought this was much of a consolation prize.

Red hair fluttering behind her, Lilian made her way over to the spot right next to Kevin, which was occupied by Lindsay. Smiling down at the girl, who was blinking up at her in curiosity, she said, in a tone that was blunt enough to make hammers seem sharp. "Excuse me, but I need you to move."

Kevin choked on his own spit. Lindsay just looked nonplussed.

"I'm sorry, but did you just tell me to move?"

"Yes."

The befuddlement on Lindsay's face was as clear as day. Her eyebrows furrowed and a small frown came to her lips. She looked at Kevin, then back at Lilian, clearly wondering about the relationship this new girl shared with her friend. "Shouldn't you find an empty seat to sit in?"

"No," Lilian stated with absolute certainty. "I want to sit next to my Beloved."

"Beloved?" Lindsay mouthed the word, not quite sure what to make of it. Meanwhile, Kevin was making choking noises, his face burning with the light of a thousand suns.

Lilian frowned for a second as the girl didn't do what she asked. A second later, she smiled.

It was a very mischievous smile.

Making eye contact with Lindsay, Lilian's green irises began glowing with an abnormal light that seemed to reflect off Lindsay's own. In return, the brunette's own eyes took on a glassy, dull quality.

"Move."

And just like that, Lindsay stood up and began mechanically walking to the nearest empty seat.

Kevin stopped his choking long enough to look confused. What... what had just happened? What was going on?

"Excuse me, Ms. Pnévma," Ms. Vis once more decided to make her presence known, it was her right as the teacher. This was *her* class, after all. She couldn't just allow people to disrupt her class. It interfered with the learning process. "What do you think you're doing? I told you to find an empty seat."

"This seat is empty." Lilian's eyes glowed as the demanding math teacher looked at her. "See?" Ms. Vis' eyes glazed over. "There's no one sitting here."

"Of course." Everyone stared. What the hell? "My mistake." Ms. Vis shook her head, her stern persona coming back in place. "Now sit down and get out your supplies. And ask Mr. Swift for the notes on my lecture. You won't be able to follow along if you only have the last half of notes for this class."

"Kay!"

Lilian sat down and class resumed, albeit a good number of boys were no longer paying any attention. They had something else to look at now.

Not that many of them had been paying attention before Lilian entered the picture anyways. It was way too early for a class like Math.

Kevin was staring at Lilian as well, but he was busy trying to figure out just what had happened a few seconds ago. How had Lilian convinced not just Lindsay, but also Ms. Vis (who was one of the strictest teachers he knew) to do what she told them to?

Seriously, what the heck was going on?

As for the girl herself, she had a notebook and pencil sitting on her desk and was now looking at him.

"Beloved?" Kevin blinked at the sound of Lilian's voice. He looked over at her, blue eyes meeting green. "Could you let me copy down your notes?"

"Um... sure..." Kevin handed over his notes before his mind snapped back into place. Then he glared at her. "Hold on a second. Why are you here? You're supposed to be back at the apartment!"

"Staying at the apartment without you is boring." Lilian began copying his notes. "You have really messy hand writing, Beloved."

"Stop changing the subject!"

"Mr. Swift, Ms. Pnévma." Ms. Vis glared at the two of them. "That will be detention for disrupting my class. I expect to see you two after school today."

"What!?" Kevin stood up from his seat, aghast. "But I have track practice today!"

"Then I suppose you will just have to skip it." said Ms. Vis, who was uncaring to his plight. "Let this be a lesson on what happens when you interrupt the learning process of my class."

Kevin grit his teeth and sat back down. God this sucked! Not only had this girl disrupted his daily life, now she was interfering with his school life! Worse still, he had just gotten detention because of her and now he was going to miss track practice! This was completely unfair!

He glared over at Lilian, who seemed to be paying attention to the lecture, writing notes dutifully in a pink spiral bound notebook with hearts on it. Where had she gotten that thing anyways? He certainly didn't buy it for her.

For the rest of class, Kevin found focusing on his teacher to be an effort in futility. His mind and thoughts were so jumbled it was a wonder he could focus on anything. By the time class ended, he was a complete mess.

As the bell rang Kevin shot out of his seat and snatched up his school supplies. He looked over at Lilian who was putting her stuff away in another item that he didn't remember getting for her: a small one-strap school bag. And just where had that come from? He didn't see her carrying it when she walked in. Without preamble, he grabbed her by the arm and dragged her out of classroom before anyone else had a chance to do anything more than look at them.

Not like it mattered. Chances were these people had already

come to their own conclusions about the relationship they shared. That was how high school students were. No one cared about what was actually going on. All that mattered were their own pre-misconceptions.

He took her to one of the more deserted sections of the school; a set of lockers that were no longer being used because of an incident last year that had ruined them. The school hadn't yet fixed the problem and the entire group of lockers were covered in graphite.

Letting go of her arm, he took several steps away from her, then whirled around to glare at the girl, who either wasn't bothered by his look, or purposefully ignoring it.

"If you wanted to get me alone, all you had to do was ask," Lilian told him. The small smile on her face let him know exactly what she was thinking. Which was pretty much the same thing she always thought about whenever he was involved.

"What are you doing here?" Kevin hissed, ignoring her play on words. He was not in the mood. His voice must have managed to convey what his expression could not because Lilian took a step back, her eyes widening and her mouth parting in a tiny 'o' of surprise. "Lilian, what are you doing here? Why aren't you back at the apartment?"

"I..." Lilian seemed to shrink in on herself in the face of his anger. Even though her ears were not out, Kevin could almost picture the way they would be drooping if they were. "I wanted to spend more time with you," she told him, her voice sounding very small, like that of a child who had just received a very harsh, angry scolding from one of their parents. "I thought if I joined your school, I could see you more often... I miss you when you go to school and leave me all alone."

Kevin had almost no time to prepare himself for what happened next. Even if he had, it was unlikely he would have been able to do anything about it.

Lilian stood there, her left arm grabbing onto her right elbow, rubbing it up and down self-consciously. An aura of sadness seemed to permeate her very being. It felt almost like she had managed to manifest her emotions on the physical plane. Kevin could literally feel the depression radiating from the two-tailed Kitsune. Her head was tilted towards the ground, but she was looking up at him. Her big, teary, green eyes were barely visible beneath her curtain of red hair as it fell about her face. It was such a sad, pathetic look that Kevin felt like someone had just punched him in the gut.

"Do... do you not want to spend time with me?" asked Lilian, sniffling. Another punch. Kevin tried not to feel guilty. He tried to remind himself that *she* was the one who barged into *his* life. That all of this was *her* fault and *he* had nothing to feel guilty about.

It didn't work out very well.

"Ugh... look, it's not..." Kevin looked away, thinking that maybe if he wasn't staring directly at her, the effects of her expression would lessen. They weren't, but it was a good attempt nonetheless. "It's not that I dislike spending time with you or anything... it's just... just..." Come on Kevin, think. "I just wish you would have told me about this first."

"I thought I could surprise you," Lilian answered, her voice still sounding very small, very soft. It was nothing at all like her normally bubbly voice. The feelings of guilt increased and brought friends. Kevin cursed himself for being so damn soft.

"Oh, I was surprised alright," he muttered, then sighed as he looked at the girl. "Just don't surprise me like this again, okay? I'm not very good with these kinds of surprises."

"So you're not mad at me?" Lilian was looking at him with such big, hopeful eyes that Kevin felt the rest of his anger evaporating like a winter breeze in the summer heat. How could he possibly stay mad at this girl? All she wanted to do was spend time with him. He couldn't hate or even mildly dislike her for that.

"No..." he ran a hand through his messy blond hair. It was getting a bit long. Maybe he should get it cut? "I'm not mad at you."

That was the wrong thing to say. Or maybe it was the right thing to say. Kevin didn't know, and probably wouldn't know until the next installment of this series.

"Thank you!" The girl's eyes lit up like a tree on Christmas morning. He didn't have much time to be affected by her stare though, because a second later she had practically jumped on him, hugging him for all he was worth. "I'm so glad you're not mad at me!"

It probably didn't need to be mentioned, but Kevin once again found himself being affected by the girl holding him in a herculean grip. Her body was pressed up against his, her breasts pushing themselves into his chest, rubbing against him in ways that generated all kinds of feelings that were both wanted and unwanted at the same time. It was enough that Kevin was beginning to feel more than a little delirious just standing there.

"I-i-it's fine." Kevin placed his hands on Lilian's shoulders and gently pushed her off him to get some distance. Anymore of that and he was probably going to pass out from all that blood that was rushing to his head. That, or die via mortification when Lilian felt the blood that was rushing to another part of his anatomy.

Neither of those options were very appealing.

Wanting to keep the girl from hugging him again, he asked, "So what class do you have next?"

"Um..." Kevin felt his face turn into a boiled lobster when Lilian reached in between her cleavage and pulled out her class schedule. Couldn't she have used one of her shorts pockets or something? "It looks like I have French next."

Wow. That was the same class he had. What were the chances of them sharing two classes in a row...

....

A feeling of dread welled up inside of him again.

"Can I see your schedule?" asked Kevin. Lilian had no objections and handed over her class schedule. Kevin held it up and began reading, his face paling as he saw what it looked like. "You have all the same classes as me..."

"I know, isn't it great?" Lilian smiled, taking the schedule back from him. "I asked the Principle if he would give me the same classes as you." She folded the paper up and put it back in between her cleavage. Kevin didn't even notice this time, busy as he was lamenting his horrible luck. "He was so accommodating."

"How..." Kevin swallowed. "How did you manage to do that? For the matter, just how did you manage to get registered with this school so quickly?" It took a lot of time to get registered with a school. He couldn't see how she could have done it in a single day, and he had no doubt this was a spur of the moment idea she came up with this morning. Lilian didn't seem like the type who thought that far ahead. Plus, didn't she need an adult to register her?

"That's simple." Lilian smiled as she grabbed his hand, entwined their fingers and began pulling the near unresponsive Kevin to their next class. "I used an enchantment."

"An enchantment?" Kevin blinked, finally coming back into himself as curiosity over came shock. "What's that?"

"It's a special ability we Kitsune have." Lilian swung their hands back and forth between them as they continued to walk. "Most Kitsune do not enjoy fighting, and we often go out of our way to avoid battle whenever possible. Enchantments allow us to do that. They are techniques that let us manipulate the thoughts, feelings and actions of others. With them, we can turn best friends into bitter enemies, make a person fall in love with us in a single glance, or even control someone's very thoughts and actions like they were nothing more than a marionette on a string."

"Wow, that sounds like a really useful power." Kevin imagined what he would do if he had the ability to manipulate others like that. He could easily get out of his homework by making his teachers think he already did his assignments, and got an A on them. Yes, school would be super easy then. He wouldn't even have to study!

Yes, Kevin was thinking about using enchantments to get out of doing schoolwork. He might be a good student, but that didn't mean he enjoyed the amount of effort that went into maintaining his good grades.

Don't judge him too harshly. If you had that ability, you would probably use it for the same thing as well.

As he was thinking this he realized what else she had said. Specifically, the part where she could make anyone fall in love with her in a single glance.

"Lilian," Kevin could not keep the trepidation out of his voice. "Did you…I mean…you didn't…"

"Don't worry, Beloved," already guessing what he was about to ask, she made to reassure him, "I would never use an enchantment on you."

Kevin relaxed. For some reason he believed her. He didn't know why (she was a Kitsune. They were supposed to be tricksters, weren't they?), and he honestly didn't have much reason to, but he did.

Of course, he went from relaxed to tense as a coiled spring when Lilian leaned into his side and his arm came into contact with her right breast. A shudder went up his arm, across his shoulder, down his spine and all the way to his toes. There's no real need to mention what was happening to his face.

"Besides," she added, either ignoring or not even noticing the way his body reacted underneath her touch. "No Kitsune worth their weight would ever use an enchantment to make someone fall in love with them. A Kitsune who needs to use enchantments in order to get a mate to fall is considered a failure among her species. We should be perfectly capable of seducing our mate without the aid of enchantments, ufufufu."

For some reason this did not make him feel any better. In fact, it made him feel worse.

It probably had something to do with that laugh of hers. It really freaked him out.

Thus, with his stomach twisting and turning, he and Lilian headed off for their next class.

***

French class was much the same as Math. Lilian seemed to be the center of attention of both boys and girls, though for completely different reasons. And because she was so intent on being with him as much as possible (even to the point where Kevin suspected her of using an enchantment on Madam Bonnet to make her pair them together for the project she assigned), he was also dragged into the spotlight.

It really wasn't a pleasant experience. Kevin didn't mind being the center of attention in certain instances, like when he was running the 100 meter dash for track and won first place or something. At least for something like that, he would have earned the attention under his own merit. But this? No, he didn't want this kind of attention.

It felt like people were trying to kill him with their eyes.

Was this the fabled Killing Intent he read so much about in his manga? How frightening.

Kevin tried to ignore the glares and do the task they had been assigned. They had been told to decide on a French play or movie, and to reenact a specific scene from it in front of the class. It wasn't really something he was keen on doing. Reenacting a scene in front of class that is, but since everyone else would be embarrassing themselves by doing the same thing as well—not to mention it would heavily influence his grade—he would grin and bear it.

It wasn't much of a surprise when he and Lilian found themselves differing on what they wanted to do. Kevin wanted to reenact a comedy, feeling that if nothing else, having his peers laugh at him because the skit had him do something stupid would be better than them laughing at him because he messed up. Lilian, on the other hand, wanted to do a romance. No surprise there.

"Look," Kevin started, "It's going to be much harder to enact a scene from a movie like La Vie d'Adèle than it would be to do one from a movie like Les Visiteur. It's easier to be funny than serious and romantic."

"But La Vie d'Adèle has a lot of kissing scenes," Lilia defended her choice, as if that was the only argument she needed to win him over. It was in her mind. What male wouldn't want to kiss their mate? "Les Visiteurs doesn't have any kissing scenes."

"And that," Kevin stated slowly, "is another reason why we should do the one I chose instead of yours." Then, as a last addendum, he added, "and besides, La Vie d'Adèle stars two women, so I couldn't play the part anyways."

Lilian crossed her arms and pouted at him. "That's a horrible reason not to reenact the movie I chose."

"Like yours is any better."

"But it is better!" Lilian insisted, grabbing the magazine where she had found the movie she wanted them to use for their project in. "Look right here." She pointed at the small lines of text in the synopsis. "This movie not only as a lot of kissing in it, but it's also got over twenty minutes of sex. We have to do this movie, Beloved."

"We are not doing a sex scene!" Kevin shouted, slamming his hands on the table as he shot to his feet, a megaton blush lighting up his face.

It took Kevin several seconds to realize that he had just shouted that out loud. He didn't need to look around to see that everyone was staring at him. He could hear them whispering well enough.

Kevin swayed dangerously as his mind began shutting down. He quickly pinched himself to keep conscious and sat back down before he could black out. He covered his face with his hands, wishing that he could hide from all the people still staring at him. He wished he could bury his head in a hole like some kind of Ostrich.

We don't always get what we wish for.

"I didn't mean we would be doing the sex scene in front of the class," Lilian chided her mate as if he had said something silly. "I would hate to have people watching us as we expressed our mutual love and attraction for each other so intimately."

"What mutual love and attraction?"

"I was simply mentioning that the movie has over twenty minutes of sex in it," Lilian continued as if she hadn't heard him. Kevin groaned exasperatedly.

"Why would you even mention it at all?"

"Ufufufu." Kevin shuddered. There it was again. That horrible, terrifying laugh. "I thought it would be a good idea. You know, so we can have a reference to use for our first time together."

"WHAT!?"

"Not so loud, Beloved. You're making everybody stare at us."

Kevin rubbed his face with his hands. She had no right to say that. This girl was bringing them attention just by existing!

The argument soon started again, albeit, without Kevin yelling out in shock this time. The two soon realized neither was going to change their position. Kevin wanted a comedy and Lilian wanted her romance.

Eventually, they settled on a compromise. The two decided on a romantic comedy called Hors de Prix. Of course, they would still have to choose a scene, which was bound to cause headaches, but at least they had managed to choose something before class ended. Sometimes you had to be grateful for the little things.

After French was Physics, which went much the same way his other classes did. Then Social Sciences where Professor Nabui kept staring at Kevin and Lilian with a confused frown, as if he were trying to figure out why one of his students, and Kevin of all people, had such a beautiful girl clinging to him.

Kevin couldn't blame his teacher. He had been wondering that very same thing himself ever since Lilian had come into his life. Surprisingly, Professor Nabui didn't say anything, thereby not forcing Lilian to use her Kitsune magic to coerce him into allowing them to sit together.

After Social Sciences was Gym. The class he had been dreading the most, which was an unusual turn of events since he normally liked Gym. Of course, he normally didn't have a girl hanging off his arm as he walked to class. If his last four classes were a disaster, then this class was going to be a catastrophe of such epic proportions that people would probably be talking about it for years to come.

It should be noted that aside from having a very over-reactive imagination, Kevin could be very pessimistic when he wanted to be.

"KEVIN SWIFT!"

Of course, he had a reason to be pessimistic in this instance. And that reason was stomping towards him with an expression on his face that was demanding an explanation.

What would he be explaining? The answer was hanging off his arm.

"You've got some explaining to do!" Yeah, he had been expecting it would start with something like that. "What's this I hear about you and... and... and..."

Kevin watched as Eric trailed off mid-sentence the moment his gaze landed on Lilian. His perverted friend's eyes glazed over and his mouth dropped. He looked like he had been struck dumb.

Kevin sighed. "Eric, this is Lilian. Lilian, this is Eric, my best friend and the biggest lech you're likely to meet."

Lilian took a single glance at Eric before pretty much dismissing him. Kevin was certain that her, "Nice to meet you," was said just to be polite because the boy was his friend.

Not that Eric seemed to care. Without a second thought, the tall teenager was in Lilian's face, causing the girl to lean back in shock as his nostrils flared like a horse. A large blush spread across his cheeks and it was clear to any potential witnesses that the boy was about to make an ass of himself in front of the new girl.

"You have the largest rack I've ever seen! Please let me shove my face in between those ginormous titties!"

With his free hand, Kevin palmed his face and rubbed it tiredly. How his friend honestly expected to get a girlfriend when *that* was his pickup line was beyond him. It was like Eric wasn't even trying to get a girlfriend, but only see how often he could get slapped.

Maybe his friend was a masochist?

"No thanks," Lilian sniffed disdainfully. "I would never let you do something like that to me, ever."

Kevin thought he saw cracks form on Eric's body. And was his skin turning gray? Kevin couldn't be sure, but he was almost positive it looked like the boy was being turned to stone.

"But... but why...?" asked Eric, a look of despair etched onto his face. He looked like his entire world view had just been shattered. Kevin's friend could be a real Drama Queen when he wanted to be.

"Because I don't like you." Lilian's blunt proclamation elicited a wail of despair from the boy, who slumped to the ground in a state of desolation. "I already have my Beloved," she continued, not seeing the way Kevin paled at the words. She looked at the boy like he was an annoying bug. "The only person I would ever let do something like that to me is my Beloved."

"Your... Beloved?"

It was only after hearing these words that Eric seemed to notice something he had missed, or simply forgotten upon noticing the gorgeous female in his presence.

His eyes traveled back and forth between Lilian and Kevin several times, finally spotting how close they were to each other, and the way Lilian's hand entwined with his friend's. Not to mention the way she was leaning up against him. And Kevin didn't doubt for one second that Eric had not managed to see the way his arm was being pressed into the valley of Lilian's cleavage.

Three. Two. One.

"WHAT THE HELL IS GOING ON HERE!?"

Chapter 13: Disastrous Meetings and Greeting

Kevin tried to ignore the way his best friend was despairing as they continued walking to Gym.

"I can't believe it.... doesn't deserve her.... damn bastard... kill him... I'll murder him dead!"

It was very hard to ignore his best friend when said best friend kept muttering what sounded like insults and death threats under his breath. Kevin didn't even need to look at the tall, lanky boy to know that Eric was glaring daggers at him. If the words being spoken weren't enough to inform him of this fact, there was the feeling of DOOM emanating from his friend that Kevin was becoming intimately familiar with did.

Just how his best friend could blame him for what had transpired was beyond him. It wasn't like he had done anything to make Lilian love him over Eric. He didn't even want her love! How could his friend possibly think this was his fault?

More and more people joined them as they got closer to the locker rooms, adding to the number of glares Kevin received from the male population of his school.

"What the hell is going on here?"

"Swift's got himself a girl?"

"How did a guy like *that* bag a babe like *her?*"

"Arg! I'm so jealous, I wish I could just strangle him!"

The not-so-soft-whispers around them were very hard to ignore. That last threat in particular made him gulp.

He looked down at the red-haired, green-eyed girl attached to his arm, taking note of the satisfied smile she wore. She looked completely at peace with the world, like she didn't even hear all the threats being directed his way or feel the glares at their backs. How Lilian remained so oblivious to everything that was going on around them was something that Kevin didn't think he'd ever comprehend.

"I don't get it. Are they a couple?"

"They do look pretty close, don't they?"

"You should have seen them in Math. According to Christy, that girl was calling him "Beloved"."

"Woah, Kevin Swift with a girl. Unbelievable."

"Does that mean he's off the market?"

At least the girls weren't glaring at him, though they did seem to be in a minor state of shock. He wasn't sure how to feel about their words. Should he be embarrassed that they seemed to think he and Lilian were a couple (it was kind of hard *not* to think that with the way Lilian is clinging to you, Kevin)? Insulted that they were so surprised he had a girl clinging to him? Or confused because he had no clue what they meant by "off the market?" What was he, some kind of trinket to be sold on a whim?

Whatever the case was, he did his utmost to ignore them as well.

"I'm surprised by how bold he's being. I remembered the last time I saw a girl even talk to him. His face got so red I thought his head might explode."

"I know, right? It was so kinda cute though."

Insert feminine giggling here.

Needless to say, ignoring the girls as they spoke was a lot harder than it looked.

When they finally reached the locker rooms, which seemed to take much longer than it should have, Kevin looked down at the girl cozying up to him. She looked so content with her head on his shoulder that he almost felt bad about what he had to say next.

Actually, that was a lie. He couldn't wait to get this girl off his arms. Maybe then everyone would stop with all the glaring and staring.

Good luck with that, Kevin.

"Lilian, you have to let go of me now."

"What?" Lilian raised her head to look up at him. "Why?"

Kevin raised an eyebrow. "How about because we have to get changed into our gym uniforms and you aren't allowed to come into the locker room with me?"

"Huh?" Lilian tilted her head to the side. All around them, several sharp intakes of breath could be heard from the male population that had been previously glaring at him. A glance around the room would have shown that every boy there was now staring at Lilian with red hued cheeks. Unlike Kevin, this was the first time these people had been subject to how cute Lilian looked when confused. "Why not?"

Kevin twitched, once. Was this girl serious?

"Because this is the men's locker room," Kevin explained as patiently as he could, gesturing to the room they were in front of. Standing by the doorway, Eric was glaring daggers at his friend. Kevin ignored him for now. "Girls aren't allowed inside."

Lilian looked at the door to see that, yes, it really was for males only. If the fact that all the males were going through that door and the females were going through another didn't tell her this, then the sign hanging above the door with the male stick figure most definitely did.

Her shoulders slumped.

"Oh..." Lilian looked truly disappointed that she wouldn't be able to join him in the locker room. Kevin wasn't sure if he was supposed to feel bad or not. "I was hoping I would get to see you do a striptease for me."

Definitely not.

Kevin choked on his own saliva at her words, his face exploding with red. A wail of despair echoed from Eric, and several other people who had heard her comment tripped over… something…no one really knows what as there was not a speck of dust on the ground. Anyways, they tripped and fell flat on their faces, their feet kicking straight up into the air, twitching.

Yes, they were in the traditional pose that all anime characters end up in when surprised. The Facefault. When shocked or surprised, often by an absurdity or non sequitur, the listener may fall over onto their face, their limbs contorted into a twisted mass above their heads. Usually, this happens when the character or characters in question hears something so incredibly stupid that it literally *floors them*. This is a very infamous pose that any Otaku worth their salt should know.

Kevin looked at Lilian, mortified. This girl… she really didn't know the meaning of the term "too much information" did she? Did she even have a filter for that mouth of hers?

Of course not. You should know this by now, Kevin.

"Just…" Kevin tried not to let himself be affected by her words. Or at least appear to not be affected. It would have been more convincing if he were not blushing up storm. "Just go into the girls locker room and get changed. It's right over there." He pointed to the door several feet away that had a sign with a very basic silhouette of a stick figure in a dress hanging over it.

Lilian sighed, clearly not wanting to do what he was asking of her, but deciding to comply nonetheless. "Alright," she looked up at him imploringly. "I'll still see you in class, right?"

"Yes," Kevin just barely managed to contain a sigh. She was awfully needy whenever he was involved. Was this natural for Kitsune? "You'll still see me in class."

"Okay."

Before anything else could happen Lilian grabbed both of his hands in a tight grip that he wouldn't be able to break out of. Kevin had just enough time to widen his eyes at the action before she leaned up on her toes and gave him a short peck on the lips.

It looks like she learned her lesson from this morning and kept his hands from being able to move so he could not use the Secret Hand Blocking Technique. Smart girl.

"I'll see you in class."

Kevin watched as Lilian walked over to the women's locker room. She paused to take one last longing look at him before entering. As she disappeared behind the door, Kevin's shoulders slumped. That girl really was going to be the death of him.

With Lilian now gone, he turned around to enter the men's locker room and get changed as well.

He didn't get very far before an arm clamped itself around his neck without warning. Forced to double over as he was pulled into a headlock, Kevin soon found a set of knuckles grinding against his scalp.

"Ouch! Wh-what the—!? Eric!? What are you doing!? Let go!"

"I'm the one who should be asking the questions here, bastard!" Eric shouted. He kept a firm hold on his so-called best friend. "What the hell is going on here!? Who was that babe!? How does she know you!? And why the hell was she getting all cozy with you when someone as amazing as me was right in front of her!? Huh!? Hu—oof!"

Kevin "tsked" as he retracted his elbow from his friend's gut. With Eric now holding his stomach instead of holding him in a headlock, the young man was free to walk into the locker room.

"There's nothing to tell. She's just some girl I'm helping out, that's all." Surprisingly enough, what Kevin said was the truth, even if he left a lot of important information out of his small summation of their relationship.

"Don't give me that bullshit." Eric straightened up as if he had not just had the wind knocked out of him by an elbow and quickly caught up with his best friend. "Hot girls don't just kiss you because you're helping them. Seriously man, what the hell is going on?"

"I don't know what to tell you," Kevin sighed. He'd been doing that a lot lately. Sighing that is. It made him feel old. "If you don't want to believe me, that's fine, but it's like I said, I'm just helping her out with something. She's just a little... erm... affectionate because I'm helping her. That's all."

Okay, so that little tidbit wasn't true. Kevin just wished it was.

"I don't believe you," Eric stated, glaring at his friend for thinking he could lie to him.

"Fine," Kevin grunted as they got changed. "Don't believe me all you want, but it's the truth."

Kevin finished putting on his gym clothes and closed his locker. He looked down at himself to make sure nothing had been put on backwards or something equally embarrassing.

The uniforms were designed using the school colors, a light shade of blue over white. They were a simple pair of blue shorts that stopped around the knees and a white shirt with blue accents that had the school name, logo, and an image of the mascot on the upper-right side of the chest.

On a side note, the mascot was a fricken' cactus. How clichéd is that?

"And what about Lindsay?" Eric continued. "Haven't you been in love with her since we were in middle school? Are you telling me you've given up on her?"

"I was—I mean, am! I am!" Kevin shook his head, the movements causing his hair to sway a bit. He really should think about getting it cut. "I am still in love with Lindsay, and of course I haven't given up on her. Do you really think I would give up on

Lindsay just because some girl I'm helping out seems to think there's more going on between us than there really is?"

"Really?" His friend sounded skeptical. "So you feel absolutely nothing for the babe, who is way hotter than Lindsay by the way, that gave you a smooch on the lips right in front of our entire gym class?"

Kevin blushed, but held firm. "Not a thing."

"You're a damn, dirty, liar, Kevin!"

"I'm not lying!" Kevin scowled. "I'm not in love with her. Lilian and I are just…we're just…" he paused as he found himself questioning his and Lilian's relationship. What were they? Really, what kind of category could he put their relationship into? Acquaintances? Temporary roommates? "Friends," he decided on after a moments thought.

"Just friends?" Eric gave him a flat look.

"Yes," Kevin nodded, "we're just friends."

"Liar. Liar, liar, liar, liar! A girl who is just your friend wouldn't kiss you like that! And no girl would press your arm in between their funbags like that if you two were 'just friends!'" Eric actually brought his hands up to make quotations when he said "just friends" as if the very notion of Kevin and Lilian being anything less than a young couple in love was absurd.

Kevin groaned. It was clear that Eric was not going to be letting this go any time soon, which meant he needed to draw attention away from him and his non relationship with Lilian and onto something else. Too bad there weren't many things that could get Eric to stop thinking about a hot female except for another, even hotter female.

His friend was pervy like that.

Well, barring the idea of changing the subject, he could always ignore Eric. He would have to put up with his best friend annoying the crap out of him if he did that, but he really couldn't think of anything else he could say or do that would convince Eric to drop his current line of inquiry.

Ignoring Eric it is.

"Whatever. I'll see you on the court." Kevin turned and began walking towards the door, completely ignoring his friend calling after him.

"H-hey! Kevin! I'm talking to you! Dammit! Don't ignore me! Kevin! KEVIN!"

***

Kevin was still ignoring Eric when they arrived at the gym. By now the lanky teen had stopped trying to talk his ear off with complaints and expletives, and was simply glaring at him instead. The rest of the male students were milling about. Most of them, Kevin noted, were talking about the hot new girl, though a few were also glaring at him.

Kevin sighed. Even when she wasn't present, Lilian still haunted him in some way.

"Beloved!"

Speak of the devil and she shall appear.

Kevin barely had enough time to turn around before Lilian jumped him. And no, that wasn't an euphemism for something. She literally jumped on him.

Blue eyes widened as Lilian's slender arms wound their way around his neck and her equally beautiful thighs and calves latched themselves around his waist, her feet locking together behind the small of his back to keep her in place. Out of nothing more than instinct, Kevin's hands went under her thighs to keep her from falling. Had he really thought about what he was doing, he would have realized that it was much better to let her just fall off him than what was about to happen next. At least, it would have been better in his mind.

Before Kevin even had a chance to speak a pair of soft, warm lips crashed into his, kissing him, claiming him, devouring him in mind and body and soul, leaving him a delirious wreck of quivering male hormones.

In other words it was hot, passionate, and definitely above a PG13-rating.

For several long seconds the only sounds in the room were the usual sounds that came from a passionate kiss. You know, lips smacking, tongues dueling, lots of moaning, those kinds of noises. Time stood still as the Law of Temporal Variability once more took effect for everyone.

Everyone except for Lilian, apparently, who continued her gratuitous display of public affection without any regard to the fact that there were over a dozen hormonal teenage males standing around. As far as she was concerned no one existed except for her and her beloved mate. Lilian had a one-track mind like that.

"What the hell do you two think you're doing!?" Fortunately, for what little remained of the chastity of Kevin's lips, help came in the form of an irritable gym coach. "Stop sucking each other's face off! Public displays of affection are against school policy!"

Upon hearing the coach's shouting, Kevin yelped and let go of the firm thighs he had been grasping as if he had been scalded. Lilian squawked for a moment as she felt the hands holding her legs up leave, forcing her to double the strength she was using to keep herself wrapped around his waist. Kevin released a strained groan as his torso felt like it was being compressed by a trash compactor. It was only after she managed to keep from falling onto her butt that the two-tailed Kitsune finally got off her Beloved.

As her feet touched solid ground, Lilian took a moment to glare at the man teaching their class. How dare this idiot interrupt them! She and her mate had been sharing a very special moment together!

It was only special to you, Lilian.

"Be quiet."

Yes ma'am.

"And don't call me ma'am!"

Kevin eyed the girl next to him oddly. Just who was it that she kept talking to?

"Alright, you maggots! Line up!"

Everyone quickly followed the coach's instructions. They knew what would happen if they failed to listen to the man. Coach Raide, like many coaches before him, was a complete hard ass. He was your average, stereotypical looking high school coach. You know, like the kind of coaches you see in high school movies and cartoons everywhere. He was a large, barrel chested man with arms and legs that made people think they were looking at Chewbacca. Aside from his broad chest and shoulders, and his extremely hairy arms and legs, the man also had a rather large beer gut. Kevin thought it made him look pregnant.

Kevin somehow found himself in the middle of the group with Lilian standing as close to him as humanly possible without incurring Coach Raide's anger. On his other side was Eric, whose hateful glare seemed to have increased several fold in the last few seconds. Probably because of that kiss Lilian had given him.

And speaking of hatred, Kevin couldn't help but shiver at all that negative energy being directed his way. He could actually see the physical manifestation of all the anger from the various males in his class being channeled towards him in the form of hell fire and ugly demons, spitting and snarling behind each boy. And was it just him? Or were their irises actually glowing a dark, sinister red?

Fearing for his life, Kevin focused his attention back on the coach. They wouldn't do anything so long as Coach Raide was present, right?

"Alright!" the coach's loud voice bellowed out. "We're going to start by doing some basic warm up exercises. When I blow this whistle, I want all of you to drop down and start doing push-ups until I say stop! Ready? Three…. Two… One!"

And that was how the first half of class went. Coach Raide would give them an exercise, blow his whistle, then they would all have to do whatever it was. They did every exercise you could think of, from push-ups to sit-ups to jumping jacks to squats and everything in between.

Most people found it to be rather grueling but Kevin actually did very well in this class. He and his friend Eric were more athletically inclined than most of the other students, being athletes on the track team and all that. Only those who were also in a sports club of some kind managed to keep up with them.

Another great surprise was Lilian. Once again the girl astounded him by keeping pace with him easily. Every exercise they were given she managed to do with the same ease that he did. Actually, it looked like she had an even easier time of it than he did. She hadn't even worked up a sweat! Kevin wondered if this was just another benefit of being a Kitsune. Maybe they had super human strength and endurance as well as special Kitsune powers?

The rest of the class did pretty poorly, even those who were athletes. At least the male portion had some serious problems during this period. The more athletic girls did fine.

Kevin knew the reason for this. Lilian, again. She was pretty much the reason for anything strange and unusual that happened here.

Not that it was her fault. She couldn't be blamed for the boys who were blatantly staring at her chest as it bounced and swung and jiggled whenever she was doing one of Coach Raide's exercises. It wasn't her fault her breasts were so big.

The blame for her breast size can be laid solely on her mom, and *Shōnen manga fanservices*, but mostly her mom.

After what Coach Raide called "warm up exercises" were done and over with they were all directed outside where they would move on to the sports they would be doing that day.

It was here that Lilian found herself taking issue with the gym coach. Once they finished their warm ups, boys and girls were split to do separate activities. Today the boys would be playing basketball on the basketball courts while the girls would be playing volleyball.

Lilian didn't like that. She had no trouble with the sport she would be playing but the fact that she would be separated from her mate, even if it was just by a few dozen meters or so. To her being separated from her chosen mate was unacceptable. The girl spent nearly ten minutes arguing with Coach Raide in what sounded like a very heated debate:

"What do you mean I can't play basketball!?"

"All the girl's are playing volleyball today," Coach Raide grunted, not appearing the least bit bothered by the angry glare he was receiving.

"I don't want to play some stupid volleyball game! I want to play basketball with my Beloved!"

"I don't care what you want. Boys and girls aren't allowed to play sports together. It's against school policy. You'll have to see him after class."

Lilian stared intently at the man, her eyes glowing a bright green. "You will let me play basketball with my Beloved."

"No, I won't."

Lilian's eyes widened in surprise. Who did this fool think he was? She would show him! "You *will* let me stay with my Beloved."

"You and your *Beloved* can spend time together after class."

"Let me stay with my Beloved now!"

"No."

Yeah, their argument went something like that.

With a scowl marring her pretty face, Lilian walked over to Kevin as he stood on the basketball court with the rest of the guys, all of whom had been watching the argument. By the time she reached him, the scowl was gone, replaced with a sorrowful frown.

She looked pretty miserable. Kevin actually felt kind of bad for her.

"I couldn't convince him to let me stay with you," she said slowly, as if she were not quite able to believe she had failed to convince someone to let her stay by his side. Considering who she was, or rather, what she was, Kevin could kind of understand where she was coming from. "Not even my enchantment worked on him."

"The rules state that boys and girls have to play sports separately, so even if he did let you stay with us, he would get in a lot of trouble." Kevin felt a mixture of relief and curiosity at her words, a strange combination of emotions to be sure, but there you go. "Still, I'm surprised he was able to resist your... enchantment." He looked around when he mentioned her power, fearing someone may have overheard him. When he saw that very few people were paying any real attention to him and those who were, were too far away to hear them, he turned back to Lilian.

"Enchantments can be resisted," Lilian admitted reluctantly. "Most humans don't have the fortitude to do so, but if there is something they feel particularly strong about, or they have a strong enough will, it can be resisted. It's just very rare for something like that to happen."

"In that case, I'm not surprised he resisted it." Kevin rubbed his chin thoughtfully. "Coach Raide has always been a stickler for the rules, and he's one of the most stubborn people I've ever met."

"Doesn't matter," Lilian's shoulders slumped. "I still don't get to be with you..."

Oh jeez. The girl looked so depressed. What was he supposed to do now? Was she expecting him to do or say something that would make everything better?

"This might be a good experience for you," Kevin said lamely. "You can get to know some of the other girls and make friends."

His words did not seem to make Lilian feel any better. If anything the red head's shoulders slumped even more. Kevin could practically see the dark, gloomy aura of depression surrounding her. It looked like a distorted wave of dark mist that wafted off her body. It sort of reminded Kevin of the steam that hot-springs or a jacuzzi would emit, only it was black instead of white.

"I don't care about making friends," Lilian mumbled lowly as she looked down at the ground. Her hair fell over her eyes, casting the top half of her face in shadow. She then raised her head ever so slightly, her crimson colored bangs parting just enough to reveal her large, emerald eyes. "I just want to be with you."

For perhaps the first time since meeting her, Kevin was very glad that Lilian had already subjected him to that look multiple times. In fact, she gave it to him so often that he was beginning to build up an immunity to it. It wouldn't work this time. He could resist her.

"Guh!"

Or not. Fortunately, while he might not have any resistance

to girls giving him a cute look, there was someone who could resist such a look, didn't care about what either of them wanted *and* had no compunctions about sending Lilian away.

"What are you two doing!?" Coach Raide shouted. "Get going, girly!"

"Shut up, fat ass!" Lilian snapped. Kevin's expression turned shocked. That was the first time he had ever heard her swear.

Was it wrong of him that he found her cursing kind of attractive?

Probably.

Lilian turned back to him. The expression on her face was very disconcerting. Her stare was very expectant, like she was waiting for him to do something. Just what that something was, he couldn't determine.

"What?"

"Can I have a kiss goodbye?"

Kevin's right eye twitched. He was honestly surprised she was even asking him that. Normally, she would have just kissed him without any prior warning.

Just what was her angle?

"I think you've gotten enough kisses to last several years at least. Besides, it's not like it really matters. You're only going to be a few meters away; the volleyball sand lot is right there."

"Oh come on!" Lilian pleaded. "Just one more kiss?"

Kevin simply pointed towards the volleyball sand lot where all the other girls were standing. It looked like they were choosing teams. No, wait. They weren't doing anything of the sort. They were actually just staring at him and Lilian as they giggled and whispered to each other.

In other words, they were gossiping about the two of them.

No doubt whatever they managed to overhear of his and Lilian's conversation would be known by the entire school after class.

How mortifying.

Lilian pouted at him. She didn't want to leave his side. At least not without getting her kiss. Still she complied with his request (demand) and started walking towards the sand lot.

Or so he thought.

A second after she had turned and he breathed a sigh of relief, she spun around, grabbed the back of his head, leaned up on her toes and simultaneously pulled him into another kiss. When she pulled back, there was a large scowl on his face, as well as an even larger blush. She gave him a coquettish smile before sauntering towards the sand lot.

Kevin watched as Lilian walked away with a sway in her hips, his face burning something fierce. He turned away from the red head who was now surrounded by a group of giggling girls and rubbed a hand over his face, not only to mask his growing blush, but also an effort to ignore the malicious presences behind him. Maybe if he just pretended they weren't there, the feeling would go away.

"Swift…"

No such luck it seemed. Dang. It looked like it was time to face the music. Kevin turned around, mentally preparing himself for what he was likely to face—

"Urk!"

—and promptly wished he hadn't, for as soon as he made a full 180 degree turn he found himself staring at the angry glares of every single male student in his class. All of them were giving him such intense looks of loathing that he was honestly surprised he hadn't spontaneously combusted. Eric was at the front of the pack, cracking his knuckles in a way that had Kevin's hackles rising.

"Ke-v-in..."

"You're so dead, Swift."

Yes, Lilian was definitely going to be the death of him. And it may be happening even sooner than he had anticipated.

***

After Kevin just barely managed to avoid getting the ass kicking to end all ass kickings in gym he met up with Lilian outside of the men's locker room. The moment the girl had seen him she'd latched onto him like a leech and refused to let go. It seemed their separation had really gotten to her. Things had gotten so bad that in their next class the fox-girl whose foxy features were currently hidden had tried sitting on his lap. It had taken almost the entire first half of class to convince Lilian that she couldn't use his lap as a seat, and even then she sat so close to him that their legs had been in constant contact.

It almost makes you wonder how she would act if they were separated by more than just a few meters.

Not only that, but after the incident which shall forever be known in Kevin's mind as "get the hell off my lap!" Lilian had used her Deus Ex Machina powers to subjugate the teacher's will and then spent the rest of their time in class trying to hold his hand underneath the table. He'd had to struggle against her each time she tried, yanking his hand out of her grip, only to have her latch back on seconds later when he thought she had given up. It had very nearly turned into a war between them. Or a game, as Lilian seemed to think of it as.

Ugh, that girl... in any case, Eric had once more tried to woo Lilian away from Kevin after gym. It hadn't worked and he'd been shot down faster than those zombies they killed at the arcades, but Kevin appreciated the attempt.

Even if, you know, Eric wasn't actually trying to convince Lilian to like him instead Kevin because he wanted to be a good friend. Kevin liked to at least *think* his friend was looking out for his well-being.

After their last class Kevin, with Lilian attached to his arm, found himself heading to lunch. Usually he would have bought a lunch from the school cafeteria, but there was no need this time. Lilian had made them both a very large lunch that morning while he had been in the shower.

He would never admit this aloud for fear of Lilian getting the wrong impression, but it actually warmed his heart that she made lunch for him. His mom hadn't made him a lunch in years and he kind of missed that feeling of someone caring about him enough to do so. It very nearly made him forgive her for all the trouble she caused today. Very nearly.

So there they were, walking to lunch. Lilian had one arm wrapped around his right arm while the other held a large picnic basket in the crook of her arm.

He didn't question where she had gotten the picnic basket. Or how it had randomly appeared in her arms after their last class when he knew for a fact she didn't have it before. Kevin just *knew* he would be better off not knowing.

That was the most intelligent idea he'd had since meeting her.

"Hey!"

Looking up as his thoughts were interrupted, the aforementioned young man saw Eric dashing towards them, waving an arm over his head. Kevin raised a hand in greeting—

"What's up Eric..."

"Good afternoon, my lovely Tit Maiden!"

—and promptly used it to palm his face.

"I must be the luckiest man in the world to see your tits twice in a single day!" Eric grabbed onto Lilian's free hand, the one attached to the arm that was holding onto the basket. He was completely ignoring Kevin. "Would you like me to suckle your nipples—I mean, would you like to have lunch with me? I'll pay."

Kevin gave a long suffering sigh and rubbed the bridge of his nose with his thumb and forefinger. Why did he even bother trying to act like things were normal anymore? They had not been normal since Eric hit puberty, never mind Lilian's entrance into his life. It was all too clear to him now that she was just the last nail in his coffin of normality.

That's a pretty defeatist attitude to have, Kevin.

Lilian yanked her hand out of Eric's grasp. This did not deter the perverted teenager, who simply looked up at her with lust clearly visible in his eyes.

What does lust look like? Good question. It's a large blush that extends across the bridge of the nose and cheeks, glazed over eyes that sweep across the female said person is lusting after, clearly stripping whatever girl of her clothes. That kind of thing.

Ahem, in any event, it seemed the fox-girl's cold act simply spurred Eric onwards. Come to think of it, every time Eric was shot down, he would become even more overjoyed and determined... after the initial period of depression that is. It was as if the act of getting turned down made him that much happier.

Kevin's eyes widened. Oh God! His friend really was a masochist!

"Hmph!" Lilian huffed. "No thank you. I plan on sharing lunch with my Beloved. Why would I want to share lunch with a perverted lech like you?"

Is this a case of the pot calling the kettle black?

"Oh, shut up!"

...That was mean...

"!!"

Shutting up now.

It was almost amusing to watch the expression on Eric's face go from its dazzling and (in his mind) charming smile to utterly depressed within seconds. His mouth dropped open as if he couldn't believe he had been shot down so harshly (even though he gets shot down like this every day). Then his eyes took on the look of a person who'd just watched someone punt their puppy across a football field. You know, the whole grimacing face with shocked, wide eyes. *Then* his shoulders slumped in despondency as he fell onto his hands and knees like someone who had just been told by their older brother that he had killed their entire family to test his capacity.

But Kevin was distracted from the very amusing sight of his friend slumping on the ground by something else he had noticed.

"Is that a raincloud?" asked Kevin, pointing to the large, black mass that floated over his friend. Tiny droplets of water were falling from it and onto Eric's head, matting down his hair and soaking his clothes. A number of flashes and sparks could be seen from inside the mass of black. If he didn't know any better, Kevin would say it looked like lightning.

Lilian looked where he was pointing and nodded.

"It certainly looks like it. And it's raining too. He must be pretty depressed for a raincloud to appear like that."

"How did it get there?" asked Kevin before he shook his head. "Never mind that, how did it even appear in the first place? Rainclouds can't form this near to the ground…and I don't think they can be this small…"

"It's probably my fault," Lilian admitted. "You see, Kitsune like myself tend to effect the Fourth Wall. Our presence alone is enough to cause small cracks in it." She gestured towards the rain cloud. "This is just a small example. I'm sure there were others earlier in this story, but you didn't notice them because my presence hadn't really become prominent until Chapter five."

Kevin had no clue what she was talking about.

"The Fourth what? Chapter five?"

"Never mind that," Lilian declared, tightening her grip on his arm as she began leading him away from the weeping sophomore and his personal raincloud. "Come on, Beloved. Let's find a spot to have lunch together."

"Ah, well, I was actually hoping to sit with my friends," he said. Lilian gave him a look that made Kevin feel the inexplicable need to elaborate. "Usually, Eric, me, and a few of my other friends from track sit together over there." He pointed to a square section of grass that held a stage underneath a modern-looking gazebo with several stone tables that had been arranged side by side.

"But I wanted to spend lunch with *just* you," Lilian pouted. Kevin turned his head away so that he wasn't looking at her. He had played this game enough times in the past to know the rules by heart. If he so much as looked at her, he would lose.

"Don't you want to meet my friends?" asked Kevin, trying a different method of dealing with Lilian than his usual straight forward approach, which was basically telling her off until she gave him The Look and he caved like a tower of cards that had been knocked over by a petulant child. If he wanted to beat this girl at her own game he would need to be sneaky and deceitful. Like a politician. "They're very important to me, you know, and it would be nice if you got along with all of them."

There was a short pause followed by a loud exhalation of breath. "I suppose if they are *that* important to you, I could at least meet them."

He let out a sigh of relief. It was temporary relief because less than a second later he felt something warm and soft and moist and horribly familiar press against his cheek.

All the blood in his body began rushing straight to his face as Lilian's lips lingered against his skin for several seconds longer than necessary. When the feel of her lush lips left his skin, he raised a hand to his cheek and turned his head to stare at her, wide eyed.

"What....?" Kevin choked as his face began to burn something fierce. Just why he was so embarrassed when he had experienced much more...passionate...moments with Lilian was beyond anyone. How this young man had not yet managed to become inured to the girl's continuous use of physical affection to express her feelings for him was simply astounding on a scale so monumental that Otaku everywhere raged at his uselessness.

This kid was really going to need to toughen his skin if he hoped to survive the sequel, never mind the rest of this series.

"What was that for?"

"Because you were being cruel," Lilian pouted at him. Kevin's look of discomfiture slowly morphed into befuddlement.

"You kissed me because I was being cruel?" He scratched his cheek awkwardly. "I'm not sure I get it."

"That's okay," Lilian patted his cheek. Kevin had the distinct feeling that she was being condescending. "You don't have to get it."

Definitely condescending.

With that small moment done and over with, the two of them headed over to the gazebo, leaving behind a still sulking Eric. It was only after they arrived that Kevin realized it may have been a mistake to have lunch with his friends after all. It had been Kevin's hope that by eating lunch in a very public setting with his friends, he would not only keep Lilian from trying anything too salacious with him, but also give his day, nay, his *entire week,* some sense of normality.

He really should have known better.

Kevin and Lilian first met up with two of his track friends, twin brothers named Alex and Andrew Streit. The moment the brothers caught sight of the pair they dropped all the food they had bought from the school cafeteria and began gaping as they looked from Kevin to Lilian to the way Lilian was glued to Kevin, then back to Kevin again.

Cue awkward silence.

"Uh... hey," Kevin greeted the two awkwardly. They didn't say anything, merely stared. Talk about creepy. "So... this is Lilian, you guys. Lilian, this is Alex and Andrew. They're twins."

"Huh." Lilian looked at the two in idle curiosity. They didn't look alike, but then, she and her twin looked nothing alike either. "Nice to meet you."

Alex and Andrew were fraternal twins as opposed to identical. Alex had brown eyes and red hair while Andrew's hair was more of an auburn color and he had gray eyes. They both had pale skin. Alex had a good deal of freckles while Andrew was freckle-less.

The twins snapped out of their stupor upon hearing Kevin and Lilian speak...and immediately begin fighting over who got to introduce themselves to the gorgeous red head first.

"As the older brother it is my right to speak with her before you!"

"You're only older than me by a few seconds! And don't you know that the younger brother always gets first dibs? It's part of the bro code!"

"What the hell are you talking about? There's no rule in the bro code that says that you idiot! You just made that up!"

"So? It doesn't change the fact that I'm going to speak with her first!"

"No, you're not!"

"Yes, I am!"

"No, you're not!"

Lilian and Kevin watched, one looking slightly curious but otherwise unaffected (Lilian) while the other sighed and began rubbing his forehead in exasperation (Kevin), as the two brothers rolled around on the grass trying to wrestle one another into submission. It would have been funny, but Kevin had long since lost his sense of humor for situations like this thanks to the girl next to him.

"Are they always like this?" asked Lilian.

"Not always," Kevin started to tell her, only to wince as the sound of flesh smacking against flesh resounded through the air. It seemed Andrew had just hit Alex in the face. "Just whenever they disagree on something," more sounds of fist meeting flesh accompanied his words, "which is most of the time."

"Hmmm..." Lilian looked at the fighting twins a moment longer before dismissing them. They weren't really important anyways.

"Oh, and that's Justin." Kevin pointed out one of his other friends, a kid with dark hair and a pale, pointed face. His friend didn't even look up from his food, just continued eating and mumbling in between bites as he listened to whatever song was on his Ipod. Probably some kind of Gothic metal band. "You can just ignore him for now. He never pays attention to anything during lunch."

"Good. That's one less support character to worry about."

Kevin blinked. "What?"

"Nothing. Let's eat."

After that she brought out the food she made that morning. Kevin had to admit it all looked delicious. He didn't know what some of the delicacies were—she said they were Mediterranean—but it all appeared incredibly appetizing.

It was as they were about to begin eating that the next set of problems during lunch came. It started with Lilian trying to feed him.

"Come on, Beloved." She held the fork with what she called Shrimp Saganaki speared on it up to her mouth, gently blowing on it before moving it next to his mouth. It was still hot, as seen by the steam rising from it. Just how it had remained so hot when it had been cooked over five hours ago was also beyond Kevin, but he didn't want to think about the impossibility of something that inane now. "Say 'ah'."

"I-I really don't need you to feed me, you know. I'm perfectly capable of feeding myself."

"Ufufufu, now don't be like that. Just open your mouth and saw 'ah.'"

"There you go with that strange laugh again. And the answers still no."

"Mou." Lilian's eyes suddenly grew big. She always had rather large, innocent looking eyes, but now they were much larger. Not only did they grow, but her eyes also began to get dewy as tear drops formed at the bottom of her eyelids, completely disregarding the fact that the tear ducts were located at the innermost corner of the eyes and not the bottom of the lid. The whole "see how adorable yet sad I am" look was enhanced by Lilian's lower lip quivering. "Please, Beloved? For me?"

Kevin felt like someone had just dropped a twelve pound bowling ball on his stomach from twenty feet high.

Several seconds later he was sitting at one of the tables, allowing Lilian to feed him. The sound of the twins fighting over who would introduce themselves to said emerald eyed beauty first was their only companion. It was during this time and just when Kevin was beginning to resign himself to his fate that another voice spoke up, one that caused his blood to chill and his heart to stop cold.

"You two are looking awfully comfy."

Kevin turned with almost mechanical precision towards the source of the voice. Internally pleading to God that the voice not belong to who he thought it did, the young sophomore student found his wish shattered the moment he turned. Lindsay Diane, his secret (or not so secret) crush. She was standing just a few feet behind him, hands on her hips, and an amused smile playing on her lips as she looked at the human and the Yōkai currently disguised as a human.

"L-Lindsay!" Kevin shouted in surprise as his rapidly paling face suddenly gained far more color than what should be possible for a human. He then realized what she had said and began shaking his hands back and forth in front of his face furiously. "T-this isn't what it looks like!"

Lindsay looked back and forth between the two of them, a single eyebrow quirked. "Oh? So this girl isn't feeding you food that looks like it kicks the crap out of the cafeteria food?" Kevin flinched. "And I suppose you aren't letting her feed you?

"Uh...." There really was nothing he could say to that, was there?

"And I'm guessing all those rumors about how close you two are, are lies as well?" Lindsay continued mercilessly.

"Guh!"

That sound came from Kevin, who had just been metaphorically jack hammered in the stomach.

Grinning, the cute, athletic teen continued. "And then there are all those *other* rumors. You know, the ones about you two trying to suck each others faces off in gym class? It's all over the school. Are you telling me those are lies too?"

"I-I was not sucking anyone's face off!" Kevin tried to defend himself. Too bad Lindsay didn't believe him, even if it was true. It probably didn't help that his face was beet red as he recalled *that* particular incident.

"Uh huh...right, because every single person who claims you two looked like you were about to have sex in class was lying."

"We were not about to have sex," Kevin mumbled lowly, his face overheating. Oh merciful, benevolent God, please just kill him now. End his suffering.

"Of course, of course," Lindsay drawled, still grinning. "You two weren't about to have sex. You were just going to shag her rotten."

Kevin looked like he was about to cry. Why wouldn't she believe him?

"Excuse me," Lilian interrupted the two before Lindsay could continue to tease her mate further. Her eyes were narrowed as she studied the brunette with suspicion. "But who are you?"

"That's right!" Lindsay snapped her fingers, a look of realization crossing her face. "I totally forgot to introduce myself in homeroom." She smiled knowingly. "Though, you were a bit too busy staring at Kevin to pay attention if I had." While said boy swayed dangerously in his seat, Lindsay held her hand out to the beautiful red head. "I'm Lindsay Diane, one of Kevin's friends."

"I see..." Lilian cast a side long glance out of the corner of her eye to see Kevin staring up at Lindsay with reddened cheeks. Her eyes narrowed imperceptibly before a large and patently false smile crossed her face. She grabbed the girl's hand and shook. "A pleasure to meet you. I'm Lilian Pnévma."

"Nice to meet you too," Lindsay smiled before taking a seat on the opposite side of the two and setting her tray of food down. She absently tucked a strand of shoulder length brown hair behind her ear before focusing on the pair in front of her again.

"But seriously, what is your guys' relationship? Are you two dating or something? How come I've never seen you around before?" She directed her last question towards Lilian.

"No/Yes," Kevin and Lilian both said at the same time. They looked over at each other, Kevin quickly looking away when the red head pouted at him.

Lindsay raised an eyebrow. She looked at Lilian. "So if you two aren't going out, then what exactly is your relationship with Kevin?"

Kevin's danger senses blared. Somehow, he just knew that if he let Lilian answer that question, she would say something potentially disastrous. His mouth opened, determined to answer the question when unfortunately for him, Lilian answered first.

"He's my fiance," Lilian told the girl bluntly, at the same time taking Kevin's right arm into a possessive hold and glaring at the cute tomboy sitting in front of them, as if daring Lindsay to contradict her.

Silence reigned for several seconds as everyone tried to process Lilian's words. Even the twins had stopped fighting when they heard the red head's proclamation. All of them seemed to be having a bit of trouble putting those words into a format they could fathom. Even Kevin was feeling a little dumbfounded, and he had been dealing with this girl for the past week.

Honestly, you'd think that after being forced to put up with Lilian's antics for so long he would have become immune to anything she could say or do. Then she pulls a fast one and Kevin once more found himself floundering as he tried to retain a grip on reality. It was like she got a kick from pulling the metaphorical rug out from underneath him.

"Oh, I get it!" Lindsay laughed as she looked between the two, a large grin on her face. "You guys are playing a prank! Good one! You really had me fooled. For a second, I actually thought you were being serious."

"I am being completely serious," Lilian actually looked angry that Lindsay would dare to think she was anything other than serious when it came to her mate. Her eyes were narrowed dangerously and her lips had formed a thin line as she pressed them together. "Kevin and I are engaged to be married."

...

...

More silence. Lindsay stared, and stared, and stared. In fact, she began staring so much that Kevin was getting very uncomfortable.

Finally...

"You're serious?" Lindsay looked at Lilian with wide eyes. "Like seriously serious?"

"Of course I am," Lilian clutched a near catatonic Kevin even more tightly to herself. This caused Kevin's face to become a strange mixture of ghost white and tomato red. Think about those clowns you see when the circus comes to town, take away the large red nose, and you have an accurate description of what his face looked like. "Why would I lie about this?"

"Wha... but..." Now it was Lindsay's turn to look completely bamboozled. A familiar wail sounded out in the distance. Kevin was beginning to feel the stress of the day catching up with him. Was it too late for him to find that hole?

Finally, after several seconds in which all time seemed to stand still, Lindsay did something Kevin thought she would never do before. Her eyes rolled up into the back of her head as the shock of Lilian's apparently honest admittance of their engagement caught up to the poor girl. Her body slumped forward and her face planted itself directly into the Chicken Ceaser Salad she had bought at the Cafeteria.

"I think that went rather well," Lilian said absently as she speared her fork into her Greek Salad and began eating.

Kevin planted his head face first onto the table and groaned. "Of course you would." It was official, this was The Worst Day Ever.

Yes, that was all capitalized.

Chapter 14: Hardships of a High School Student

"So when did the two of you meet?" Leaning forward on her right forearm, her cheek resting on the butt of her left hand , Lindsay looked at the red-haired, green-eyed beauty sitting opposite her and next to Kevin. Her eyes were alight with interest. It was clear that she had every intention of interrogating her fellow female until she was well and truly satisfied with what she had learned.

Upon waking up and realizing that, no, she wasn't caught up in some crazy dream and yes, Kevin really had somehow managed to bag himself a beauty who apparently considered them as good as married, the athletic brunette decided it was time for her to do something that she had never done before: gossip.

"And how come we've never met until now?" Lindsay was sure that if her friend had a fiancée this hot, she would have known about it long before now. It should have been all over the school! So how was it that she hadn't even heard about Lilian, much less met her, until today? That was what she wanted to know. "Did you go to another school or something? Long distance relationship?"

"The reason you haven't heard of me is probably because my Beloved and I haven't known each other for very long," Lilian informed the brunette. "As for when we met." She looked over at Kevin, a smile creeping onto her face like the dawning sun as it began to cast it's brilliant luminescence upon the Earth as she thought about the day she met her Beloved. It was an absolutely breathtaking smile, to which every male there could attest. Even Lindsay, who was a completely heterosexual female with no interest in the same gender, was feeling a little hot under the collar at that smile. "We met last week."

At least she had been hot under the collar, until her mind fully processed the last part of what was said by the red-haired vixen. Then her eyes widened.

"Wait, wait, wait, wait! Hold up! Slow down! Time out!" Lindsay held her hands up, forearms crossed in an X pattern as she stared at the girl incredulously. "You mean to tell me that you just met him last week and you're already thinking of marriage?" At Lilian's happy nod, Lindsay gawked at the other girl. So did the others, but they aren't as important to the story right now. "Isn't that taking things just a little too fast?"

"No," Lilian was incredibly succinct in her answer. There was no hesitation in her voice. "I know that my Beloved is the one for me. Why would I want to wait to make sure he is "The One" when I already have the answer?"

"Well," Lindsay looked a tad unsure of herself. "I guess you kind of have a point," she conceded, more from a lack of being able to think up any kind of counter argument than because she actually agreed with Lilian.

The brunette shook her head. Regardless of her own beliefs on marriage, or the fact that she felt the redhead was taking things too fast, she couldn't really argue with the girl. And it was clear to everyone that Lilian wouldn't be dissuaded from her beliefs.

Onto the next question then.

"So when did you realize he was the one for you?"

"Just a little while after we met." Lilian's eyes lit up at the thought of sharing the story about her first meeting with her Beloved. It was one she would obviously be cherishing for a long time to come. "I was injured when my Beloved found me, brought me to his apartment and tended to my injuries." She sighed, a dreamy expression on her face. "He was so gentle and treated me so tenderly that I couldn't help but fall in love with him."

"Wow," Lindsay whistled, impressed. Meanwhile, Kevin had buried his face in his hands to hide his growing blush. "That almost sounds like something you'd read about in a romance novel."

"Or a manga."

"Or a manga," Lindsay agreed with her fellow female.

"Or a fanfiction."

"Yes, or a... wait. What?"

"Never mind."

"Right." Lindsay eyed the red head oddly. Shaking her head a second later, a grin spread across her face as she leaned forward. "So tell me more. How did you get past Kevin's shyness around girls?"

"Urk!"

For those who are wondering, yes, that was Kevin who just started making random choking noises. The reason for this could be due to the water he had been drinking going down his air passage upon hearing Lindsay's question. Or it could be completely unrelated to what the girl said. Who can say for sure?

"His shyness?" Lilian tilted her head, her delicate eyebrows furrowing in thought and her lips pursing slightly. Eric, who had joined the group at some point during their conversation, had to cover his nose upon seeing that expression. Yes, he was nose bleeding. And to think, this wasn't even an anime where such things were commonly expected from most male characters, especially ones as perverted as him. "He's not that shy."

"Not that shy?" Lindsay guffawed. "Kevin can hardly even talk to a girl without looking like someone shoved his head in a stove." Said boy blushed brightly at her words. He wasn't that bad, was he? "He even has trouble talking to me, and I've been his friend for years."

"Really?" Lilian frowned. Lindsay nodded.

"Really."

"There's no way he could be that bad," Lilian defended her

Beloved. "I mean, it's true he gets all cute and embarrassed sometimes." He's also passed out several times, but naturally, Lilian thought it had more to do with him just not feeling well than because of any shyness of girls. Plot Devices are convenient like that. "But I don't think he's ever been particularly shy."

That's because you tend to ignore all of his negative traits.

"I do not."

Yes you do.

"Be quiet."

...

"Lilian?" Lindsay looked at the girl oddly again. "Who are you talking to?"

"I ask her that all the time," Kevin quipped. "She'll never tell you."

Lindsay raised an eyebrow. She opened her mouth to say something to the young man, but before she could give voice the question on her lips, Lilian spoke again.

"No one."

"See what I mean?"

"Anyways, where was I?" There was a slight pause as Lilian tapped the index finger of her right hand against her lower lip, her head raised slightly so she could look up at the ceiling of the gazebo in thought. Alex, Andrew, and Eric all gulped as they stared at her lips, soft jawline and the elegant curvature of her neck. "Oh, right," she snapped her fingers. "We were talking about my Beloved being shy." Gracing her fellow female with a look, she said, "There's no way he could be as bad as you say." Lilian nodded to herself, as if affirming her own thoughts on the matter. "Why, just the other day he and I were making out on the floor of his apartment."

The term "silent as a grave" came to Kevin's mind after Lilian dropped her bombshell on his friends, for that was how quiet it became after Lilian finished speaking. Not even the crickets were chirping.

"He was really getting into it."

Several crows cawed in the distance, breaking the silence.

It was a testament to his development as The Main Protagonist that Kevin was able to speak before anyone else did. "When did that happen!? I don't remember this!?"

Naturally, because it hadn't happened the way she said it did. Lilian had been doing all the work. Kevin had been practically insensate.

"And there was also that one time he and I shared a bath together."

"That never happened either!"

"I got to wash his back."

"Don't tell them such an obvious lie! And stop ignoring me!"

"We also sleep together every night."

Everyone turned to look at Kevin, who suddenly found himself in the spotlight. The boy's cheeks went off like a flare in the night in response to all the expectant stares being sent his way. Dang, they really knew how to make a guy feel uncomfortable.

"Um... that is one actually is true," he admitted reluctantly. "B-but the rest are complete lies!"

Naturally, no one believed him.

Lilian's lips quirked into a triumphant smile. "If my Beloved was as shy as you say he is then he wouldn't have been so brazen with me." She crossed her arms under her chest, which caused Eric to begin nose bleeding... again. "So there."

"I can't believe it," Lindsay whispered in shock. Her eyes had also gotten pretty wide. "Our shy, little Kevin is all grown up and doing perverted things to his future bride."

"She's not my bride!" He paused, then blushed. "And we haven't been doing perverted things! None of that stuff happened!"

"Does your mom know about this?"

"Geh!"

"I'll take that as a no," Lindsay shook her head in equal parts amusement and surprise. "Who knew our little Kevin was such a bad boy." She snickered at the look on said 'Bad Boy's' face. "You rebel, you."

"Ugwa."

"Stop making funny noises for no reason, Beloved," Lilian said. Kevin glared at her. If he was making strange noises, it was her fault!

"Kevin!"

A hand landed on his shoulder. Kevin turned around to face Eric, Alex and Andrew. All three of them were staring at him with something akin to awe, and jealousy, but mostly awe.

They were also crying. As in, really crying. No, seriously. There was even snot coming out of their nose they were crying so hard.

Well, except for Eric. He still had blood coming out of his nose.

"I hate you so much right now." Manly tears were running down Eric's face, pouring out of his eyes like two massive waterfalls as he spoke. "But at the same time." He raised his free hand and gave Kevin a thumbs up, a cheesy grin plastered on his face even as the tears continued streaming down. "I'm so proud of you!"

For some reason Kevin imagined Eric standing on a cliff overlooking the ocean, the setting sun at his back and waves crashing against the rocks as the gleam from the sun 'pinged' off his teeth.

It was all kinds of creepy.

"Don't say that so happily!" Kevin spat, his face red. "And aren't you supposed to be angry at me or something!?"

"I still am." Eric tried to stem the flow of manly tears with his arm to no effect. There was no stopping tears like that. When a man cries, he cries hard. "But I also feel this strange sense of pride! Does that make sense?"

"No!"

"So what's sleeping with Kevin like?" Lindsay was now letting her imagination run wild. Who knew her ridiculously shy friend had it in him to sleep with a girl he had only known for a little over a week? It was the scandal of the century! And her inner gossip (which had been conveniently hidden away until just this moment) demanded to know more!

"Don't ask questions like that!"

That was Kevin, again. The two girls ignored him, again.

"It's amazing." Lilian held her hands to her cheeks as she thought about those amazing nights they slept together on the bed... erm... couch. It didn't matter if one of them was an unwilling participant and the other snuck in only after the unwilling one had fallen asleep. At least it didn't matter to her. For Kevin, it was an entirely different story. "My Beloved is so warm and cuddly, and it's so nice to rest my head on his chest and listen to his heartbeat as I fall asleep." She grinned a devilish grin. "And I like that he doesn't sleep with a shirt on."

"Eep!"

"It is kind of disappointing that he won't let us sleep naked,"

Lilian added with a pout. Kevin 'eeped!' again. Lindsay gaped, the twins stared, and Eric began crying that much harder. "I don't know why he won't let us sleep naked together. I mean, we've done it before."

"WHAT!?"

"What do you mean you two have slept naked together!?"

"Have you gone all the way?"

"What my brother really wants to know is if you two have fucked yet?"

"Kevin! How could you do this to me!? I thought we were friends!"

Bombarded by voices asking questions and making accusations, Kevin cried out to the heavens.

"Why me?!"

***

It took a good deal of time for everyone to calm down and allow Kevin to try and explain the situation to them. He couldn't, not because he didn't try, but because no one believed him. As far as they were concerned, everything Lilian had just told them was true. The fact that he had admitted to him and Lilian sleeping together had done little to help his case.

It made Kevin want to cry again.

"I still don't get it," said Alex. Judging by the frown on his face, he was a tad annoyed. Just what was annoying him was something no one could figure, though from the way he was glaring at Kevin it most likely had something to do with our Hapless Hero. "How is it that out of all of us here, you're the one who managed to get a hot girlfriend? We all know you can't talk to a girl to save your life."

"That's right," added Andrew. "If anything, I'm the one who

should have gotten the super hot girlfriend before any of you. I am the most handsome, dashing and charming among us, after all."

"Like hell you are!" Alex growled, throwing his brother a scathing glare. "I'm way more handsome than you are!"

"Ha! Don't be an idiot, brother. We all know who the better looking twin is, and it sure as hell ain't you!"

"You wanna go!"

"Bring it!"

"I don't think I'll ever understand how those two can constantly fight like that," Kevin sighed. Shouldn't twins have that weird twinergy thing that allows them to know each other so well they could finish each others sentences without even thinking about it? These two certainly didn't have that.

"Who cares about them!" Eric cried out as he gave Kevin an accusing glare. Now that his episode of manly tears and pride was over he was back to feeling nothing but hate towards his best friend. "I can't believe you would do this to me! Have I not been your best friend ever since we were in second grade? Haven't we done everything together? You promised me that you would help me find a hot girl to date after you and Lindsay started going out! Now look at you! Not dating Lindsay, *and* you've somehow got the hot girl you were going to hook me up with for yourself!"

"Would you keep your voice down!" Kevin hissed. He cast a glance over at Lindsay to make sure the girl hadn't heard them. When he was sure that the brunette was too embroiled in her own conversation to be listening in on theirs, he looked back at Eric and glared. "And I never remember making a promise like that before."

"Okay, so I made that part up," Eric admitted. His glare returned. "Still, I thought you would have my back. You know, bros before hoes and all that."

"And how many times have you ditched me to chase after a girl?" Kevin asked. He didn't give Eric time to answer. It was a rhetorical question anyways. "I don't think you have any right to tell me that I'm supposed to put your well being and happiness before a girl. Besides," Kevin stabbed his fork into the Shrimp Saganaki and absently stuck the food in his mouth, chewing thoughtfully. It really was quite good. He wondered where she had gotten the shrimp though. He didn't remember having any shrimp in his fridge... "It's not like I actually want her following me around every where I go. Like I said, I don't like her like that."

"Che, yeah right," Eric grumbled angrily. He crossed his arms over his chest. "And what about all those times she's kissed you, huh? I didn't see you doing anything to stop her then?"

"That..." Kevin flushed as blood rushed to his face. "That's just because she caught me by surprise! That's all! It-it's not like I wanted her to kiss me!" Against his will, his right hand came up to touch his mouth. With the mention of all the passionate kisses Lilian had given him, including the ones Eric didn't know about, Kevin felt a pleasant tingle like that of phantom lips over his own. Needless to say, it was a very distracting feeling.

Eric growled. "I don't believe you. You know what I think? I think you've been pretending to be some kind of girl-shy boy all this time! All the while you've been secretly hiding your true womanizing nature, waiting for the moment to take advantage of some poor girl!"

"Are you sure we're not talking about yourself now?"

Ignoring Kevin's comment, the lanky teenager stood up rather abruptly, startling those present and paying attention, meaning Kevin, Lilian and Lindsay. The twins were too busy beating each other up to notice, and Justin was still singing under his breath as he ate, ignoring the world outside of his music. Of course, the girls went back to their own conversation the moment they saw that it was just Eric, leaving Kevin the only one listening.

The lanky sophomore pointed an accusing finger at Kevin. "That's it, isn't it? You've used your playboy ways to seduce the beautiful tit maiden, Lilian, in order to have your lustful way with her."

"Don't put me on your level," Kevin grumbled. "And if you're going to say something like that, don't mention her tits!"

His words fell on deaf ears. Eric wasn't listening.

"Don't worry, my lovely tit maiden!" Eric cried out, drawing the attention of the girl in question and Lindsay again. "I'll save you from Kevin's vile ways! Then you'll be so grateful to me that you'll... hehehe... and then we'll... kekekekeke!"

Lilian wrinkled her nose in disgust as the perverted sophomore devolved into a cacophony of lecherous giggling. Deciding not to waste any time wondering why the idiot was babbling, or even figure out what he was yapping about, she turned her attention back towards the conversation she was having with Lindsay. What were they talking about again? Well, not like it mattered. She was just scouting out the competition.

"Sit down, Eric," Kevin grumbled, grabbing onto the lanky teens sleeves and yanking him back into his seat. "You're embarrassing yourself."

Eric grumbled as he was forced back onto the bench, but he thankfully didn't try getting back up. Kevin sighed as he listened to his friend continue to complain and grumble and curse his name upon being forced to sit down.

"I can't believe a bastard like you managed to convince a girl with such a beautiful pair of knockers to date you over me! What do you have that I don't!? Huh!?""

Yeah, like that. Having already gotten used to Eric's complaints, insults and death threats from gym class, Kevin ignored him.

"I should kill you and dump your body in a ditch! Then I could offer Lilian some comfort and we'll... hehehe... then she will... kekekekeke..."

Kevin's right eye began twitching violently as he continued to eat. Maybe if he just ignored the insanity happening around him everything would return to normal. Not even he believed his own thoughts, but the small hope that burying his metaphorical head in the equally metaphorical sand would bring back his old life was all he had.

At least this day couldn't get any worse. Right?

He had no idea how much he would come to regret those thoughts later on.

***

After lunch Kevin was subject to more classes with Lilian. It was even worse than his first few classes of the day because his first class after lunch had Eric in it as well. Normally, this would have been great as they could talk about, you know, guy stuff. Things were different now. With all that had happened this day, Kevin and Eric weren't really on speaking terms.

This may have had something to do with the way Lilian was 'still' clinging to Kevin. Even now the red head was sitting at the table, completely ignoring the computer in front of her as she rested her head against Kevin's shoulder and watched him as he typed away on the keyboard. Yeah, Eric's decision to not speak with his best friend and simply glare definitely had something to do with that.

Jealousy kills friendships faster than herpes.

Thus, Kevin was forced to deal with more of the same thing he got during gym and lunch. It was even worse because they were all sitting right next to each other.

Then there was the teacher. Ms. Nestato, a crotchety old woman with scraggly white hair. She had come over to berate them and tell Lilian to start typing. Naturally, the fox girl had just worked her Kitsune magic and the woman had not looked at them since.

"You really should think about actually doing some of the work," said Kevin, trying to subtly convince Lilian to let go of him and stop distracting him with those two round globes on her chest. He still hadn't been able to figure out if she was doing this on purpose or not, though he supposed it didn't change the fact that it was keeping him from being able to properly concentrate on what he was doing.

"Why?" Lilian asked plaintively, clearly not understanding why she had to work when she could just use an enchantment on the teacher to make the old woman *think* she had done her work.

Besides, it wasn't like she would ever have any use for this class. She had never even used a computer before and couldn't see herself needing to learn how to use one any time soon. The only reason she was even here was so she could be with her beloved.

"Because everyone else is staring at us."

Lilian took her head off his shoulder to look around the room, thereby missing Kevin breathing a sigh of relief. When she noticed that, yes, everyone in class was staring at them, and in the case of boys, glaring at Kevin, she put her head back down on his shoulder, missing the look of complete dismay on his face as she scooted her seat even closer to his. "So?"

"So?" Kevin sputtered for a moment, ignoring the mutterings of rage from his friend next to him. "So can you just act normal for once?"

"This is normal," Lilian told him in a matter of fact voice. She sighed and gently rubbed her cheek against his shoulder. Her Beloved made a really comfortable pillow. "Couples are supposed to do this, aren't they? It's perfectly natural for us to be close like this."

"Not in class it's not," Kevin muttered before his right eye twitched. "And we're not a couple."

"Of course we are." Once again, Lilian was speaking with that accommodating voice she used when she thought he was being silly. "You're my mate. In human terms, we might as well be married. That makes us a couple."

Kevin just slumped in his seat. That was it. He was giving up. There was just no winning with this girl.

Instead of trying to convince the beauty using his shoulder as her head rest that she should at least try and do some of the work, Kevin focused on his own work, hoping it would distract him from said girl. It was very difficult: between Eric's grumbling and heated glares, and Lilian doing what she always did, concentrating on anything was a challenge. Still, he managed to muddle through his lessons somehow.

The class was called Computer Programming. It was an elective class that taught students how to use programming languages like C++ and JavaScript. Kevin wasn't really sure what he would use these skills for, but since the world they were in had entered the digital age several decades ago and the internet was the largest network in use, he felt that knowing this stuff would be useful.

Surprisingly, Eric was incredible at this class. The guy was a computer whiz. At least when he wasn't busy trying to discreetly surf the web for porn.

It really was a good thing for him that his dad was the Principle.

***

When the last class of the day finally ended Kevin was forced to trudge his way towards Ms. Vis' class instead of the locker room where he would have gotten changed into his track uniform and hit the field. He was not happy about that. The only silver lining to this whole situation was that Lilian was going with him. Since he blamed her for what happened and really didn't want to spend anymore time with the girl, it wasn't much of a consolation.

"I'm glad you two made it here so quickly," Ms. Vis said with a sniff as the pair entered her classroom. "It shows that you at least know how to be prompt. Now, if you could just learn not to disrupt my class." Kevin winced while Lilian simply looked indifferent. "And since you are here, we can get started on your punishment."

She directed them over to the chalk board. Kevin honestly didn't know why this woman still used something so nineteenth century. Most of the other teachers used newer technology. He guessed she was just old fashioned that way.

"You can start by cleaning the chalk board and dusting the erasers. After that I'll find something else for you to do. We'll continue doing this until I've determined that you've learned your lesson." With that Ms. Vis walked towards her desk, sat down, and began grading homework assignments.

"I can't believe this," Kevin grumbled as he got started. "I didn't even do anything wrong." It wasn't like he had asked Lilian to cause a scene. Why was he getting punished for something she did?

The one who had actually caused the scene was you, Kevin. All Lilian did was show up at school without telling you before hand.

"Hmm?" Kevin looked up for a moment, his eyebrows furrowed. "Why do I have the sudden urge to strangle someone?" After a moment he shrugged the thought off and resumed work. That board wasn't going to clean itself.

Kevin ignored Lilian as she stared at him while he was cleaning the chalk board. If she didn't do something soon, she was going to get in trouble.

"And I'm going to miss practice," he sighed. His coach wasn't going to like that. The man hated when his athletes couldn't make it to practice for *any* reason. They could have a doctor's note stating they had bronchitis and he still wouldn't give two squats.

He also seemed to like working Kevin harder than the others, so it would be worse for him. He didn't doubt the man would throw a fit at their next practice and give him a long lecture on why he couldn't afford to miss a single practice. Then he would force Kevin to run laps around the track until the young man was ready to drop dead.

Life was so unfair sometimes.

"Are you okay, Beloved?" Lilian asked in concern.

"No, I'm not okay," he snapped, making Lilian flinch. Kevin felt a bit guilty when he saw the look on her face, but his frustration currently overrode his sense of guilt.

"Is… is there anything I can do to help?" Lilian sounded surprisingly meek, her posture and expression downtrodden. Clearly, she was feeling the pressure of her Beloved's anger.

The guilt came back and brought friends. Kevin opened his mouth to give her some reassurance that it wasn't her fault. And it really wasn't when he thought about it. It's not like she had caused a scene. All she had done was show up. He had been the one to blow his top and get them detention.

So good of you to finally notice Kevin.

Before he could speak up he was interrupted, however, and by the last person he would want interrupting him right now.

"Excuse me." Kevin nearly groaned as Ms. Vis stood up from behind her desk and marched over to them. "Why aren't you two working? Are you done? Should I give you more work to do?"

Kevin's eyes widened. He opened his mouth to try and come up with some excuse as to why they weren't working that wouldn't get them into trouble, when Lilian did it for him. A good thing too. With Kevin's inability to tell a good lie, it would have likely only caused more problems.

"We were working," she told Ms. Vis, who turned to stare at her. Big mistake. "But you already knew that, didn't you?" Lilian's eyes glowed as she stared deeply into the stern math teacher's own irises. "You were watching us the whole time."

"Yes..." Ms. Vis blinked, her eyes glazing over. She then nodded to herself. "Right, my mistake. Carry on."

As Ms. Vis walked back to her desk, Kevin turned to Lilian with a new light in his eyes. He had a plan to make it to track practice now. All thanks to this girl.

"Lilian," he said slowly. "Do you think you could do that Kitsune enchantment thing to get us out of trouble with Ms. Vis?"

"Of course," Lilian tilted her head cutely before smiling. It was a very mischievous smile, one befitting a Kitsune. "Just give me a second and I'll get us out of here in no time, Beloved."

At that moment, Kevin couldn't help but think that she had the most beautiful smile he had ever seen.

Chapter 15: The Fine Line Between Interest and Obsession

"Swift!" Coach Deretaine shouted the moment Kevin arrived at the track field. Said boy just barely managed to contain his wince as he looked at his coach. He knew the moment Ms. Vis gave him detention he would be in trouble with his coach, but that did not prepare him to actually face the man.

He wondered if it was too late to turn back.

Coach Deretaine was a lot different than PE teachers like Coach Raide. Where that man was large, hairy and had the biggest beer gut he had ever seen, Coach Deretaine was small, thin and wiry. He had actually been mistaken for a high school students a few times because of his small stature and youthful appearance.

Not that any of the track and field students would admit to thinking that. The man may be short and thin, but that thin body was packed with wiry muscles of the kind you would expect on someone who coached track and field. Kevin often wondered if the man had been an Olympic runner or professional athlete at some point. He had the kind of body type that Kevin was striving to attain.

Unlike Coach Raide, who taught Physical Education, Coach Deretaine taught Health, which they all took freshmen year. It was knowledge based rather than physical work based. In that class they had learned about the human body, puberty and nutrition. They were also taught about the importance of having a healthy and balanced diet, and learned about muscle groups and their purpose. It was all very informative, if a bit boring.

"Yes, coach?" asked Kevin, even though he already knew exactly what the man was going to say.

"You're late!"

There it was.

"I'm sorry," Kevin apologized, but didn't offer an excuse. Coach Deretaine wouldn't care for any excuse he made. He could have gotten a note from Ms. Vis and his coach *still* wouldn't have cared. "It won't happen again."

"See that it doesn't," Coach Deretaine growled. Kevin also sometimes wondered if the man had been a military instructor in a past life. He certainly acted like it sometimes. "I can't have any of my runners getting lazy and fat from slacking off! Now join the others and start stretching!"

"Yes sir!"

Kevin quickly did as told and ended up standing next to another person who did the 100 and 200 meter dash, as well as the 500 meter relay like him. This boy had dark brown nearly black hair, black eyes and narrow features. He was a few inches shorter than Kevin and quite a bit skinnier. He actually looked really scrawny, like a stiff breeze would blow him over, but Kevin knew better. This kid was his biggest contender for title of fastest student on the track field.

"Chase."

"Swift."

The boy's name was Kasey Chase. Despite his small size he was actually a year above Kevin, a junior. Ever since Kevin had joined the track and field team, he and Kasey had formed a rivalry that could become pretty intense at times. They had never come to blows, but there were numerous instances when the two would stay out on the track field well after everyone else had left in order to see who was faster. They had actually been chased off the track field one time by an officer who had been in the area after a report had been filed about vandals making noise on the track field.

After the quick greeting and by now traditional glare, the two boys did their best to ignore each other. They would save their rivalry for the field, where they would try to prove once and for all who was the fastest student.

Kevin focused entirely on his stretches. Stretching both before and after any kind of physical exertion was very important, especially when running. The likelihood of injury greatly increased if the body wasn't loose and limber when running as fast as possible for 100 meters.

It was while Kevin was stretching out his hamstrings that another problem in the long series of problems that had happened this day occurred. The problem started when a string of mutterings broke out among the track members. Kevin ignored them at first, but he would only be able to keep to himself like that for so long.

"Swift!"

Kevin sighed. "Eric. Still mad at me?"

"You're damn right I'm still mad at you!" Eric looked livid as he stomped up to his friend. "Not only did you steal those busty bazungas from me, but now you're parading them around to everyone on our track team?"

Kevin gaped at the boy for several seconds as he tried to determine what his friend was talking about. He couldn't, so asked, "what are you talking about?"

"I think he's talking about the girl with the really big boobs over there in the bleachers with the large sign that says 'Go Beloved!'" Kasey said, pointing over to the bleachers.

Kevin's eyes widened. Oh no. No, no, no! Please don't let her be here! He told her that he would meet up with her after he was done! Surely, she had done as he asked and was even now waiting for him at the school.

Craning his neck towards the bleachers, Kevin nearly broke down and cried. Just like Kasey said, Lilian was there, standing on the bleachers, holding the aforementioned sign above her head and she was waving it around with great enthusiasm.

"Hey, Kev." Justin came up to the group, now without his

headphones in his ears and wearing his track uniform. "Who's the girl? Do you know her?"

"You would know who she was if you didn't spend all lunch listening to music and ignoring everything around you."

Justin had the decency to look sheepish.

"I take it you know her?" That was Kasey

Kevin sighed. "You could say that."

"Could say that..." Eric grumbled hatefully. "You make it sound as if you hardly even know the girl."

Eric received a glare from Kevin. "I do hardly even know her. We just met last week!"

"Don't believe you," Eric growled. "I don't fucking believe you! Even now you're lying to me!" Then, inexplicably, he began crying. "What happened to best friends, huh!? HUH!?"

"You know what," Kevin's shook his head, "I give up. I'm done. Just... think whatever you want."

"Hehehehe... someone's angry. Are we going to see a fight between friends?"

Kevin pointed a finger at Justin. "Quiet, you."

"You should probably deal with her before Coach Deretaine gets upset."

Kevin's shoulders slumped. He hated Chase for his words. He hated him even more for being right.

Quickly sprinting to the bleachers Kevin reached Lilian. The girl smiled at him, but he was doing anything but smiling.

"What are you doing here?" he asked before she could even open her mouth. "I thought I told you to wait for me at the school."

"But it's so boring at the school and I want to spend time with you," Lilian pouted cutely at him. The look just caused Kevin to rub his face tiredly. "I came to this school to be with you. There isn't much point in me going to school if I'm not spending my time with you, is there?"

"That doesn't mean you need to spend every waking second with me!" Kevin argued. There had to be something seriously wrong with this girl. There was no way a normal girl would be this needy. Was it some kind of Kitsune thing that he didn't know about?

"Did I do something wrong?" Lilian began sniffling. She looked like she might cry any second now.

"Look," Kevin sighed as his anger left him. He couldn't be mad at her for this. He couldn't even blame her. She had been home schooled and had never lived among humans before. She probably just didn't know how to act around them. "I just don't want you to get in trouble with my coach. He's kind of strict."

"So you don't mind me being here?" The look of unabashed hope on Lilian's face ensured that whatever small amount of resistance Kevin had built up (meaning none what so ever) was crushed. His shoulders slumped in defeat.

"No…" he sighed wearily. "I don't mind you being here."

"Don't worry," Lilian was suddenly all smiles now. It was almost as if the whole 'I'm so depressed, pity me' act was just that, an act. But there was no way she would do something like act sad to manipulate his emotions.

Right?

"I won't interrupt your training or anything."

Too late for that, Lilian.

"You won't even notice I'm here."

Also too late for that.

"Kind of hard not to notice you standing there with that big sign in your hands," Kevin pointed out dryly. He then adopted a confused expression. "And just where did you get that sign anyways?"

"I took it from my Extra Dimensional Storage Space."

Kevin blinked. Once. "Your what?"

"My Extra Dimensional Storage Space," Lilian repeated. Kevin scratched the side of his head in confusion.

"Is this, like, some kind of Kitsune power or something?"

"Of course not," she chided in a voice that asked "how come you don't already know this?" Kevin twitched. "All women have an Extra Dimensional Storage Space. It's all right here in this book." Lilian pulled out a large, red book titled "100 Rules and Laws of Anime" and began flipping pages.

Kevin watched the girl, gawking. At the same time, Lilian began muttering to herself as she perused the book in her hands.

"Let's see... Law of Inverse Lethal Magnitude... no... Law of Transient Romantic Unreliability, I think that one is talking about us! No, never mind, it's talking about that idiot Minmei. I just thought it was talking about us because it had romance in the title... now let's see... ah ha! Here we are! The Law of Extra Dimensional Capacitance!" Lilian coughed to clear her throat, then began reading out loud. "It says here that all anime females have an Extra Dimensional Storage Space of variable volume somewhere on their person from which they can instantly retrieve any object at a moment's notice." She then held the book out to Kevin so he could see what she had read. "See?"

"This isn't an anime!" Kevin shouted, smacking the book away from his face.

"I know that." She put the book away, which involved her shoving it back into her cleavage, something that Kevin noticed right away. "That's why I also have these."

Two more books randomly appeared in her hands. The one in her right hand was a book that looked like it had been taken straight out of an RPG, which was ironically titled Dungeon Master's Guide. The book in the left hand had an image of a demon statue with various mythological species underneath it called the Player's Handbook.

Kevin's right eye began twitching. It couldn't be good for him to gain a tick like that at such a young age.

"This isn't Dungeons and Dragons either!"

"I know that," Lilian pouted. "But they're still useful. I've been using the knowledge in these books for the past week and everything's turned out perfectly."

Kevin had to wonder what was wrong with this girl to think anything that had happened so far was perfect. And just what advice was in those books for her to follow anyway? Didn't they just explain rules and game play for D&D?

"Swift!"

"Oh crap!" Kevin turned around, his face ashen as Coach Deretaine stomped up the bleacher stairs to where he and Lilian were talking. This was *so* not good. He was really going to get it now. "Coach—"

"Don't you Coach me!" Coach Deretaine scowled. "What the hell are you doing talking to this girl? I thought I told you to get started on your stretches!" The track and field coach didn't give Kevin enough time to reply as he whirled on the red head. "And you! I don't know who you are, but I want you to stop distracting my runners and get off this field! You got me!?"

Kevin began sweating bullets as Coach Deretaine tore into them. He had never seen his coach this angry before. Annoyed, yes, but never angry. This was not good. Annoying Coach Deretaine often resulted in you running laps until you couldn't stand anymore. He didn't want to know what actually pissing his coach off would do.

Thankfully, he wouldn't be finding out today.

"I'm really sorry sir," Lilian said, her eyes going impossibly wide as she stared at Coach Deretaine. Said eyes began watering and her lower lip started to quiver. The watery eyes managed to block out the way they glowed. "I didn't mean to disrupt your practice. I just wanted to support my boyfriend while he trained."

Kevin's track and field coach reared back as if struck. "Ah… well…" the wiry man scratched his buzzed head awkwardly, an easily noticeable blush staining his cheeks. "I suppose that's okay. Just make sure you don't disrupt my student's training again."

Kevin gaped. He didn't know if he should be amazed, impressed, or displeased that Lilian's looks seemed to work on his coach just as easily as they did on him.

"Don't worry," Lilian smiled brightly. "I won't."

As Coach Deretaine walked back down the bleachers in something of a daze, Kevin turned to look at Lilian with a raised eyebrow. "That enchantment ability of yours is an awfully convenient power."

Lilian actually looked a tad smug as he said this. "I know."

"No. Seriously," Kevin insisted, "it's like a poorly disguised Plot Devise or a "get out of jail as many times as you want" card."

"And that," Lilian began succinctly, "is why the Laws of Anime, the Dungeon Master's Guide and the Player's Handbook are so useful."

Kevin didn't respond. Really, what could he say to dispute something like that? Nothing, so he didn't bother.

***

Practice went by quickly after that small moment on the bleachers. Or relatively quickly. Lilian's presence still caused a few problems with some of the boys who couldn't seem to get over her beauty, but for the most part, practice went normally.

Of course, Eric was a bit of a problem. But Kevin had known he would be the moment Lilian had shown up, so it didn't bother him too much.

The twins were also a problem, but it was one for Coach Deretaine to deal with, not him. No way Kevin was getting in between one of their brawls.

"I guess we'll have to find out who's faster during our first track meet," Kevin frowned at his rival. Once again, the times they scored on the 100 meter and 200 meter dash averaged out to a near tie. Kevin had done better on the 200 meter, while Kasey had one-upped him on the 100 meter.

"I guess so," Kasey narrowed his eyes. If this were a cartoon or some kind of anime, this would be the moment where their rivalrous glare physically manifested itself in the form of sparks. This wasn't a cartoon or anime, however, so the sparks didn't happen. "You'd better bring your A-game next time, Swift, or I'm going to kick your ass."

"You should worry more about yourself," Kevin shot back. "You might want to stay here and practice some more. It would be embarrassing if you lost to a rookie like me."

"Hmph!"

"Beloved!" The glaring match between the two came to an abrupt halt as Lilian walked up to Kevin and smiled. She was holding out a bottle of water, which Kevin knew she had not been carrying before. Was this more of that storage space stuff she had been talking about? "Here, this is for you, because you worked so hard."

"Uh..." Kevin's glare disappeared as he turned to look at Lilian. Kasey used this opportunity to walk away, though not before sending one last glare towards his rival. "Thank you."

"You're welcome," Lilian smiled lovingly at him as he unscrewed the cap. Not wanting any of his peers (all of whom were glaring at him with DOOM in their eyes) to see the color change on his face, Kevin took a long drink of water, finishing it all in one go.

Wanting to get off the track field as quickly as possible, Kevin was about to head out with Lilian when a voice interrupted them.

"Oh, my beautiful and large breasted tit maiden," Eric had appeared before the two of them. He was holding Lilian's left hand in one of his while the other stroked her knuckles. Both of them had to wonder how he had gotten there so fast. They hadn't even seen him coming! "Will you grace me with your ginormous bazungas and walk with me to the locker room?"

"Ugh, no," Lilian wrinkled her nose as she jerked her hand out of his and quickly wrapped her arms around Kevin's right arm. The smaller of the two boys just sighed and rolled his eyes as his best friend slumped to his knees in defeat. "I'm going to walk with my Beloved, not you."

"Damn you, Kevin!"

And so, Kevin walked with Lilian on his arm, Eric trailing behind them as he glared at Kevin's back. The young man had to admit he was not too fond of being glared at. It had been growing more and more frequent as the day went by, and seeing his friend giving him the same glare as everyone else really bothered him.

They reached the locker room with minimal fuss. Other than the glaring.

"I'll wait for you here," Lilian smiled, then wrinkled her nose a bit. "You need to take a shower."

"Yeah, well, I did just do a lot of running," Kevin reminded her. "I'm pretty sweaty."

"I know," Lilian frowned, "That's the only reason I haven't jumped you yet."

"Eep!"

"The only kind of sweat you should be getting on you is the kind that comes from the two of us sharing intensely erotic moments with each other."

"Eep!"

"Now, get cleaned up so we can go home and begin practicing procreation."

A wail of despair sounded behind them. That was probably Eric, judging by the volume and pitch. Kevin ignored it.

"Would you stop saying things like that!" He hissed furiously.

"Ufufufu..."

"And don't laugh like that either!"

"Relax, Beloved," Lilian soothed. "I'm just kidding." Somehow, he didn't believe her. "I just want to go home so I can cook you dinner and then we can play that Residence of Evil game."

"Resident Evil," Kevin corrected, sighing. "Honestly, you have the Player's Handbook and the Dungeon Masters Guide and you can't even remember the name of a video game."

Lilian pouted as Kevin went inside to get shower and get dressed. He finished quickly because he was afraid some of the older students would try to start something with him because of Lilian. They had given him the evil eye from the moment he walked in.

Ha... even when she was not actually around him that dang Kitsune was still causing problems.

Kevin was thankful when no one actually tried to kick his ass. His track mates just stuck to glaring, which he supposed was the best outcome he could ask for.

It did kind of bother him that Eric was ignoring him, but knowing his friend as he did Kevin was sure the perverted sophomore would be back to his old self tomorrow.

He left the locker room dressed in a pair of tan shorts that went down past his knees and a black band T-shirt. Lilian was waiting for him exactly where she said she would, right outside the door to the locker room.

When her eyes found him they lit up like a million watt bulb. She quickly latched onto his arm the moment he was within reach. Kevin barely managed to contain his long suffering sigh as they began walking down the hallway. Every guy seemed to be insanely jealous of him for being with Lilian, but they really didn't realize how much of a pain she could be. She was just too clingy.

As they walked down the hallway, Kevin had no clue that in a few seconds he would run into the first of many problems that came from being involved with a Kitsune...problems that were unrelated to Lilian's unhealthy level of affection for him, that is.

"SWIFT!"

Turning around, Kevin found himself paling as the large, hairy and ridiculously muscled body of Chris Fleischer stomped up to them. The older boy's face was a snarling visage of hatred and barely restrained rage as he glared at the two of them, though just why he seemed to be glaring at Lilian with such vitriol was beyond the currently scared out of his wits sophomore.

"I THOUGHT I TOLD YOU WATCH WHO YOU HANG OUT WITH, BUT YOU DIDN'T LISTEN! NOW YOU'RE GOING TO GET IT!"

Chapter 16: Dogs of War? Or Should it be Dog of War?

This must be some kind of karma. There was just no other explanation for what was happening. It was the only logical conclusion Kevin could come to for how he found himself being faced with this new, frightening, and hairy problem.

Emphasis on the hairy.

Now it was just a matter of finding out whether he had been a psychopathic killer or something equally horrendous in his past life. After all, only someone who had done something truly evil could possibly find themselves with karma bad enough to be in this kind of predicament.

What was the situation? What could possibly be so horrible that he would wonder about what evils he must have committed in a past life?

Oh. Right. Now he remembered. He got into this situation because that stupid jerk turned out to not be human. Even now he could still recall what happened after running into Chris outside of the school lockers.

***

Kevin stared at the large, hairy figure of Chris Fleischer in shock and more than a little fear. He had no clue what the older student was talking about, but supposed that it didn't really matter in the end. Whatever the reason was didn't change the fact that this person looked like he was on the verge of murdering him, or at least beating him so badly that he would be hospitalized for the rest of his life. Neither option was very appealing.

"B-beloved," Lilian's fearful voice was accompanied by her grabbing a hold of his shoulder and shaking him. "We need to leave. Now!"

Turning his head, he looked over at the girl and saw that she was frightened. No. Not frightened. She was petrified. Her face was drawn and pale. Those lovely green eyes were wide and quivering in barely masked terror, and even her pupils had become dilated in unadulterated fear.

Why was she so scared? Was it because of Chris? Kevin was scared too, but not to the extent Lilian was, and he actually knew just what the large teen was capable of, unlike her.

Keep thinking that, Kevin.

"Beloved," she repeated more urgently. "We need to run now—what are you doing!?"

"I don't know," Kevin replied honestly as he stepped protectively in front of her, keeping her from Chris' hate filled eyes. "I have no clue what I'm doing." He shrugged uncertainly. "I just know that I don't like the way this guy is glaring at you."

Kevin wouldn't be able explain what he was feeling no matter how hard he tried. His thoughts were so jumbled with confusion, fear, and a million other emotions that not even he knew what was going on in his own head. All he knew was that there was something inside of him telling him he needed to protect Lilian at all costs.

Chronic Hero Syndrome is an affliction found in particularly idealistic-protagonists, which renders them unable to say "it's somebody else's problem." Every wrong *must* be righted, and everyone in need *must* be helped.

While this desire to help others can be, at times, admirable, this unquenchable need to help everyone can have a negative side-effect on the hero and those around him. Such heroes will often wear themselves out in their attempts to help *everyone* around them, or they'll become distraught and blame themselves for that *one* time they were unable to save the day. Severe cases of this trope may even end up devolving into a full-blown Martyr Without A Cause.

Fortunately for us and Lilian, Kevin only has a very mild strain of this affliction. It really only crops up when his friends and loved ones are in danger, or when The Plot demands it.

"Beloved..." Lilian's eyes widened at his words. Her heart was hammering in her chest. Despite the situation, she couldn't help but feel incredibly touched that he felt strongly enough about her that he would put himself in harm's way to protect her.

"So, the little shitstain is trying to protect the fox, eh?" Kevin's eyes widened in surprise. How did he know about Lilian!? "That's fine with me! I never planned on letting either of you get out of here alive anyways!"

Wait! This guy was going to kill them!? What the hell!?

Lilian's shaking grew more insistent as her fear rose to new heights.

"Beloved! Beloved, we need to get out here! Now!"

But it was too late to run. Fleeing was no longer an option. Before either of them could even think about getting the hell out of dodge they were forced to watch in growing horror as Chris began to change. His body started growing, lengthening and shifting and morphing into something that no longer looked even remotely human other than bipedal in nature.

Chris' face was the first to change completely. It had stretched out and scrunched up into a mean looking muzzle filled with rows of sharp teeth. Hair began growing out of the pours of his skin, thick and blackish brown with several white spots interspersed across his face. The ears on either side of his head moved up, stretching and elongated from human ears to large, floppy ears that rested against the top of his head. As he stared at Chris' face, Kevin could not help but be reminded of a pit bull.

More changes erupted from the rest of the junior's body. The hair on his legs and arms grew thicker, even the hair on his chest puffed out of his shirt. The shirt itself stretched across his bulky frame before ripping as his muscles bulged. His hands became chubby and clawed, looking like a strange amalgamation of paws and human hands. His legs transformed to strange, hind-looking legs, thicker at the base and thinner near the calves. Meanwhile the shoes he was wearing tore open to reveal padded looking human feet with sharp, claw-like nails.

With his transformation complete, Chris looked like a Werewolf gone terribly wrong. Like someone had tried to crossbreed a lycon with a pug and got this monstrosity as a result. Needless to say, ugly did not begin to describe how truly horrendous Chris now looked.

"What the... what is this?" Kevin whispered in horror. Just what the heck was Chris!?

"Now I'm going to tear you and your little Kitsune apart, shitstain!" Chris growled, his voice sounding like thunder rumbling in the distance. It was deep and harsh, and seemed to contain an unquestionable lust for blood. It reminded Kevin of those Overlord type characters in some of the video games he played. **"No one's going to save you or that damn fox now!"**

Just as he said this a large, bright ball of light struck him in the face, sending him stumbling backwards as steam rose from the spot he was hit.

"Gah! You bitch!"

Kevin turned, shocked to see Lilian standing behind him, her hand extended and slightly clawed. Her fox ears were out as well, pointing straight up on her head as they quivered and shook much like the girl herself. Even her tails were out, and they were shaking even more than the rest of her.

"Lilian?"

"Let's go!"

Lilian grabbed his hand and took off at a pace that had Kevin nearly falling flat on his face. It was only thanks to his reflexes and talent for running at high speeds that he managed to keep from being dragged behind the girl like some kind of rag doll.

"Lilian!" Kevin managed to right himself after several seconds of stumbling behind her. He quickly began pacing her as she tore out of the hallways with the kind of panic of someone who'd had her tails lit on fire. "What's going on!?"

"Don't worry about that! Just run!"

And that was how Kevin found himself in this horrible situation.

Truly, Karma is a bitch.

***

And so they ran. They ran as fast and as hard as they could. Even now they were still running. Both of them were afraid, *terrified*, that if they stopped for even a second, Chris would catch up to them.

Kevin gasped for breath as he ran, his lungs burning as they were deprived of oxygen quicker than he could take it in. His body was slick with sweat, and his clothes were caked to his skin. His eyes were beginning to get irritated as sweat broke out on his brow and dripped into them.

He didn't dare close his eyes though. Even now they were open, searching frantically, looking at everything around him, almost as if he expected Chris to pop out of the wood work without warning.

They had made it out of the school and were now running down the street. The completely empty street that was devoid of cars, pedestrians and anyone else who might have been able to help them.

Which was very strange, considering it was rush hour right now. The roads should have been packed with people returning home from work.

"Where..." Kevin gasped. He had no idea how long they had

been running, but it felt like hours had passed. His lung were burning and his legs felt like they were on fire. "Where is everybody!?"

He honestly didn't expect an answer, but ended up getting one anyways.

"It's probably because of The Author," Lilian informed him helpfully. She didn't seem to be having the same trouble breathing that he did, even though she was running just as fast. Kevin would have been jealous, but was too busy fearing for his life right now. "He likes to use the power known as Convenient Plot Device in order to further The Plot without hassles like, say, getting rid of any potential witnesses who could see us being chased through the streets by an Inu Yōkai and call the cops."

"Oh..." a pause for breath. "What?"

"Just keeping running." Lilian actually rolled her eyes at him in a way that was completely Out of Character for her.

Kevin decided his questions could wait for when they were out of danger. And speaking of danger...

"You fucking bitch!" The two paled as Chris came running up behind them, looking for all the world like a human... erm... inhuman bulldozer. **"I'm gonna fucking rip those tails out of your ass and strangle you with them!"**

"Dammit....!" Kevin swore, a first for him, but he felt the situation warranted it. He had been hoping they would have lost Chris by now. Lilian had done a pretty good job of catching him off guard with that strange light ball of hers, and he thought that would have given them enough time to lose him. It looked like his optimism was misplaced.

"Don't worry," Lilian smiled grimly. She must have been even more terrified than him, yet somehow she still managed to keep her cool. "I've got a few tricks that should help us lose him." As she said this, her two tails pointed straight up in the air. Two compressed, yellow balls of light no larger than a baseball appeared on the tips.

Without preamble, the tails jerked forward, or backwards as the case may be, and the two balls of light were launched at Chris.

"HA!" Chris shouted as he swatted the two balls of light away like they were nothing. **"That shit won't work on me twice, you fucking—"** His words were cut off when another ball of light suddenly struck him right in the face. Lilian had launched a third ball hidden behind the second in such a way that made it appear that there were only two. **"GWA! FUCK DAMMIT!"**

"Hold on tight, Beloved!"

Lilian's grip on his hand tightened.

"What? Lilian, wait — Holy craaaaaap~!"

With no further warning, Kevin found his arm practically pulled out of its socket as Lilian suddenly took off at a speed that caused the world to pass them by in streaks of light and color. The wind smacked him in the face, his eyes watered, and his lips peeled back and began flapping like a dog when its head is sticking out of a moving car.

This must be the famed Ludicrous speed he had heard so much about in that Star Wars parody he had watched a few years back! How frightening! They were moving so fast he could barely think. He could hardly even breath! In fact, getting oxygen to his brain seemed to be nearly impossible! The air was whipping by him far too fast to take a proper breath! If this kept up, he was going to pass out!

Fortunately, they stopped soon after they started. Kevin gasped, bending over with his hands on his knees. His stressed lungs were heaving as they tried to take in as much oxygen as they could. Meanwhile, Lilian pressed herself against a wall, her panting even more frantic than Kevin's.

It was only after regaining his breath that he realized they were hiding in some kind of alley between what looked like a convenience store and an ice cream parlor. Just how far had they traveled?

"What... what the heck was that?" asked Kevin. He didn't give Lilian a chance to say anything as he continued. "What is going on? That speed? And Chris? What is he? Lilian, what —"

"Beloved," Lilian cut him off by placing an index finger against his lips. Kevin's eyes crossed as he got an up close look of her delicate finger. "I love you, but if you want me to answer your questions, I need you to shut up."

Kevin blinked. That was the bluntest thing she had ever said to him. She must have been really serious if she was telling him to shut up like that. He was so shocked that even if he were inclined to speak up, he wouldn't have.

Lilian sighed and leaned against Kevin, using him as support. Her head came to rest on his shoulder and her hands held his arm in a vice grip.

It was only after she had done this that he realized how tired she was. Her body, her legs in particular, were trembling with exhaustion as much as they were fear.

"To answer your questions, we are currently being chased by an Inu Yōkai, a supernatural creature that takes the form of a dog. Inu are the mortal enemies of us Kitsune. In fact, all Kitsune hold a great... dislike of Inu Yōkai."

That answer actually made sense to Kevin. He had wondered if there were other Yōkai out there after meeting Lilian. It looked like he now had his answer.

But that Inu looked nothing like he expected it to. Weren't Inu supposed to be *Bishounen* pretty boys like that Sesshomaru character from that anime he once saw?

Heedless of his thoughts, Lilian continued answering his questions. "The speed you saw me use was a Kitsune technique known as enhancement. It's a very difficult technique to master because the youki requirements needed to use it are massive. Most Kitsune have to wait until they have gained their third tail to use it properly. I myself can only use it in short bursts." She paused in order to suck in a deep breath. "Essentially, enhancements are the ability to strengthen our bodies to inhuman levels. Lastly, that person, Chris, is an Inu that has obviously been hiding at your school."

"There are Yōkai at my school?" How come no one ever found out about this before? Surely someone would have discovered a youki hiding out in his school. Right?

"Beloved, there are Yōkai all over the world, most of them hidden among humans." Lilian actually managed to crack an amused smile despite the situation. "It's not so unusual for one to be disguising itself as a human at your school. I wouldn't be surprised if there were more than just that Inu hidden at your school and this city. A Yōkai could be anyone and anywhere, and you would never know it. Chances are you've interacted with a Yōkai or two on a regular basis and never realized it."

"I... I had no idea there were youki so close to me..." Kevin whispered in shock. How many people had he interacted with that were like Lilian and Chris? Yōkai hiding out among humans? Were any of his friends Yōkai? Questions. Lilian was giving him far more questions and not anywhere near enough answers.

"Of course you didn't. A Yōkai wouldn't be doing a very good job of hiding if you knew what they were."

Lilian's hands let go of his arm and went around his torso. Kevin blushed when she pressed herself against him, but he soon realized she was not hugging him to show her affection...or to try and seduce him with her feminine wiles. She was exhausted and her hug was merely her attempting to keep herself upright.

He decided to help her by letting his arm move around her waist in a tight embrace that kept her from falling. His chivalrous act earned him a grateful, if tired, smile.

"Thank you."

"You're welcome," Kevin mumbled lowly as he tried to ignore the feel Lilian's body against his own. This wasn't the first time they had been in a situation like this (meaning a situation where she was pressed against him, not them getting chased by a mad Inu Yōkai) and she was wearing more clothes than she usually did when this happened. Really, compared to those times, this was nothing. "So how come you revealed yourself to me? I mean, if you're supposed to remain hidden from humans..."

"You are my mate," Lilian answered. "So it's okay to reveal what I am to you."

"There you go with that mate thing again," Kevin sighed, but decided not to argue with the girl. He had a feeling such an argument would be a lost cause, so instead he refocused on the situation at hand. It was the larger problem for the two right now anyway. "Do you think we lost him?"

"I don't know," Lilian looked pensive as she bit her lower lip. "Inu have a very strong sense of smell. They're very good at tracking down other Yōkai and humans. I ran away as far and fast as I could, but...."

"There you little bitches are!"

Two sets of eyes widened in horror as they stared at the end of the small alley. Chris was standing there, looking just as hideous as Kevin remembered. The sun's rays reflected off the left side of his face. The hair had been burnt off and his skin was blackened and cracked, the results of getting hit by not one but two of Lilian's light spheres (he got hit with the first one when they were near the locker rooms and the second when they were on the run). It gave his hideous visage an even more terrifying appearance.

"It looks like the fox has finally been caught by the hound."

"Ugh, that was a really lame pun," Kevin murmured softly enough that no one except Lilian could hear him. "And a bad Disney reference." Were the situation any different Lilian might have giggled.

"I'm going to enjoy killing you two."

Chris stomped into the alley, his feet pounding harshly against the pavement, causing it to crack underneath him. Where his feet left, a small imprint with gouges from his clawed toenails could be seen on the ground to mark his passing.

Kevin and Lilian began walking backwards as the ugly dog monster came closer and closer.

They soon found their backs pressed against a wall. The giant mass of hair and muscle stopped barely a foot away from them, a fang filled grin on his face as he lifted a clawed hand to strike them down.

Kevin's eyes widened as he saw that Chris was going for Lilian first. The girl who, for the past week, had been one of the biggest annoyances in his life. The girl who had snuck onto the couch he slept on after he had so graciously allowed her to sleep on *his* bed. The girl who had stolen his first kiss and many kisses after that. The girl who dragged him into a lingerie store and posed for him in the skimpiest, sexiest clothing he had ever seen.

...The girl who had cooked for him. The girl who enjoyed playing video games with him. The girl who claimed he was her mate. The girl who told him that she loved him.

Kevin was positive that he did not love Lilian back. As beautiful as she was, as nice and kind as she was, he did not love her. And yet at the same time, he didn't dislike her either. He might find her annoying, and some of the things she did and said made him downright embarrassed, but just because she tended to leave him chagrined didn't mean he didn't like her. Over the past week he had gotten to know the girl who claimed to love him. He had gotten to know her quite well, intimately well, a little too well in fact. One of the things he had learned about Lilian was that she was a sweet girl who was kind (to him at least) and devoted (again, this really only seemed to extend to him), and that any guy would be lucky to have her as their girlfriend, even if he didn't want her as *his* girlfriend.

She didn't deserve to get killed by this brutish, ugly looking monster.

Chris' raised claw came down, snapping Kevin's mind back to the present. Without even thinking about what he was doing, the high school sophomore pushed Lilian out of the way, causing her to fall on her rear.

A loud scream echoed in the alley. Kevin didn't know who it came from. It could have come from him, or Chris, or Lilian, or maybe even all three of them. He didn't know. He couldn't know. All he knew was pain. All he could feel was immense agony ripping at his chest and a slick wetness soaking his clothes.

Kevin pressed a hand to his chest, feeling the strange, wet and somewhat sticky liquid cake to his palm. Pulling his hand away, he saw that his entire hand was covered in crimson liquid that glistened from the small amount of refracted sunlight in the alley. Blood. But whose blood? Was that his blood?

"Beloved!" There was another shout. Someone was shouting at him. At least he thought they were shouting at him. Wasn't there someone he knew who called him Beloved? The voice was familiar, even though he couldn't quite recall who it belonged to. It sounded like it was coming from across a vast distance.

Kevin felt himself falling backwards, his back hitting a wall. His legs gave out and he slid down. Why was everything getting so blurry?

"Beloved! Beloved!"

Soft hands pressed against his cheek. His head was lifted up. Tear filled green eyes stared into his. Who was this girl? Why did she look so familiar? Her lips moved. She was trying to tell him something, or maybe she was speaking to someone else? He didn't know. He couldn't hear anything. Come to think of it, he couldn't see much either. His vision was fading. Everything was getting darker.

The last thing he saw was a pair of luscious red lips opening in a silent scream.

***

Lilian's breathing all but stopped when she saw Kevin's eyes close. "Beloved?" His head lolled back as she grabbed onto his shoulders and began to shake him. "Beloved!?" He didn't respond to her calls, nor did he respond to her shaking. The only movement he made was his head lolling back and forth and side to side as she shook him, and the expansion and compression of his chest as he breathed, and even that was rapidly slowing down.

She didn't know what was worse: the way his body seemed to be growing cold, how shallow his breathing had gotten, or the blood. Dear Inari the blood! It was pouring out of the four slash marks on his chest like a river! They were deep, gouging wounds that looked like Freddy Kruger or Wolverine had gotten their hands, claws, on him.

Lilian was at a loss as to what to do. She knew there was a way to help him, but in her panicked state of mind, she couldn't remember what powers would help. The only thing she could think to do was try and stop him from losing anymore blood.

Unfortunately, staunching the flow of blood from a wound *that* large was pretty much impossible. Even after she had torn the shirt she was wearing off and pressed it's wadded up remains against his chest, the four wounds continued to bleed copiously. Soon the cloth that had once been a shirt became so soaked in carnelian liquid that her hands were also stained red.

It should be noted that as a Kitsune, Lilian actually has the ability to heal his wounds, although it takes time. However, in her state of panic from seeing the vermillion liquid gushing out of her Beloved's broken and battered body, the young two-tails could hardly even use the higher and more complex thought processes her mind was normally capable of making. All conscious thought fled her in the face of this horrendous and gut-wrenching scenario.

"Aw...." The voice of her tormenter made Lilian stiffen. **"Upset that you lost your little human toy. Don't worry. You'll be joining him soon enough."**

Starting from her tail, traveling down to the base of her backside and going all the way up her spine before reversing direction and making it's way down to her toes, Lilian's body shuddered.

It was not fear. Not this time. It was anger. This monster had hurt her mate. He had to pay.

"You..." Lilian whispered harshly. "You hurt my mate... you hurt my Beloved..."

"What was that?" Chris growled. When Lilian didn't answer, he took a step forward... and promptly received a ball of compressed light to the face. **"Bitch! I'm gonna fucking kill you!"**

"The only person who's going to die here is you!" Lilian snarled, her features shifting. Her face became longer, her nose taking on a more streamlined, muzzle-like form. Three whiskers materialized on each cheek and a sharp looking pair of canines were easily visible jutting out from her upper lip. Even her fingers changed a bit, gaining a nasty looking set of claws. "I'm going to kill you for hurting my mate!"

"I'd like to see you try!"

Famous last words. The moment Chris opened his big mouth, his world erupted in a blaze of light, and from that moment on, the only thing he knew was pain.

For the sake of the ego of men everywhere, the epic beat

down Lilian gave to Chris shall not be mentioned. Just know that the beatdown he received would have made men everywhere shudder in fear and slowly inch away from the nearest female just in case they decided to follow suit.

And so, several minutes and one incredibly epic ass kicking later, Lilian was standing over her fallen foe, who looked like someone had thrown him into the sun and it spat him back out. His now hairless skin was burnt and black. Blood was leaking from several massive cracks on his body and his skin looked more like an overcooked steak than skin. What's more, there were several spots on his body that had burst like overripe fruit. Imagine a lemon left out in the summer heat for several weeks. Now imagine that lemon being shot at point blank range multiple times by a 9mm pistol, then stuck in an oven at 350 degrees for several hours and you'd have an accurate image of what Chris looked like. Not a very appealing picture is it?

Lilian was breathing heavily. Her face once again looked more human and her hands no longer clawed. She stood over the unconscious and twitching body as it groaned and whimpered pitifully, emerald eyes glaring down at the damn dog that had attacked her and her mate.

A ragged breath drew her attention away from her fallen foe and back to the reason she had unleashed her prodigious ass kicking ability on Chris to begin with.

"Beloved!"

She rushed over to Kevin and dropped to her knees, her hands glowing with a bright healing light (she just now remembered she was a Kitsune and had healing powers). She pressed them against the wounds on her Beloved's chest, unmindful of the blood that was caking to her skin.

Slowly but surely, the wounds began healing, muscles reforming and skin knitting back together. It was a strange sight, sort of like watching someone sewing, only without someone actually there to sew.

For many minutes, too many in Lilian's opinion, she crouched there, willing her powers to heal her mate. Eventually, the wounds became nothing more than thin red lines that only leaked a little bit of blood.

It wasn't the best of patch jobs, her mother, matriarch, and older siblings could do better, but it was a right sight better than before. At least now her Beloved wasn't in any danger of bleeding out. She could heal the rest of his wounds after she got him home.

"Come on, Beloved." Lilian's two tails wrapped gently around Kevin and proceeded to lift him up like he weighed less than a feather. "We're going home."

As she walked out of the alley, Lilian calmly and none too gently stepped on Chris' head. The Inu Yōkai whimpered as his face made an indent in the cement from the youki reinforced heel stomp.

Yeah, Lilian was vindictive like that.

Chapter 17: Lessons of the Past

Kevin woke up to the familiar sight of his bedroom ceiling and the by now familiar weight on his chest. He blinked several times as his eyes adjusted to the room's lighting. It wasn't all that bright out, but it was still nowhere the perpetual blackness of unconsciousness and therefore required some getting used to.

A glance out the window revealed it was nearing night. Dusk had set long ago and the world was now cast in twilight. Heavens canvas had been painted in a pale glow of dark purples and blood reds as the sun hid itself behind a mountain range. The sparse amount of light it provided just barely penetrated the thick, parted curtains into his room.

With his bearings now set, the blond-haired, blue-eyed, high school sophomore glanced down at the "weight" on his chest. He was not surprised to see the mass of red hair that belonged to Lilian. You could even go so far as to say he had been expecting it.

It was impossible to see her face, hidden as it was by her hair. Only the crown of her head was visible. He couldn't see much of the rest of her body either, but that didn't mean much. Kevin could feel the way she was wrapped around him. Her arms were holding him tightly, as if afraid he would disappear if she let go, and her legs had latched around his left thigh in a grip of herculean proportions. It was a very good thing he had strong leg muscles, or his thigh would have looked like a tube of toothpaste that had been squeezed by one of those fabled Super Sayains he often read about in his manga.

Lilian's face was pressed against his chest. Each breath she took sent shivers down his spine and created goose bumps on his skin as the hot air she released with every exhale hit the naked flesh of his pectorals.

And that was to say nothing of her generous bust. Pressed against his stomach as they were it was impossible not to feel them, and each time she breathed the pair of large mounds seemed to squash into his chest even more, creating a pleasant yet highly embarrassing sensation that Kevin would rather not think about. The only good thing he could take from their position was that Lilian was at least wearing a shirt, which was surprising as she had never bothered before.

Doing his best to ignore the girl cuddling with him, Kevin took this time to try and figure out how he got back to his room. He remembered Chris and learning that the beefy junior was not human. He remembered getting chased and being cornered in an alley with Lilian by said Inu Yōkai. He remembered feeling indescribable pain, and then nothing. It was most unfortunate, but he couldn't recall what had happened after that or how he got back home.

It may have had something to do with the fact he had been unconscious and therefore wouldn't have any recollection of getting home. Just a guess.

He tried shifting a bit, wanting to get more comfortable, yet for some reason his body did not seem to be working properly. He couldn't move much, if at all. It might have something to do with how tired he was. There was an unusual kind of exhaustion he had never felt before. It was difficult to properly describe, but if necessary he would probably have to say it felt similar to how those zombies in Resident Evil felt after rising from the dead.

You know, if reanimated corpses were capable of feeling.

He even wanted someone to put a bullet in his head just so the headache that was currently splitting his skull in half would go away.

"Mmm..." Kevin stilled as a moan escaped the girl using him as her body pillow. A part of him was very afraid of how she would react upon realizing he was awake. Another part had already predicted how she would react and was dreading it. Hopefully, if he remained perfectly still she wouldn't stir anymore and go back to sleep.

Luck was not on his side it seemed. The girl stirred again, mumbling something incomprehensible and lifted her head.

Sleepy green eyes blinked blearily as they met light blue. After several seconds those lethargic, half lidded eyes widened, as the girl they belonged to realized he was awake. To complete this adorable picture of astonishment, the girl's mouth parted in a tiny "o" of surprise.

"Umm..." Kevin looked at the surprised girl unsurely. What do you say to someone who woke up on your chest after the two of you had been chased by an Inu Yōkai and nearly killed after said dog went Freddy Kruger on you? "Hi?"

That, apparently. How eloquent.

"B-beloved?" she whispered in shock, as if she couldn't believe what she was seeing. "You...you're okay..."

"Y-yeah, I'm — H-hey! What are you...?"

All words left him as the young Kitsune pressed her face against his chest and large drops of water fell upon on his bare skin. Lilian was crying. The tears ran from her eyes, dripping down her cheeks to fall on his skin, making a trail down the flesh of his torso before dripping onto the bed, soaking the sheets underneath him.

"You're really, really okay! I-I was so worried! And scared! You were bleeding all over the place and you weren't moving! I thought you were dead! I didn't... I couldn't..."

Kevin felt increasingly uncomfortable as the red head cried into his chest. No. That was an understatement. He felt downright awful. Tears and this girl just did not mix. Actually, tears and any girl did not mix as far as he was concerned. It was just made ten times worse because this particular girl was someone he knew most intimately, much as he might wish otherwise.

"Uh... look... I uh, I don't really know what's going on, but I'm fine, see?" Kevin tried to reassure the girl by patting her head.

Tried being the keyword here. His arms felt like someone had injected several tons of liquidized lead into them. He couldn't even lift his hand, much less use it to pat Lilian reassuringly on the head. The most he got out of his arm was a twitch. Not that this stopped him from trying to make the red-haired beauty stop crying. "So could you... uh... could you please stop crying? Please?"

Yes, he was pleading with a girl to stop crying. Kevin was kind of pathetic like that. On another note, Eric would be most disappointed that his friend had not taken advantage of this situation to offer the girl some... ahem... succor.

Actually he would probably be glad since it meant Eric still had a chance to take Lilian's virginity.

...

...

Yeah. Right. As if *that* would ever happen.

***

Several miles away, Eric was at his home, alone. His parents were still at work. Well, his dad was likely at the nearest bar with some friends and his mom was at work, but that didn't matter much for this story. The point was, Eric was alone, sitting on the couch, playing video games.

You probably find it strange that he was playing video games instead of watching porn or something. Don't forget that even perverts need some down time from perving, especially after a day filled with disappointment.

...Right.

Anyway, it happened just as he was about to strip a girl of her clothes in his newest *eroge* (eroge is the Japanese word for video game porn, in case you were wondering). There was no warning. He just stopped playing and dropped the controller as feelings of intense jealousy overtook him.

A moment later Eric was on his feet, shaking an angry fist at the heavens as he cried tears of mixed anger and pride.

"Damn you, Kevin Swift!"

We now bring you back to your regular program.

"I'm sorry." Lilian sat up on Kevin's waist, her lovely thighs straddling his hips. Not that she was aware of this, busy as she was sniffling and getting the last bit of tears out of her system, but Kevin sure was.

He supposed he should just be glad she was actually dressed this time. Sure, she was only wearing what looked like a pair of white, lace panties and a large t-shirt that looked way better on her than it ever did on him, but at least it was something.

He decided not to say anything about her choice of clothes or complain about their compromising position. At least this time. It was clear that his red-haired roommate had gone through a traumatic experience while he had been unconscious. The tears she cried may have helped him realize this. In any case, since she was clearly feeling very emotional right now, he decided just lie there and give the girl some time compose herself.

"I didn't mean to cry all over you," Lilian mumbled as she wiped a few errant tears from her cheeks.

"Ah, no," Kevin was quick to assure the girl. He was just nice like that. "It's not that it's bad or anything. It's just, ah, I just don't really like seeing a girl cry... you know?"

Lilian perked up, her tears seemingly forgotten so she could scrutinize him properly. Her gaze narrowed in contemplation and her lips twitched slightly. The near 180 degree switch was enough to startle him.

"Oh? So you dislike it when a girl cries in front of you?" There was something about the tone in Lilian's voice that made the hairs on the back of his neck prickle. He didn't know what it was. He just knew it didn't bode well for him. "Does it make you... uncomfortable, perhaps?"

"Uh... yeah, a little, I guess."

"Ufufufu, that's good to know. Very good indeed."

Kevin gave the girl on top of him a weird look. "I know I already asked this before, but what's up with that weird laugh?"

A smile and a pat on the cheek was her answer. "Don't worry about it, Beloved."

Kevin frowned, but Lilian changed the subject before he could inquire further.

"So how are you feeling?" Her concerned gaze moving across his body to check for any lingering injuries that she may have missed had Kevin blushing even more surely than if she were giving him a look that promised unfathomable amounts of pleasure. "Are you in any pain? Does it hurt anywhere?"

"No, not really," Kevin actually had to think for a moment before he answered. His body felt kind of numb, so it was hard to tell if anything hurt. "Just tired." His stomach then rumbled loudly, alerting them both to another problem. Kevin's face began to heat up like an oven while Lilian giggled at him.

"You're also hungry it seems," she commented lightly, "Why don't I make you something to eat?"

Before Kevin could answer, Lilian climbed off him and left the room. The door closed behind her, leaving him alone.

With nothing to do, Kevin was pretty much forced to stare at the ceiling, counting the patterns he could make from the lines in the white plaster ceiling. He had gotten to thirty-five with the last pattern he found being something that resembled a cat when the light "thump, thump" of bare feet on carpet signified Lilian's return. There was a soft "click" as the door opened, and a second later the girl in question walked in carrying a tray bearing a plate of steaming food. The smell wafting towards him told him that whatever the red head had made it was very cheesy.

As in it smelled of cheese, not the euphemism used to describe something. Like, for example, corny pick up lines.

"It's kind of basic," Lilian defended her choice of food as she set the tray over his lap. "But I thought you would appreciate something fast and easy. Sorry if you wanted something else."

After saying this, she helped Kevin sit up because he couldn't do so himself, allowing him to see that she had cooked up macaroni and cheese.

Well, at least now he knew why the food smelled so cheesy, and it was definitely basic compared to her normal fare.

"This is fine," Kevin assured her, "I like mac&cheese." His words caused her lips to curve into a delightful smile.

"I'm glad. Now, eat up."

It was only after Lilian spoke that Kevin realized he had another problem. His entire body, including his arms, were incapable of moving. He could hardly even get them to twitch, much less lift them to grab the spoon she had provided so he could eat. Even his hands weren't working properly.

"Is something wrong with the food?" asked Lilian, concerned whether or not the food would adequately satisfy his palate. What if he didn't actually like it and was just telling her that he did to be polite? Was he waiting for her to leave so he could dump it all out and then claim he ate it?

It seemed that Lilian sometimes had an over reactive imagination as well. At least whenever her mate was concerned.

"Do you want me to make you something else?"

"No, no. This is fine," Kevin assured her quickly. "It's just... my arms..."

"Huh?" Lilian tilted her head to the side, confused. It was only after she took a look at his arms that she realized what the problem was. "Oh!" Her eyes widened, right before a gleam entered them. Kevin did not like the strange glint that entered her eyes at all. "You can't lift your arms to eat, ufufufu." And there was that scary laugh again. It caused a chill to run down his spine. "Don't worry, Beloved. I'll feed you."

"Ah, ah ha, y-you know," Kevin stuttered as she sat down on the edge of the bed and grabbed the spoon she had given him for his mac&cheese. "Suddenly, I'm not really feeling all that hungry anymore. Ah ha! Hahahaha..."

"Now don't be like that. There's no need to be embarrassed. It's just us here." Lilian smiled as she took a spoonful of macaroni and brought it to her mouth. She gently blew to cool it down, her red, moist lips puckering up in the most enticing of ways.

Kevin felt his mouth go dry and his face turn red. That had to be one of the most sensual acts he had ever seen involving food, and he was positive she was doing it on purpose.

She wasn't, in case you were curious. Doing it on purpose, that is. Lilian, despite all her sexiness, was just a bit too pure and innocent to do such an act consciously. Surprising, right?

"I'm not embarrassed." Kevin looked to the side, cursing his own body for giving him away. There was no way Lilian would believe that, and not just because he was a terrible liar. If the way his face felt like it had been set on fire were any indication, she could probably see the megaton blush that felt like it had traveled from the crown of his head all the way down to his chest.

"Ufufufu. You're so cute."

"Okay. Seriously. What is up with that laugh?"

"Ufufuf, don't worry. That's just a part of my character

concept."

"What? Character concept? — eep!"

Kevin squeaked when he turned his head around to look at the girl and found himself staring into gorgeous green eyes that were less than four or five inches from his own. Lilian had somehow closed the distance between them in the short amount of time he had looked away. She was leaning towards him, her face and body close enough that not even the overpowering scent of macaroni and cheese almost right underneath his nose could block out the pleasant, sweetened smell of honey and vanilla that was Lilian's natural scent.

Lilian held the spoon full of Macaroni and Cheese up to his mouth. "Come on, Beloved. Say 'ah.'"

Kevin's mouth clamped shut, refusing to open it even when Lilian prodded his lips with the spoon. The lovely, red-haired Kitsune looked mildly exasperated by her Beloved's stubbornness. She removed the spoon from its position near his mouth and gave him The Look.

"Now don't be like that, Beloved. Open that mouth and let me feed you." More head shaking was her answer. It seemed that even The Look was not enough to compel her mate to do what she asked of him this time. Lilian sighed. "You are being very stubborn. Do you want to go hungry?" When her mate obstinately refused to open his mouth and let her feed him, she decided that it was time to bring out the big guns.

She pouted, and in doing so managed to make Kevin cave like a Goomba after Mario jumped on its head. This wasn't just any pout. Oh no. It was The Pout to End All Pouts. One of the most powerful weapons in a woman's arsenal when it comes to convincing people to do their bidding.

Her eyes grew wide, wider even than the normally innocent "Disney Princess" look that seemed to be her natural state. Kevin found himself falling into the depths of those eyes, like two pools of an endless emerald ocean.

If that were all he had to deal with, then he might have been able to resist...maybe. But on top of the large, wide eyes, Lilian's lower lip had begun trembling as it stuck out in a small pout that enhanced the lovely features of her angelic face.

With such a horribly adorable expression on her face, Kevin didn't stand a chance.

The way she was leaning over him, causing those two large, round *things* on her chest to sway enticingly didn't help. Not at all.

"Won't you please open up and say 'ah', Beloved? For me."

"Guh!"

That was the sound of the last bit of Kevin's resistance shattering like a vial of glass after being dropped from a fifty story window. There was simply no way someone like him was capable of resisting a Pout like that. Especially not when that kind of pleading tone was used in conjunction with it.

It was like something out of this one manga he read. Only that one had been about a vampire who used a similar tone and expression on the Main Protagonist, another boy of the Hapless Hero variety, to put him off-guard so she could suck his blood.

At least this girl didn't want to suck his blood. She just wanted to suck him off. Which honestly wasn't much better in his opinion, but at least it wouldn't kill him if she ended up sucking too much.

Unless he died from embarrassment, of course. Knowing him, such a thing was not outside of the realm of possibility.

Slowly, ever so slowly, as if his mind was trying to fight his body's instinctual reaction, Kevin opened his mouth. The smile that came to Lilian's face lit up the room in a way that the light fixture on the fan could never hope to accomplish. It was like a slap to the face. As much as a part of him felt ashamed for falling prey to this girl's admittedly powerful abilities of persuasion, another part felt like a jerk for being so stubborn. Lilian just wanted to help him. Was he really so dead set against allowing her into his life that he would willfully keep her from helping him when she just wanted to be useful?

Yes. Yes he would. Regardless of how kind, pretty and devoted she was to him, it didn't really change the fact that she had barged into his life and destroyed a good number of his perceptions about the world. He would resist her until the bitter end.

Or at least until she brought out her more fearsome techniques. That pout was no joke. Seriously.

In any case, there wasn't much he could do to resist her now, not after she pulled out what he hoped was the most powerful ability in her arsenal.

So he opened his mouth and allowed her to place the spoon full of cheesy goodness inside. He then closed, allowing her to pull the spoon away, chewed, and swallowed. It was a process that repeated several times until the plate of cheesy noodles was nearly gone.

Eventually, he even got used to her feeding him. It even felt kind of nice, having someone take care of him like this.

Not that he would ever let Lilian know these treacherous thoughts. There was no telling what kind of chaos that would unleash.

"Lilian?" He asked after he finished swallowing a bite of food. Lilian, who was mid-process of blowing on the utensil bearing another spoonful of packaged All-American goodness looked at him, her eyes blinking.

"Hm?"

"What happened after I lost consciousness?" When Lilian just looked at him, he quickly clarified. "I mean, I don't remember much of what happened after we ran into that alley. I was just wondering about how we got out of there alive... and what happened to Chris."

Lilian sighed as she put the spoon down and set the tray aside. She had finished feeding him for the most part anyway. And with the tray out of the way, she could move in to snuggle with her mate, which she did not hesitated to do, much to his consternation.

"After you passed out I was so worried... and angry," Lilian admitted after she had gotten comfortable, her body tucked into his side and her head resting on his shoulder. One hand absently came up to his chest and her index finger began tracing patterns against his pectorals. Kevin shivered at her touch. "That damn dog nearly killed you. If I hadn't had my healing techniques, you could have very well died."

As she said this, her finger traced a line where his wounds had been. They were gone now, not even a scar remained, but she remembered how bad the damage had been. How horrendous the four large slash marks had looked. The blood that had gushed from those wounds in such copious amounts that the only reason she hadn't hyperventilated at the sight was because her mate's life had been in danger. That was not something she wanted to see again, to experience again. Never again.

Kevin felt his blood run cold at the words passing Lilian's lips, his face paling. The thought of death was not fun for anyone, much less someone as young as him. He still had so much he wanted to accomplish before kicking the bucket.

Like getting together with Lindsay for starters. He couldn't die, not until he at least told her how he felt.

Makes you feel kind of bad for Lilian, doesn't it?

"So what happened to Chris?" Deciding that the best course of action was to steer this conversation away from his possible death to something a little less unnerving, Kevin asked about the one who had nearly done him in. Which probably wasn't a good topic to discuss with Lilian either, but he was curious.

Lilian sniffed derisively. "He won't be bothering us anymore." It took Kevin a few seconds to work around her statement and realize what she meant.

His eyes widened. "You didn't... I mean, is he...?"

"I didn't kill him, if that's what you're asking," Lilian assured him. Kevin breathed a sigh of relief. He didn't want someone's death on either of their hands. "But he won't be in any shape to contest me again. Even the famed durability of an Inu Yōkai won't be enough for him to recover from the wounds I gave him. A good deal of the damage I did to him was internal and will require someone with healing abilities to fix." She gave him a fanged smirk. "And Inu don't have any healing techniques. He won't die, and he'll be able to live the life of a normal human, but his days of torturing others with his immense strength are over."

"I see." Kevin was glad to know he wouldn't have to worry about Chris anymore, especially since they went to the same school. The last thing he needed was to have someone constantly trying to kill him because of his association with Lilian.

He frowned a second later, however, when he realized something else. "Wait, if you could have beaten him, why didn't you just do that sooner? You know, like when he first transformed? Or even before he transformed?"

"Ah, well..." A small tinge of pink appeared on Lilian's cheeks as she smiled sheepishly. "Us Kitsune don't like Inu very much," she admitted reluctantly. "In fact, most Kitsune are downright petrified of them. I'm not!" she hurriedly added, though the way her body seemed to shake as she spoke did nothing to convince Kevin about the sincerity of her words. "But a lot of us are."

"Why is that?" asked Kevin. Now that he had found his curiosity growing, Lilian literally conforming herself into his side didn't bother him... much.

"It all started a long time ago, like, one thousand years or something, when a Kitsune fell in love with a human." Kevin raised an eyebrow. Lilian saw this and smiled. "It's not unusual for a Kitsune to fall in love with a human, is it?" When he flushed and looked away, she giggled before continuing her story. "Anyways, this normally wouldn't have been a problem. Plenty of Kitsune have mated with humans before, but there *was* a problem when she fell in love with *this* human. You see, this particular human already had a companion. An Inu Yōkai."

"So, what?" Kevin furrowed his brow. "Did he cheat on this Inu after he met the Kitsune or something?"

"No. Good heavens no." Lilian giggled as if he had said something funny. Kevin pouted at being laughed at. It wasn't that funny, was it?

The girl finished laughing at his expense, then continued speaking. "Back then Inu rarely ever used their human forms. They usually preferred to stay in their hybrid form, which is what you saw that ugly mutt transform into, or their dog form, which just makes them look like a regular dog. This particular Inu had been in dog form and the human in question had thought it was just a normal dog. It wasn't, and when the human started spending more time with the Kitsune, the Inu became jealous. In a fit of rage, it killed the Kitsune in a brutal and violent manner, then killed the human for his betrayal. Ever since then we Kitsune have had issues with Inu Yōkai."

"Oh, well, I guess that make sense." He wasn't really sure what to think of that story. In some ways, he could sorta, kinda see where the Inu was coming from. Kevin was sure he wouldn't like being ignored in favor of someone else by the person he loved.

At the same time, killing both the Kitsune and the human just because they fell in love was really extreme. Besides, it wasn't their fault they fell in love. These things just happened some times.

Of course, if that Kitsune had been anything like Lilian, he could see why problems would have arisen. But surely not all Kitsune were as... um... devoted (read, obsessive) as she was when it came to their mates, right?

"Besides, it's like I told you before, we Kitsune aren't fighters." Kevin's eyes focused on Lilian. "We prefer avoiding fighting whenever possibly, unless, you know, it furthers The Plot in some way."

"The Plot?"

"Inu, on the other hand, are born fighters," Lilian continued without answering Kevin's question. If he didn't know any better, he would say she was ignoring him. "You could say they're natural warriors. Born and bred for combat. They revel in violence and bloodshed. It's in their nature to fight."

"I can kind of see that," Kevin admitted. "Chris was on the school wrestling team. While I've never seen any of the wrestling matches—" because, you know, watching sweaty men grappling each other wasn't really his thing, "— I've heard that some of them have gotten really violent. I remember this one rumor about how Chris was nearly expelled from the team because he had almost broken another boy's spine during a match once."

"I'm not surprised," Lilian wrinkled her nose in barely concealed derision. "Inu have always been a bunch of mindless, violent brutes."

Kevin shrugged. He was sure her perceptions of Inu were colored by her own nature and dislike of them, but seeing as he had never met any Inu other than Chris — at least he didn't think so — and that boy had done nothing to make him think the red head was wrong, he couldn't really say anything against her.

Either way it was time to change the subject.

"So what was the power you used against him?" asked Kevin, "You know, that strange ball of light?"

"That was my specialized ability."

Kevin tilted his head.

"Specialized ability? Is that something unique to you?"

"No, all Kitsune have specialized abilities." Lilian sat up a little straighter so that she could look at him. The action ended up inadvertently pushing her bosom into his arm. Kevin squeaked, causing her to look at him for a moment before shrugging off the strange noise and continuing her small lecture. "All Kitsune are born with a special affinity to a specific element. There are thirteen specialized affinities that come in three tiers, or levels; Lower, Middle and Upper."

"The first, or the Lower tier consists of what we call normal elements. They are Fire, Earth, Water, Air and Lightning. The Middle tier contains Ghost, Forest, Magma, Ocean and Ether. And the last tier, the Upper, only contains two specialist affinities; Celestial and Void."

"I'm guessing your power is... Celestial?" he asked tentatively. Lilian smiled, telling him he was right.

"Yes, I am a Celestial Kitsune. My powers are those that are said to be the closest to the Divine. Among Kitsune affinities, ours are supposedly one of the strongest because the only other beings who are capable of wielding Divine powers are the Gods and their servants. No other race of Yōkai can use Celestial powers. Every other affinity, including the Void can be used by the other Yōkai races to some extent."

"Of course, that doesn't mean the other affinities are weak," Lilian continued. "Fire for example. It's in the lower tier of Kitsune abilities, but I don't think anyone can deny the destructive power of fire."

Kevin rubbed his jaw as he tried to absorb all this information. His mind absently went back to how Lilian shot those strange balls of light at Chris. "So those balls were your specialized powers?"

"Uh huh. That particular technique is called Kōkyū, or Sphere of Light, if you want to use English," seeing Kevin's blank look after she told him what her technique was called, she added. "Not very original, I know, but it gets the job done."

"I guess."

"Normally, a Kitsune won't start learning how to use any specialist techniques until they've gained their third tail." A proud look crossed Lilian's face. "But I happen to have such a high affinity with my Celestial powers that I was able to learn a number of techniques shortly after gaining my second tail. Right now, it's limited to just those Light Spheres and basic healing techniques, but I know of a few others that I'll be able to learn once my youki is high enough."

"Youki?"

"The energy that all Yōkai use."

"Energy? Like chakra?"

"Chakra?" Now it was Lilian's turn to look questioning.

"Mmm." Kevin nodded. "Chakra is this one internal energy source in the human body that I read about in one of my manga."

"Ah! You mean Shinobi Natsumo." Lilian nodded her head thoughtfully. "Yes, I suppose there are similarities to those two powers. But there are also a lot of differences too. In Shinobi Natsumo chakra comes from an internal network similar to the veins that carry blood through the body. All of a Kitsune's power is contained in their tails. That's why Kitsune dislike keeping their tails hidden. It's also why most Kitsune can't use enhancement until they've gained their third tail at least. We don't have any network like those chakra pathways so we have to pretty much pump our bodies full of youki, which not only costs more youki than it's worth, but is also a very inefficient method of strengthening ourselves."

"I see." Kevin nodded, then blinked. "But wait. You can use enhancements and you only have your second tail."

"Yes, but only use in short bursts," Lilian informed him. "Anymore than sixty seconds of using the enhancement technique and I'd burn through all my youki."

"Oh." Kevin looked contemplative. "It's still a pretty cool ability though. Almost makes me wish I was a Yōkai." Lilian beamed at him. If she were a peacock, he was almost sure she would be fanning her feathers out.

Which, by the way, really wasn't needed. Her chest was large enough as it was.

An awkward silence soon engulfed the room. Well, Kevin thought it was awkward at least. Lilian didn't seem bothered by it at all. She just lay there, all smiles as she snuggled contentedly against him. Yes, she was perfectly happy just to let the silence ensue and enjoy the feel of her mate's body conforming to her own.

"Hey, Lilian, do you think you could, you know, let go of me? At least until I go to sleep?" Normally, Lilian would wait until he was asleep to sneak onto his couch. He still didn't like it when she did this, but at the very least it meant he wouldn't have to deal with her until he woke up the next day.

"Not a chance." She nuzzled her face against his chest. It sent all kinds of strange feelings and shivers down his spine. "I almost lost you today. There's no way I'm letting you go now."

Kevin sighed. Couldn't blame a guy for trying, right?

It looked like it was going to be a long night.

***

Located in a small apartment in a rundown apartment complex was none other than the Inu Yōkai that Lilian had so thoroughly thrashed with her Celestial powers: Chris Fleischer. He had woken up in that Gods forsaken alley the fox bitch and her boy toy had left him in several hours after the sun had gone down. It had been a miracle no one had found him, but that could have just as easily been due to some kind of illusion that red-haired whore had placed over him to make him invisible to the eyes of others.

After waking up, he had managed to get himself back to his dingy little apartment. It had taken him hours to get there, dragging his broken and battered body inch by agonizing inch across the ground. His fingers were bleeding from the many rocks and cracked surfaces he had cut himself on, and his body wasn't in much better shape, covered as it was in scrapes, scabs and burns, both from the dragging and from that damn fox's Celestial attacks.

The high school junior was currently staring up at the cracked and pitted ceiling of his bedroom, his eyes glazed over and unseeing, his mind lost in limbo. His entire body felt like someone had dipped it in boiling lava, like his cells were being ripped apart molecule by molecule. Never in his life had he felt so much pain. Nothing, not even the fights he'd had with his sister or old man could have prepared him for the agony he was now feeling. The pain was unfathomable.

None of that mattered to him. The pain, the agony, the torture of his body being invaded by a thousand needles piercing his skin due to the Celestial powers of that bitch who had nearly killed him. None of it. All that mattered was the agony of his defeat, the knowledge that he had lost to a Kitsune. A Kitsune of all creatures! He was an Inu! A proud warrior! A fighter of incredible strength and power! A creature that all Kitsune were supposed to fear! And yet that fucking little whore of a fox had nearly killed him! Him! He who was the son of one of the greatest Inu to have walked the Earth in a thousand years! A Yōkai whose strength was known far and wide to match those of the legendary Kyuubi! To suffer such a defeat from a two-tails (of all things) was a disgrace to his heritage!

The mere thought of that fox bitch made his wounds burn like nothing else, yet he did his best to ignore this as he focused not on his defeat, but on how he would get his revenge. He didn't know why that bitch had left him alive. Maybe she had been too worried about her toy, or perhaps she was just one of those soft-hearted little sluts that couldn't bring themselves to kill another living creature.

Not like it mattered either way. Whether the two-tailed bitch had let him live as an act of mercy or because she was just too soft to kill him didn't matter. The only thing that mattered was that he had been given an opportunity to exact his revenge, and he would not be wasting it.

He would need help though. As much as it pained him to admit it, that red-haired slut was stronger than she looked. Those strange light balls of hers packed a serious wallop.

Fortunately, he knew exactly who to get in touch with in order help him. While he didn't particularly want to call *her* for a favor, he didn't have many options. If nothing else, he knew *she* would get the job done.

Laying there on his bed, his body still black and crispy, Chris began to laugh a devious, diabolical laugh. "Hehehe... Hahahahaha... HAHAHAHAHA... MWAHAHAHAHAHAHA—ack! Gods fucking dammit! My spleen!"

Okay, so maybe he shouldn't try the Evil Villain Laugh until *after* he had fully healed.

Printed in Great Britain
by Amazon.co.uk, Ltd.,
Marston Gate.